The Trap

The Trap

by

Ana María Matute

Translated by

María Jose de la Cámara
and
Robert Nugent

Latin American Literary Review Press
Pittsburgh, Pennsylvania
Series: Discoveries • 1996

The Latin American Literary Review Press publishes Latin American creative writing under the series title *Discoveries*, and critical works under the series title *Explorations*.

Library of Congress Cataloging-in-Publication Data

Matute, Ana María, 1926-
   [Trampa. English]
   The trap / Ana María Matute ; Robert Nugent and
María José de la Cámara.
   p. cm.
   ISBN 0-935480-81-1 (pbk.)
   I. Nugent, Robert. II. Cámara, María José de la. III.
Title.
   PQ6623.A89T65 1996
863.64--dc20   96-17096
                               CIP

Cover photograph by Egidio Lunardi
Book design by Connie Mathews

Latin American Literary Review Press
121 Edgewood Avenue • Pittsburgh, PA 15218
Tel. (412) 371-9023 • Fax (412) 371-9025

Acknowledgments

This edition has been translated with the financial assistance of the Spanish Dirección General del Libro y Bibliotecas of the Ministerio de Cultura.

This project is supported in part by grants from the National Endowment for the Arts in Washington D.C., a federal agency and the Commonwealth of Pennsylvania Council on the Arts.

…they deal in chains, they enslave men, they trade in the truth, they sow dishonor, what will grow…?

Taras Shevchenko

Contents

PART ONE

Surrounded by Plants
and Weeds

Disordered Diary

The course of time is there, a hand with delicate fingernails, a little bird's claw, which I hated so much. Why does hate also wither? Hate is old, yet the fingers do not tremble as they carefully peel apricots. I always eat apricots whole, with their skin, with a mixture of teeth on edge and desire, with a definite, naive, cruelty. Then, some time ago, she decided what was proper and what was not proper, at table as well as in the world for which she destined me. Nevertheless, she once speared three or four gherkins together with the point of her knife and ate them up. She was aseptic, implacable, vulgar and Olympian. I remember her hand holding the knife like a lance, the blade worn out and sharpened by use, like a razor blade. I remember her, infringing on us her codes of behavior, her admonitions, her law. I still see her, now, and she keeps on appearing to me, just exactly as she was then, breaking the law and exemplary.

She is peeling the apricots, on that hot June night. Neat and fierce, I do not know if what she is doing is orthodox or not. Just that I witness something similar to the spring being skinned of its leaves. Within a few days she will celebrate once more the holiday, the extraordinary day on which she gave a shout (the first and possibly the last one) on the face of the earth, because she is the only thing that truly and tangibly exists.

At times—now, for example—I say to myself if it is certain that only she is alive, as she prolongs indefinitely the time for dessert, on the eve of her great commemoration. Because that commemoration is the only incontestable thing of all that surrounds us in this house, in this island within the island.

How is it possible that she has achieved it? What were the cunning artifices that she used to bring us, scattered and distant, together here, for the sole purpose of celebrating the decisive year, the surprising, sarcastic year, with which she has been threatening us for how long?...I don't know. She is ageless, she is time. Always the same, alive and mortal, an eternal paradox. The white wave above her forehead no longer rises up. It had been so long that I had not seen her, had not heard her, and suddenly the distance between us has melted away, it is she who monopolizes everything: the world is she. The rest of us, next to her, seem to be excluded from the world. I did not see her grow old, but I know that a lot of time, a lot of years have passed since that year, the last one in which I had seen her.

She has to grow old, necessarily. Even though it might be internally, the way trees do. Death will climb through her arteries, it will appear one day in the grey of her eyes: even though death may be in the nature of a challenge, or of an epigrammatic promise. It is necessary to say to her: "You have not changed, the years don't go by for you." And it is true. The calendar, the course of the sun and the moon, the equinoxes and the solstices, have nothing to do with her. Not on her big day, twelve months before her authentic centenary. Nor within a week, when she will savor the gluttony of her ninety-ninth birthday; when all of us will be present on that ironic, teasing new year, with which she seems to scourge us out of pure and melancholic mockery. For sadness— I am beginning to call it melancholy—has never left her, it was always a part of her since the first day I saw her. At times in my memory (at the time when I was getting older) her disparaging gesture had become simple sadness. Perhaps this might be the secret, the reason why my hatred dried up.

Nobody knows, as I do, why she brings forward the celebration of her hundredth birthday by one year. ("I have to move the date up. If I wait to celebrate my hundredth birthday party, I will never complete that year.") I know the course of her thoughts because she is not mysterious for me, but like an empty glass. She has a taste like that of life that is whimsical, cruel, killjoy. She fears that her real hundredth birthday will not come to pass. Let her whim take her away to the miserable and splendid place where the dead are waiting, ecstatic, some memory, some word which can bring them briefly to life, among vague, alien phrases. Words that they would not understand, even if they returned to life.

Seated in her portable chair (not a wheelchair, she doesn't like that word: it is simply portable, like a typewriter or a transistor) she will, once again, triumph over us: those of us who are living and those who have died, Uncle Alvaro, Jorge de Son Major, Big Grandpa, my mother...We are the ones who grow up, dry up, die. She is the one who triumphs, quietly and solemnly, without amazement or delight, without apparent well-being. She triumphs because she has always triumphed; at the moment of her birth, in her youth, in her old-age. Because her words drag silence along, as certain boats drag along behind them a foamy trail, followed hopefully by sharks, ready to devour the leftovers which some kitchen help might throw overboard. She has the gift of fabricating silence, of making it flow, like a spring. She provokes confusion, distrust, fear, admiration, hate...What does it matter? Above all, she provokes feeling, silence. It is difficult to burst out speaking, after she has spoken, even when it might be a question. She is frighteningly prevailing.

And she will pass this birthday and possibly reach, without greater difficulties, her centenary. Perhaps, as I look at her through the conversation (which faintly favors her) I can discover her decay. From my place at that table—the same place I have always had—silent, perhaps I might return to my lost childhood. Staring at her and silent, as in the time when she reproached me for both things. Thus, I try to make sure now, as I did then, that "no one notices me, that no one remembers me." In this peaceful and certainly cordial family dinner, seeing how she devours soft and golden apricots, while I look on as her interminable desserts appear, I shall discover her decay.

But this decay did not appear as her years came on. Like sadness (or melancholy) it always existed. Yes, there, in that heavy column amongst ruins, as though embraced, by all kinds of wild plants and remains of ivy, that she outlives, spring after spring, one apricot after another apricot, apple after apple, I imagine the column in the long winter; shameless and cold nudity, trampled by the rain, profaned by far-off inscriptions of obscene little boys, a column vaguely captured by skeletons of leaves, thorny stems, curly ghosts of flowers. At another time past...

She will never give the sensation of feeling captured. Neither by her own old age, nor by the death of her close ones, nor by those of her enemies, nor by the births of those who, more or less, can legitimately carry her blood. She is like a stationary mockery of life and death. A sedentary outrage, without any emotion, in the presence of life and death. It makes one shudder to think that she refuses to die, fearless and irrational, possessor of considerable earthly goods, spectator of the ruin and the ashes which surround her obstinate body. Unharmed witness of the ephemerous kingdom of the blue bell-flowers, the bougainvilleas, of those humble and frothy heads of hops. Tyrannizing all life around her, with the appetizingly sweet promise of her death. As if in each of her thick silences she would say (and I am now thinking of you, Borja): "Patience, serenity. After all, one day I will die."

She has finished the apricots, the moist little pits shine on her plate like a little girl's dark eyes. I remember the picture of St. Lucy that used to upset me in the past. Antonia smoothly removes the portable arm chair away from the table, brings it to the sitting room where the coffee is steaming. She does not keep a strict diet, nor does she feel any discomfort other than that of not being able—I suspect it's more not wanting to—to move forward on her diminutive and swollen feet.

Her cup, filled and black, is an insult to the pale camomile infusion that Aunt Emilia takes, humiliated by diets and interdictions. Aunt Emilia already deprives herself—she is truly falling to pieces, like a limp shawl on a carpet—of the few and miserable joys which old age brings: gluttony, avarice, laziness... Perhaps she still has laziness left. But, according to what she said to me before, she suffers from insomnia. Sad reward for her obedient and punished body. Aunt Emilia sips resignedly from the edge of the little cup because—I remember it so well—she can not bear excessively hot beverages. (Oh, that bottle of cognac, that red crystal glass that you kept in the chest of drawers in your room! It is not right that you should have paid such a high price for your condition, while she, the great sampler, is oblivious to matters of vital organs and chronic complaints. Injustice upon injustice, this house keeps on, built on the arbitrary distribution of good and evil which characterized it. I feel a vague irritation—the injustice continues, since hatred, on the other hand, has spent itself towards Aunt Emilia. A dried-up, blond doll, she would have wanted to become an easy-going, greedy, grandmother; one of those who carry candy in their purses and fall asleep over the newspaper. But life has flown by and keeps on denying her all that it could have done to make her moderately happy—even being an orphan. She would have been a chubby and nice little grandmother, with her skin still in good condition: yellowish velvet, drooping and good-natured cheeks next to her still greedy mouth, sensual in a middle-class way. She probably would have given bicycles as gifts when exams came around and, from time to time, she would have told the story of Rapunzel (the only story she knew). But there she was, without grandchildren, without coffee, without candy, without cognac and without Marie Brizard. Without cigarettes, with glasses and with insomnia. Her body slips from her, like a dress from its hanger. She keeps only her eternal consent. Day after day she acknowledges her irresponsible character, her dim wit, her excessive acts of indulgence towards her son who is a bachelor and a squanderer. Year after year, she acknowledges that she is absolutely lacking the energy with which she should sustain her dignified state of widowhood of a national hero.

I have the feeling that her husband looks at her spitefully, from that photograph which, in the past, made me uneasy. I believe that men like Uncle Alvaro were born in order to die violently. His long scar, his lean face, his eyes clinging to a rigid and strict idea of the world. As a child, I had imagined him to be distant, brutal, mysterious. Now that old portrait, in its place on the little table as always, offers me an insipidly obvious face. And his great justification: it was not true, he had scarcely any money. This man, about whom I always had heard ferocious virtues (both military and civil), was half-ruined. Evidently (although at that time no one said so), he very much liked to play poker. Now I know from whom Borja inherited the same liking and weakness. Dear Borja, you were the one who took it on yourself to enliven, with your last remnants of inherited wealth, your disrespectful—it must be confessed—orphanhood. Borja, you too have not changed. On the contrary, alas, did that man who had anybody he chose to shot, did he ever exist?... What is certain is that he died consistent with himself. On the ground (as expected) and at the gates of Teruel. Contrary to the examples of his life, there was nothing barbaric in that death. It turns out to be a natural, reasonable death. To tell the truth there is no great violence in it. I do not believe that he left medals, although he was awarded them. It is evident that, except in and for gambling, his was an austerity bordering on avarice. In this portrait, now, he only appears disillusioned. As if he had missed a last hand in cards on which he counted. In my recalling of that night, I can even reconstruct the silence that fell after his death: about mortgages, debts and indigences. About Aunt Emilia, obedient to his subtle order that floated alongside her: she must not find out about anything. It was, apparently, her mission in this world. To be, as was incumbent on her, stupid, good and resigned. Thus, nothing altered the natural order of things.

But the old column kept on dominating among the ruins. Ordering, classifying, selling, paying, deciding. What importance does the course of human events have for her, the empty spaces where time flows as in a vessel with a broken bottom? Nothing. Nothing matters. Ruin is never her ruin. Death is never her death. Misfortune is never her misfortune. What does not happen to her does not happen to anybody. In this regard, she does not recognize children, parents, brothers or sisters. So nothing matters. She, after all, is the world. All the known world (like the maps of antiquity). Everything returns to her and takes shelter in her; she accepts or rejects according to her understanding and her interest. I suspect, therefore, that she never hoped for or desired anything else: not from Uncle Alvaro, not from her daughter, nor from her grandson. That everything happened just exactly the way she foresaw it should happen. Her house, her family—her world—kept on as always; nothing changed.

And you, Borja—perhaps you sometimes remember these

things—you had already forgotten the old seashore; you were amazingly given over to growing up, gently unsubmissive, politely rebellious, flatteringly selfish. Borja, dear friend, dear brother, at times I have thought that these two women who loved you and who still love you—each one in her own way—did not expect a different behavior from you. It is easy to understand, tonight, in this house, that you were loyal. You did not break accepted patterns, you acted in accordance with conventions and customs. And there was (and there still is) a sweet promise in the air, which brushes against your ears, your gaze, your hope: "Patience, one day or another I will die." She never became angry or complained about your life, Borja, the way you become indignant and waste away because of her delay in dying. A death that tomorrow she will ridicule with family festivities, by piling up one more year of life on top of ninety-eight years (even though she pretends that it really is her hundredth birthday). The last time, I saw you Borja, you had become a little rigid: I could guess the false pretenses of your neglect, sitting down on the armchair. I know you, Borja, I can even recognize a thousand alert lances under your shoulders of a make-believe young man. The eyes of that boy who cried once, on a certain daybreak, no longer exist. They have turned yellowish with the years. No one could any longer believe them to be golden, or pale green, like this June sky.

She, too, waits for you impatiently. She has been waiting for you for two nights. She looks furtively at her watch, while she scatters words about. She knows, and she has always known, how to speak about one thing and think about another. She is thinking about you. The two of us are thinking about you tonight. More than your mother thinks of you. More than I do about my son. Although you are both equally late. And now I know why she and I agree almost always. These things have nothing to do with love nor with human interest. These things are irremissible facts in time, in our short life (in the portion of selfish, mean time, that behooves each one of us). It is possible to lie— one is used to lying—about these things. But no one believes them.

And I repeat myself again and I state once more that, after all, that white wave no longer rises up on her forehead. Now her forehead reminds me of the sand where the sea is about to die: as though it were to die truly and forever. But I know that all the waves will go on, fading away or choppy, one after the other. Dying waves, now, over a distant splendor of gold (those that were sought-after conches, maritime shells, with which to string together necklaces and bracelets of an oceanic princess; blurred ghosts of some creature that possessed a garden in the shape of a sun in the deepest part of the ocean; a garden furrowed by shadows, wandering reflections of shipwrecks; a deep sea of mud and emerald, where skeletons of ships are still floating, in a sonorous wind; an almost mineral sea, abysses through which descend, spinning upon themselves, awkwardly and very slowly, ships and dead sailors. They are similar to certain mills made of paper that are no longer manufactured. Mysterious descents with the smoothness of feathers, which recall the last snowfall inside an abandoned crystal ball).

I ponder on that necessarily old head and I know how useless it is to wonder, with a hook in one's hand, like someone who is looking for scraps in the sand. That head brings back to me the mirage of my childhood; but the sea is distant, lapping the coast of an island that I never came to understand.

I do not reach many things tonight. Things that made me suffer, laugh, think, grow. Now we are grown up, Borja. And we have forgotten. Our wandering childhood road, our perverse, bitter-sweet childhood heart. Although sometimes—yesterday, ten years ago, perhaps tomorrow—we believe that this heart is kept in some place (as when a box, found unexpectedly, is opened, and on the other side of the lid, on the tiny, speckled mirror, the ghost of eyes that will never return, frightens us). In all our acts there is something similar to an ambush, isolated and always the same.

This is the way it is, I imagine (along with loneliness) that one arrives at the age of reason. I can reconstruct, tonight, the first time of loneliness: a dramatic separation from the world, a sweet, fearful and impatient distance from the surrounding world.

The ultimate loneliness—the present one—is a pathetic and un-controllable immersion in the surrounding world. There exists no other notable difference between that moment and this one. Moreover, people acquire vices, virtues that are more or less conventional. An understanding and silent attitude in the presence of imbecility, injustice or ugliness. A greater tendency towards silence. In any case, I think that if the first loneliness appears somewhat like an island, the ultimate loneliness—the ultimate island—belongs to an abundant archipelago. If I were to wonder for what reason I have come today to this house, which I detested in the past, I would find it difficult to confess: because I wanted to. But that's the way it is. Once I saw a dead beggar on the outskirts of a town. He was really close to the wall of the cemetery where a white, flowering branch peeped out. On another occasion, I saw a murdered man stuck to the back of a boat.

I know perfectly well why I have come here. I know very well why I can not free myself, nor will I ever know how to free myself from the tyranny. I was born in tyranny, I will die in it. Perhaps, even, with a certain comfort, supposing myself to be exempt from all guilt. Perhaps I am still too much immersed in the last stage of loneliness, or perhaps I am a little bit more indifferent than I was last year, yet nevertheless...

I know, in a clear although invisible way, that something is opening up under the ground. I do not know if it is under my feet: in any case, it is very close to me. Since I have returned to the island the feeling of a hidden snare does not leave me, and I believe I can guess, however gratuitous it may seem, the presence of some inaudible scream between these walls, as though someone had just been trapped. Right here, now, at this moment. It is a fleeting guess, scarcely formulated, already disappearing. But, no longer believing in it, I surprise myself turning my head, looking around me with distrust.

I should never have returned here. It had been a long time, a very long time, since I had thought of these people, and of my childhood; since I had thought about any one of these things; about the house, or about this room. Nor about the island. I have only needed something so simple, so common, as reading her call: "I am going to be a hundred years old, I want to gather you around me" (and a tenuous, ironic promise in the last sentence: "Perhaps for the last time"). Perhaps. Perhaps. I do not understand how she is able to reach ninety-nine years of age and say: "Perhaps this is the last time." She is the last time. Perhaps is not a word to be pronounced by her. For there was no perhaps, probably will never be a perhaps for her. Here still lies an infantile anger, diluted, still turning around without a destination. Poor Borja, with your velvety eyelids above your tiredly eager eyes; in the past, vague and promising phrases tyrannized you too: favored heir, beloved boy. If you had not hoped for anything, you would not now come at her call (but you will come; although late, you will come). Perhaps you would not have consumed your life in hoping, hoping. You would not have wasted away energy and talents (in the numismatic sense) waiting. Now I suspect that the realization of the desired promise would come to you late. What we long for always arrives late, that is true. I will never understand human beings, I can only hint at desires, moments of impatience, disenchantment, emptiness. Where does fame, that they talk to us so much about, go? Where does the fullness that we were longing for? Borja, despite everything that happened, all that which will happen or can happen, you and I are united by a thin cord. It is possible that we are joined by some tenuous, unbreakable love, from one end to the other, from one extreme to the other of this thread, wherever we might go. It is certain that, at times, we feel a painful tug. I have read in your veiled eyelids, as I always did. Possibly you only wait for a nostalgic future, heavily sweet, because possessions take too long to arrive. There is no longer a remedy, nobody can return to the time past. Today, yesterday, is late. Tomorrow has not arrived, but it is already late. My dear Borja, an opulent maturity awaits you, without the sharp, piercing pleasure of the original splendor, of the first profligacy. You lost it, you can not even remember it.

Years, people, facts, cross between you and me. We have seen each other from time to time. Within a few days we will see each other again. We will renew the usual timeless conversation. I believe that the warmth of our last argument still has not gone out. (At least, this has been saved.)

I have the gnawing sensation that at some time I wrote a true diary. Naturally, it would not be a methodical and faithful document, a daily and exemplary exercise of minute details and observations. Not a normal diary (something similar to when my old Mauricia looked at the sweaters that she knitted for me and said: "when I was doing the sleeves, you had the scarlet fever," or "when I was doing the elastic for this sleeve, we had that cold spell when we went and lost the tomatoes"). No, it would not be like that, the hypothetic diary that I imagine to have written; but I am convinced of the existence of some echo, perhaps of some tone—the tone of a voice, of a phrase that persists and gravitates over my acts and in the rare memory of what is still to happen—something I did, or believed, or lived at some moment (this early morning when I can no longer close my eyes), seems to me entirely vain. How will the past reality be found again? The day that some future Edison—as an example—gives it to us in crystal bubbles, within the reach of a little switch, the malaise from bearing witness to our passage through life will lose all value. Meanwhile, people will resort to knitting sweaters, intimate diaries, works or art, buildings, dirty tricks...One day not one of these things will be necessary; it will be possible to eliminate, like dirty dust, the deliquescent memory.

If I were to begin now, in this stupid and sleepless early morning hour, in this same room—rooms closed off at that time, belonging greatly to the great and feared Great Grandfather who frightened me as a child—a solemn and conceited diary, a hypocritical diary, full of the best good faith and innocent analytical spirit, it would be one of the many free acts of my life. But I am here, hearing the "scratching of the pen on the paper" (as must be said in a real diary). This, that I am writing now, could be the fruit—after seeing her, Aunt Emilia, and Antonia—of a doubtful recovery; so faded and dull that I fear it has no use for me. Sometimes, fascinated, I contemplated the ruins of cities and landscapes, overrun by the centuries, theft, war or earthquakes. Silhouettes in the wind, symbols of a distant beauty, of a lost glory, of a pain that does not return. And I can not avoid saying to myself that heroic deeds, cruel acts of slaughter, when contemplated from some cold and high region, would probably be confused with pilgrimages or invasions of tourists. From my early memory wells up a glance of reproach: "What have you done with me?" I do not keep childhood photographs. At the mere idea of writing a real diary, a frothy fear comes over me; as when, on some occasion, I ruminated vengeance and the moment arrived of putting it into practice: I did not put it into practice. It must be true that writing is one of the thousand forms of vengeance—not too arrogant—that are given to us humans. The gods had other more satisfactory methods: and there are their shadows, in the grass. Without arms, without a nose, winding around in the sun, among inflamed nettles. The shadows of the gods, the already withered acts of vengeance, have escaped like smoke from the marble, from the bronze. The gods have died in scholarly theses, in the propagandistic pamphlets of the firm of Bayer.

All this is pure palaver by means of which I can elude my true malaise, the reason why I now find myself disposed to write about my feelings. Almost always I tried to deceive myself about the true motive of my acts. This was the great trick on which the development of my feelings was built (my intellectual formation never mattered, since a woman does not need certain kinds of baggage in order to establish herself worthily in the society for which I was destined), my education as a creature born in order to initiate a mean and gentle struggle against the masculine sex (to which I was inexorably destined). Thus my most important weapons were the veils with which to conceal selfishness and ambition, ignorance and helplessness, laziness and sensuality. Veils capable of filtering anything, in such a way that everything might appear licit or illicit (according to what suits the occasion). But I was no longer a slow and inquisitive child, nor a silent and terribly sad girl, nor an apathetic and forgetful woman who observed, with a sacred amazement at the world, the passing by of people. I am, on this early morning, a creature without age, without any capacity for judgment or resentment, without any fame, without great shortcomings. I remember that, when I was twelve, fourteen years old, I imagined that one day I would know something brilliant and splendid (although feared) that would give me the key to the world. On this early morning hour I experience the deceptive feeling that the world exists uncomplicatedly; that it turns, inanely, without any sense; fulfilling its cycles with the dehumanized pleasure that provokes, for example, the yawning of some gods.

If, on some unknown map, I could mark the country (on the road we call age there are so many countries travelled through, loved, forgotten) where I definitely lost soundness of mind—which is not in any way adulthood—it was there that I said to myself for the first time: "There is no reason to hate her. She is my grandmother and, when all is said and done, she took charge of someone as unfortunate and as unpromising as I." If this were a real diary, and if it were necessary to choose a departure point—that is to say, the suitable departure point where it may be possible that people began to take me into account—I would start out from the moment (from the country, to express myself better) where I was when I loathed her again. I think this so-called diary, written or remembered across gaps and empty spaces, can not be anything else other than a patching together of visible and invisible realities, of past and present, somberly superimposed. An authentic diary, a truthful accounting of present realities is probably not possible without counting on the ghosts of other realities (future, past, forgotten, immediate). It will not be possible to write a real diary, I, perhaps, am less able than anyone. I can not believe that the events of a life are simply events. Nothing is its name, just that; nothing so insecure as looking for, more or less honorably, self-justification.

One day I hated her again. That is why the absence of hate tonight surprises me. That is why I am so confused tonight. After all is said and done, what difference does it make to me that she reaches a hundred, or two hundred, or nine hundred years of age? I will no longer be a spectator of her years. I have given up being so, a long time ago.

I reconstruct the day that I hated her again. I remember exactly the day that hatred returned, mature and ripe (not the sour and tender hatred I had at fourteen): it was the day that the first letter from my father arrived. The war had ended, we were living in Barcelona; the whole house was floating in the euphoria of victory. And when no one appeared to remember him, his letter arrived from the University of Puerto Rico. My father wanted to have me with him, and the astonishment of knowing that some-one wanted such a thing prevented me, suddenly, from having any feeling whatever of love, gratitude, or rancor. I only know that she (of course, she had already read the letter before I had) looked at me in silence. I remember my hands holding up the letter, the trembling of my fingers, my infinite astonishment. I remember that slender handwriting which seemed to me, just the greatest expression of human sadness.

When my father sent me to the countryside with old Mauricia, I did not have a mother or even a memory of her. On the other hand I could describe with great exactitude the old house, the woods, the creaking of the doors. As for my father, I knew that he was thin and dark like me and that—unlike me—he had very pretty ears. Years later I saw some just like his in a Handbook of Anatomy for Draftsmen. My father's ears were, then, my father. Delicately dark, anatomically perfect, deaf to me (a situation which, paradoxically, conferred greater perfection on them). Generally, that is the way a child's mentality is , and I can not falsify it.

For many years his real profession—before the war he was an associate university professor—constituted a mystery for me. Then a moment arrived when I understood that the man, absent and rarely mentioned, had allotted his life, his health, his money and my mother's money (in addition to her happiness, or, at least, her conjugal happiness) between politics and literary illusions. (It seems that he was rather better known in the first than in the latter). Since he did not belong to the victors, but to those who had been conquered, he disappeared from my life together with the last mists of the war.

Only she (once in a while) spoke to me of him whom the others tried never to mention. She alone, in psychologically peda-gogically-suitable moments, gave me an image of a man whose most frequent attributes were: communist, Mason, libertine, Jew, and possibly if he had been born in Catalonia or in the Basque Provinces, a separatist. As we were living in a time when those adjectives turned out to be rather usual, they did not impress me in any special way, (Almost everybody who did not think or act as she thought opportune could be considered as entered in this register.) But the tone of irremediable fatality with which she referred to him did indeed affect me: as though it had to do with a guilt that weighed over me. An indelible stain, which I was supposed to wash out at whatever price. Definitely, my father, the one with the soft and velvety ears, if he did not exactly personify the devil, was a faithful representative of what she considered his followers. The devil's followers, hardened militants in the ranks of error, were worse than the devil, since they lacked the prestige—subtle, but indubitable—that such a legendary character exercised in the minds that programmed my bringing up. After all (the class spirit prevailed), the devil came from a good family. The followers, on the other hand, are ridiculously pretentious people, upstart lower class, laborers of the evil, but indubitably royal Satan. If I had been Satan's daughter (and sometimes I thought so, alone, in the bitter night of the boarding school, between moments of held back tears) I probably would have felt a certain relief. But the Partisan—so I called him and even today I call him so to myself—whose ears were like seashells, ruined my early youth and inspired in me a vague but poisonous rancor that I had a great deal of difficulty to lay aside.

The Partisan was—and always had been—very far from suspecting that his ideological adventures had embittered me up to such a point. He always belonged to the race of the angelic ones, capable of seeing die alongside of them the one they love most without being aware of it. Those capable of strangling what they love most, of total self-destruction without being aware of it. Poor Partisan, afterwards so beloved: always on the way towards a complicated Truth that (apparently) he alone was in a position to reach; determined to redeem, the World, as a whole, to be the World. Poor Partisan, how uselessly I love you still.

I know exactly the day when I hated her again, after the first news about my father, from his distant University. On that day (she had already kept the letter in her drawer, she still had not commented on it), that same day—it was time for after-dinner coffee and she was glancing through a magazine—she said, unexpectedly, in her curious syntax: "Look, like these shoes, just the same, your father wore them." Her finger pointed out, without compassion, some horrendous, two-tone, yellow shoes. And I knew that, with that, she awoke in me an ignoble shame, hopelessly sad and ridiculous; and that the shame, like dirty foam, was growing; and that it erased perhaps, any memory, or a nice word, or a distant sign of affection. What I did not know was that, in addition to shame, hate came back too. She opened the drawer, took out the letter once more and threw it in my lap: "Go on, read it again and think about it. After all, you are his daughter." Over the thin letters which had formerly moved me, over the timid call: "come with me, my daughter," intervened, irritatingly, a pair of vulgar, yellow shoes. I could not manage to forgive her for it.

In the first years of my life my character was undisciplined and rebellious; but in my second school (where I was a boarder as soon as the war was over) I changed completely. From being a naughty little girl I became a respectful, timid adolescent and a passable student. The former tendency to chatter, the insolence, the bad behavior that had characterized me, softly gave in; and silence, a great silence, arrived in my life. This is as much as I can remember now, in this early morning. I suppose that my true story begins in silence; on that day, I do not know for sure which one, when, like the protagonist of a children's story, I lost my voice.

Wasting Time

Beverly explained to him how his life had come to be, and, in general, the life process of any other being. Delicately vociferous she slid the ineffable and vast gamut of her vowels into his child's ears—a child who spies on the garden wishing that something might immediately occur. Some exciting event that might turn the world inside out, like a purse. Bear had discovered some time ago (and understood it perfectly) the inexistence of Paradise. There was no Paradise for Beverly, nor for Mother, nor for Grandfather Franc. Nor was there any Paradise for Bear. Very well. But, could a Paradise not exist for Puppy? Puppy had just been squashed under the truck that delivered the milk, orange-juice, and ice-cream. Under the enormous wagon of vitamins had Puppy really ceased to exist? At that moment Beverly supposed that it was appropriate to speak once more about the time in Bear's life when Bear began to exist, there, inside mother's womb. Bear should know the right, exact importance that life holds. Bear imagined himself, then, inside a womb; scarcely a repugnant lump of tapioca. And he confused vaguely the devastating absence of Puppy with the marvelous mystery of life.

Bear was born when Father had gone to fight far away, for indubitably just causes (although they already reached him, there on the plains beaten by the wind, at the little pink and white house, and to the red flowers of the hedge, deprived of their own meaning). Beverly put on her heavy leather gloves, took a hook painted green and turned over the earth, searched in the ground (while he tried not to roll about on the lawn from the pain because of the unnatural disappearance of Puppy). Beverly spoke at length and clearly of the mystery of life, of children who exist secretly in the womb of wise and loving mothers. "Like the same earth that I now turn around in order to sow it with beautiful flowers." Beverly did not want Bear to remember Puppy. Things must be accepted this way, and he must understand that the world is filled with infinite Puppies which, in their turn, breathe like gelatinous lumps in some maternal dog womb. Upon arriving at this point Bear, without any apparent reason, began to vomit.

But all this went back to other times. Fragments that arrived now, without any special reason. Now, when the impulse emerged to go out into the street, to abandon the apartment, the elephantine, broken down furniture (as on the point of some strange inauguration). "It is like living in a warehouse of packed up years," she said to herself once. But they decided that living there, sporadically cared for by Leandro's daughter, was better than living in a comfortable hotel room. How was she going to argue about certain points? There are things that are not worth arguing about. When Bear would cross the main door, he would smile at Leandro (who had known Mama and Grandmother Maria Teresa: he even remembered the latter leaving the house, dressed as a bride). Even though Leandro was then almost a boy, as he himself hurried to state. All of Leandro's words caused him malaise. Words which sent off a heavy perfume of fidelity. A damp, animal domestic fidelity. At the end of two years, he still had difficulty in adapting himself to the new system.

Beverly was different. And Grandfather Franc, too, was different. Bear felt invaded by unease. As though some old affection, already outdated, already useless came back to him. Just as at the sight of some objects that he refused to throw away (on that day when he packed up his things and travelled to this country which Grandfather Franc called the Homeland). Grandfather used to cut flowers with delicacy comparable to their names. And he also placed those names in invisible, earthenware vases. On other lips, his words could irritate, perhaps bore, or simply not exist. With Grandfather Franc, everything gained an air, a tone, that saved him from ridicule or anger.

And now, when he least suspected it, Bear felt impelled to leave the house; to hear no longer, even for one more minute, through the open window, the announcer's voice on the TV. He left the book open, he did not pay attention to the telephone call (even though the call was perhaps urgent or perhaps came from those who were the only ones who mattered to him: Mario, Luis, Enrique or the others). He went out, almost running, down the street, along the wrought iron fence, in the silence of 3 o'clock in the afternoon, in the sleepy peace of a garden unusually saved among the modern buildings. Here, the gardens were scarce. Here, the demolishers, punctually and periodically, arrived; the saws arrived and severed the tree trunks. In place of them, they raised red, white walls, interspersed with venetian blinds of a remotely Japanese type. Mother said, when she saw the house again: I would not have recognized it. But Mother had scarcely lived there. Grandfather Franc took Mother and Grandmother Maria Teresa to Madrid. Then, (according to what Grandfather said), Madrid was a high and distant city, like a tower. To go away to Madrid, from that street, among the half-extinguished wild bellflowers of the east garden, must have been something like absenting one-self from the world. Grandfather Franc said that. Listening to Grandfather Franc awoke useless curiosity (as if for something heard many times and, nevertheless, impossible to retain.)

At the present moment it turned out to be absolutely neces-sary to leave the book, jump from the chair, dash downstairs, smile at Leandro and keep on running down the street. At such moments he covered kilometers and kilometers of asphalt. He discovered streets, solitary squares, forgotten fountains, the re-mains of a park, tangled among the thorns; the torso of a statue, a lumber warehouse, clinics, industrial blocks. As in a fleeting film, he himself changed into a ghostly and dizzy camera: until he felt his legs were stiff and, unexpectedly, a great tiredness overcame him, sweat dripped down his throat, arms and legs. Then, he would enter some bar or another and he had a drink or a cup of coffee. A cup of coffee and a drink to which—after two long years—he could not quite get used to. At those moments, Bear felt disconcerted and extraordinarily alone. An unusual thing, because in the past he had no friends, as he did now; and in the past he had never become conscious of his loneliness. Enrique, Luis and even Mario seemed to him, at such moments, unreal beings: scarcely some references (like the causes of life related by Beverly, or the mystery of death, in the absence of Puppy).

Then (as now) Bear felt a foreboding (like an invisible iron collar, a prison). There came into his memory the young black woman who threw herself from the window when she saw approaching the women's dorm a white group with hoods (a group which was, simply, heading for a festive "initiation" ceremony in an adjoining sorority). When he hurried towards streets still unknown to him, something similar impelled him (and he feared that all the streets of this city, of this country, of this Homeland, would always appear to him in this way, unknown). A blind, terrifying fury (just like that of the young black woman) impelled him. Such a useless death, so stupidly pathetic, that of the young black woman, like his flight down the street: towards nowhere.

When he was a very small child, Beverly caught him with the fingernail scissors, cutting a little frog into pieces. Beverly convinced him of the unsuitability of this act. Truly, Beverly always convinced him of the uselessness of all kinds of unsuitability. With her guttural sweetness, her serene determination, Beverly gently took away from children's hands sharply pointed objects, expertly washed away all vestiges of blood, until no trace was left. Blood is cruel (and, above all, dirty).

Down the stairs, down the street, Bear is homesick and flees, contradictory, to a shining, unpolluted, transparent bell. And when, finally, he awakens (it was, really, like an awakening) aching, tired, revived, sweaty and happy, he goes into a bar. Then the moment comes of repeating mentally: the crust comes off, finally, the odious membrane which encloses, like a fetal placenta, is finally slashed, and it is possible to escape from the net, from the enormous trap...

Step by step, day by day, he became aware of a vast cowardice, crouching everywhere (like ants or lizards). "And I am grateful to that cowardice, to everyone. To Mother, to Uncle Borja, to my father, including Grandfather Franc (almost no one knows it, that he, too, is a coward). I thank them for that cowardice, that has allowed my first action."

But that action, unawarely desired, only began to take on shape, on the point of being realized, beginning with friendship, then camaraderie, then the complicity of Mario and the other boys. "One action will precede another action." In those moments there existed the conviction that and unknown equilibrium came back to him, to Bear. (Bear without friends, Bear without love, Bear without Paradise.) A dark hidden balance, that he had lost some time before (perhaps in the mists of the first crying, perhaps when he was only a viscous and negligible lump of tapioca).

In the half-shadow of the bar, surrounded by dirty formica, by bottles, by fans which had been turned off, next to a man who was half-asleep, Bear asks for a cup of coffee and loses himself in the mists of thc TV. Shaking to and fro, he travels in an old heap that is falling apart, with a cigarette between his lips. He scarcely catches anything else but noises, mingled with one another, almost metallic; unexpectedly swollen, like rags floating on the sea, like a buzzing of insects, or whistling that leaves him amazed, floating on a hard and phosphorescent sea. Everything turns out surprisingly logical. Even more, convincing. He likes to listen to the mingled coming and going of sounds, where, very rarely, is inscribed a melodic fragment; syncopated, like a parody. "Much more agreeable than any organized symphony or melody." He lets himself be rocked, voluptuously, in the swarm of sounds: wandering, like an insect. "I feel exactly that," he devotes a kind smile to the ceiling, "an insect around the light, stupefied, rocked, comforted and relaxed." Above all, relaxed. He is living in an organized tiredness; perhaps lodging in him, from his most distant instincts, up to the concrete and palpable point of his feet. At times, in this tiredness, he believes that he feels in peace with something or with someone. As one who fulfills some law, handed down form the highest and unknown branches, uninterruptedly. On occasions like this (smoking in silence, rocking back and forth in some sound or in some emptiness) he supposes that his extended tiredness (much older than his age) is not an easy and banal tiredness but a very elaborate and thought-out state to which the babbling of other very primitive beings lead, generating him, from one to the other. A tiredness, he conceded, finally, through branches and branches more or less busy or preoccupied; and in it he, Bear, lies, deposited (like the sediment of this poorly strained coffee), on the bottom of the cup. It is not a fatigue which is

rapidly achieved. It can only be attained after much waiting, boredom, uncertainty. "I am, sieved, strained, what is left." The ash
falls on his chest, and he becomes aware that he has not smoked,
that his cigarette wasted away by itself.

It turned out to be paradoxical, almost humorous, entering
Mario's world by way of Uncle Borja.

When he finished his studies in W. High School, he was seventeen. Beverly gave him the Dodge as a gift, and everything
seemed to happen without excessive complications. He was always careful not to set himself apart from the others, neither in
good nor in evil. To be like everybody, not offering any bothersome evidence of thoughts and desires was, generally, the attitude most recommended. Once he was on the point of becoming
an idol because of baseball. But he stopped in time. He liked to
walk alone, among the oaks and sycamores that surrounded the
College, to love lightly (better, to let himself be loved lightly), to
speak of just what was necessary (better, what was indispens-
able). In fragments, treading on the yellow leaves with which
the autumn invaded the ground, he reconstructed a diffuse, lost
feeling that, perhaps, had a great deal to do with the origin of
indifference (but it was not possible to specify and Bear abandoned the idea.) It is not very advisable to dwell in the foggy
past—even in such a recent past as seventeen years can offer—.
He returned to F., to Beverly, to Grandfather Franc and to his
University: to the squirrels and the maples; to the garden shining
under the sun. He felt comfortable in F. He did not share the
obsession of so many companions that fled frenetically from their
place of birth and enrolled in Universities the farther away the
better. It would not have mattered greatly to him to enroll in the
University of F. (that would always be for Bear Franc's University, in spite of the fact that Grandfather Franc constituted but a
tiny cog, without any importance, in the great machination—).
"Perhaps," he thought, "it is a question of some atavism." Also
Franc was different from his companions and from most of his
compatriots. They ran, without respite, from University to University, panting from Department to Department, from state to
state. They crossed from East to West, like packs of hunting dogs:

astute, farsighted, hopeful and exhausted. Bear remembered Franc, disoriented, in the last MLA convention (the famous "Slave Market"). Pushed by Beverly, he debated with himself in his room in the Sheraton, drunk from telephone calls, from martinis, from "appointments," "Papers," and "Reports," dizzy, disoriented by offers, insinuations, confidences, visits, intrigues…Poor Grandfather Franc, staggering at the exit of the Oak Room, clutching Bear's arm, saying to him: "Let's go home, Bear." "Casa." (Home did not have a translation, upon becoming acquainted with the hearths of this Homeland) It was already, only, the office of his beloved Spanish Department, the beloved Campus of scarlet and gold autumns; the beloved chattering, intranscendent and comfortable, with Beverly (rigorously programmed beforehand, of course), the great friend, and already the only woman friend. Bear smiles at the memory. "Will I be like Franc, perhaps? I never felt like wandering; I am sedentary." But he is not in love. He did not love F., he does not love the Tulip Trees, he did not love any country nor any woman. He will never love anything, or anybody. His affections are honorably reasonable, bearable.

But one day Franc (he must say Grandfather Franc, "why did they all call him Franc?" Including his daughter-mama-including himself, they call him simply Franc. With Beverly it was different: it would bother Beverly beyond measure that he should call her Grandmother), one day, then, Grandfather Franc revealed his secret that he had long dreamed about. At times, in his memory, Bear regains the recondite trembling of his voice upon pronouncing the name of this country. In those moments Bear recovers the strange, inner mysterious direction that forced him to listen in silence (although without believing in his words, nor in his feelings, nor in his ideas). Carried away by diffuse, languid curiosity; by a blurred respect that no one would tolerate profaning. Just the idea that someone could smile at Franc's words—of Grandfather Franc—made him keep at a distance (from the plain house of white painted wood, from the little garden with two single oak trees), all his friends and acquaintances or companions. Just the idea that someone could smile, even tenderly, at the words (inane, absolutely deprived of sense) of Grandfather

Franc, would have brought him coldly, consciously, to murder. Nevertheless, Bear does not love Grandfather Franc either.

The secret cherished year after year by Grandfather Franc was revealed one Sunday morning in the garden, next to the oak-tree. Grandfather Franc asked him, once more, what was his vocation, what were his plans. But Bear understood that this time was the time (not as when he was ten and Franc laughed so much on hearing him answer: Nothing, I do not want to be anything when I grow up). When he insisted on "what did he intend to do in this life," Bear knew (because, even though it appeared practically impossible to understand older people, Bear understood Grandfather Franc as no one else understood him: neither mother, nor even Beverly, who loved him so secretly), he knew that for Grandfather Franc to do something in this life could not be separated, in any way, from some university activity or other. And as he well knew (and he was still the same old Bear, the one who cut frogs into bits and permitted, with absolute docility, that they clean the blood from his fingers), he saw at that moment, on the little table in the garden, on the beautiful and damp lawn, carefully cut by Grandfather Franc, a magazine where one found out about great architectural projects, impressively photographed, referring to the new and dazzling city of Houston. Bear said: "Architect." Grandfather Franc said: "Good." It was perfectly fine, anything whatever (within the university world) would have been all right. Bear knew it that Sunday morning. And now, too, he knew it, in the slipcovered house where—evidently—Mother had been born; and he knew something else: I will be a good architect. (In the same way he knew that he would have been a good whatever; anything whatever seized at random, on a table, or under an oak, at the moment of the question: "What are you going to be in life...?) That morning he answered Grandfather Franc and looked somewhere over his white head (that did not bother Grandfather Franc, as much as it bothered them.) He was, at this moment, contemplating the leaves of the oak tree, when grandfather Franc unveiled his old and cherished desire. When he spoke to him about all that: of going back to the Homeland— how can one go back to a place where one has never been before?—to validate previous studies and to enroll in an unknown University, in a distant country, in a distant language? (Nothing. I don't want to be anything, he thought, and only that, staring at the oak tree.) But he did not feel any rebellion. The now known rebellion had not arrived yet, not by a long shot. Since that morning when, looking at the oak tree over Grandfather Franc's white head, he secretly communicated to the leaves his absent vocation. What an uncontrollable time those two years appeared to hold!

Grandfather Franc entered his sabbatical year. Propitious year (apparently) for Bear to know old Europe. (The Europe Beverly "did" every two years, for three or four weeks. The Europe of Beverly's photos, Beverly smilingly superimposed on cathedrals, bridges, towns that seem to her as burned by torrid catastrophe.) There, in Franc's intimate and self forbidden country, in Franc's secret and frightful land (where, for now, I will not return), Bear was supposed to study, Bear was supposed to live. What was that thing, the Homeland?

Grandfather Franc's oak-tree is no longer here. When he speaks, Bear no longer looks over the other person's head. Bear does not have a Homeland, Bear does not have friends, Bear does not have (for a very long time) Paradise. He never called anyone Puppy again: he carefully excluded this possibility. Although the so-called Homeland might be waiting for him, for Bear. This was what Grandfather Franc said; but Grandfather Franc did not cross the frontier. He was growing old stubbornly, in the boundary of his country, sabbatical year after sabbatical year, and was astonished and indignant that others who were (or had been) like him, were separating themselves slowly from his side, like the fallen leaves of an implacable autumn, of a clinging obstinacy. Stubborn, beautifully undaunted, he contemplated how others were separating themselves, gently and inexorably, from the austere branches: they returned, they even bought parcels of land from a forbidden and beloved country. They even wanted to die in it, to disintegrate in it, forgotten, melancholically docile (perhaps indifferent). Ashes of an old and extinguished hearth, they returned, they came back: like reasonable, false and late young men, disposed to begin again, to forget, all together. Anger (his only anger) then shone in Grandfather Franc's black eyes. Bear observed him, saw him withdraw, more and more, an elusive and tight island, far out in the sea. An island that backed away in some sunset, splendid and ultimate; behind the sun, an island of a day that was already only memory. Deeply wounded, remote in life, symbol of some old, heroic and inconclusive battle; his hand raised, clutching the ebony cane, threatening (no longer to men, but to a time) because not everyone has a grandson whom he can send, like a challenge, like a warning, like a cry that reminds one: I have not yet died off. Bear saw himself, then, like a dusty, defeated and loyal banner of some unshared contest.

Here in this line, on the edge of these words and of this desire, Bear's understanding brusquely stopped. He does not yet achieve deciphering that delivery of which he is the object, the message-challenge of which he is the object by the man who has forbidden himself the ultimate possible happiness. Those words, and that contradictory challenge, proves to be "too much Grandfather Franc" for him.

They travelled together to Europe and Mother met them in Paris. They crossed frontiers, went through cities, peoples, languages, cathedrals, museums, stones, trees, rivers, misery, splendor, history, meanness, death. One night, Bear returned—but how could he return to where he had never been either in his thoughts, or in spirit, or even in understanding?—He crossed the frontier in dispute, at the end of which, an old man (suddenly extraordinarily similar to an oak tree) held back, his cane in the air, the unforgivable, immodest tears. He crossed the line of the ultimate and stubborn dignity of Franc, under the rainy November sky; on a night train, full of creaks, next to my distracted mother, indisposed, surrounded by magazines and useless squabbling.

Bear arrived at the old city, the old house where only the slipcovered furniture was waiting for him. At the place where he now found himself rooted, an unquestionable element in the framework of a net which he no longer desires to break. Bear smiles at his memories as he would at a playmate who is difficult to recognize. It was difficult for a boy accustomed to speak secretly with oak trees and sycamores, to enter the new land. There were exhausting days, strange like a skin which does not belong to us, eyes that do not look at us with our eyes, an understanding that does not fit in with our understanding. A concept of the world, of men, different from our concept of life and of the beings that breathe in it. Bear started out, in a mute stupor, on the discovery of an alien world, absolutely different, absolutely foreign.

A little after arriving he took part, in silence, in complicated plans, vast cities of words, of which he alone was the inhabitant. At breakfast time, in the city where Mother and Uncle Borja met by chance (Mother and Uncle Borja repeated a thousand times their jokes of former children who, grown old, meet again and who do not seem eager to forget that childhood passes, or, even worse, breaks down, foul-smelling, like one more cadaver), he said: "I would need someone, a guide, a person who would orient me during these months, before enrolling." His own words were already lost, too, in the uproar of setbacks and advances, of memories and worn-out jokes—jokes monstrously infantile in beings who already exceeded forty, ignorant of the short duration of tenderness—. Under the downpour of recommendations and plans, in the splendid future that for the young Bear (who is going "to rejoin our Homeland") exploded all around him. Bear closed his eyes, softly, gently (over the delicate aroma of orange marmalade, above the torrid and thick brew that in the Mediterranean they drank for coffee; over the pale sunlight that lay on the tablecloth and already foretold a raw and damp season, in spite of the fact that the city boasted of a warm and mild winter; Bear closed his eyes or, at least, half-closed them, over the tablecloth (carefully washed, ironed and hand-embroidered). A question he withheld danced in his question; in his ears, in his eyes; it made its way through his memories, through phrases he had heard before. ("A hand-embroidered tablecloth for what reason?") Apparently uncle Borja was aware of all his fears, doubts or hopes. He said: "Of course, naturally. I'll fix it.")

Validate my studies. Enter the School of Architecture. Someone Who Might Orient Me, Seventeen, Almost Eighteen years old, Homeland, I Don't Know Anyone, I Don't Want To Be Anything.... The world has turned itself into a succession of shell-like phrases, absolutely empty. Bear felt himself to be a cloud, an indifference he had regained—and he recognized it, the indifference, as he recognized, at times, a solitary tree, or a house on the line of the horizon—.

To be precise, the old world appeared to him to be dirty and small.

In reality, not even Uncle Borja knew Mario. He knew Enrique, because Enrique was "Fernando's boy." In his imagination, Bear could have been able to reconstruct his conversation in the Club, on any morning, before setting out for the ocean. Uncle Borja's friends must suffer from the same love of the sea as he: if not, they would not be able to be his friends. He said it once, clearly: the ocean was the only way that could unite him to another human being, lead him to whatever affection or friendship. Undoubtedly—he could not deny it—it was the ocean also that united the two of them. In spite of everything, Bear had to admit this fragile and special understanding. "Bear, you belong to a race of sailors." Bear knew the touch of a disquieting, perhaps bothersome pride. But real. "Bear, you belong to a race of sailors." A few days later Uncle Borja said: "Ah, for sure, you now have the person you are looking for: he will orient you, guide you, as you say—whenever he referred to Bear's words or the words of anyone not yet over thirty, Uncle Borja stressed with an incomprehensible irony: "as you say." He is a good person, I believe that he is an assistant professor at the University. He's been helping a lot Enrique (Fernando's boy) who failed twice in a row. With those classes, he helps support himself; because, you understand, don't you, they are proud people, without money... I believe that he is preparing for competitive exams or something like that and, on top of everything, he is supporting his sick mother. Well, Fernando's boy is delighted. I even think they are friends..." How strange that explanation sounded to Bear, how strange that kind of talking. Uncle Borja gave him a card, a telephone number. "Here, call Enrique. He'll bring you up to speed."

This is the way it was, in an anodyne way, almost stupid, how he entered into the only stage in his life that made sense.

In This City

She smiled, thinking: "Happiness is a word invented by some sadist so that we all might feel damnably unhappy. She was calmly smoking, stretched out, pretending to look at the ceiling. When, in reality, she felt herself a spy, her own self a pure, living ambush.

She contemplated Mario from the corner of her eye. He was quiet, not even smoking as he did at other times. Immobile, with his eyes closed, as though dead. Isa pulled the sheet up to her neck. She felt an ancestral modesty after love, she could not avoid the idea that love, when all is said and done, was an immodest act. Someone had told her—years ago, obviously—that this modesty came from very far back, from the expulsion from Paradise ("and they covered themselves because they saw themselves naked," etc.) She no longer believed in Adam and Eve, but the same words, the same concepts, continued to ferment at the bottom of her conscience.

Mario continued with his eyes closed, surprisingly young for his age. No one would have thought that he was thirty and some— "nearer to forty than thirty—." No one would give him more than twenty-eight. But he did show that he was tired: of her, of living, of himself." Who knows, perhaps he is thinking of another woman. Shakespeare says: green eyed monster. Green or of a nasty color, nevertheless a monster. Why does jealousy exist? This jealousy that I drag along, provincial jealousy like all that eats me up. She sighed, almost softly. "But everyone is more or less provincial. And, after all is said and done, what importance does it have? I'm provincial. OK I'm full of faults, of eagerly crammed together prejudices, and, on top of that, an army person's orphan. Nothing is lacking in the lots: but I have escaped from my surroundings, I have arrived at the city I dreamed about (there is a film called that, I believe), and although I am not especially educated, I can trust my intuition. I am astute, and (a quality not too often found) I know myself. Not like this poor

Mario, who knows it all, except about living, about knowing himself. Not me. I know what I am, I know my slow reflexes: I am limited, but profound in what I know. Because of these things I'll dominate you. If I were not domineering, I would not have you, and I was born to have you. I want you, just the way you are, weak and doubtful, young-old, a born loser. But not with me: I belong to those who twist destinies, to those who change life and turn it inside out, like a sock. I shall win out, I always win out, although at times I remain raging. Mario belongs to me, Mario belongs to me. I will make his life, and I fabricate mine everyday. The world does not belong to the weak, theoretical, vulnerable, intelligent Marios. The world belongs to the mediocre and the strong, like me. I do not deceive myself, I know how to face up to the mirror, I know myself, I know how to attack myself, how to attack others. Mario is mine, and no cause, woman, or anything else will take him away from me, because no one has my strength. I have invented myself, Isa, for Mario, for him I have patiently fabricated my personality; in order that he might want to be with me, although he may not love me. Mario will not love anyone, ever. He can't. Mario, you know that it is difficult to fight against people like me. We are like vinegar, always floating on the surface.

Now the landscape of childhood, of past youth, remains far away, very far away. Stretched out alongside the man in whom all that is desirable in the world has come together, Isa rids herself of all that seemed to her to be her clear destiny: a destiny bent over, extorted by her will and rebellion. The little Isa remains far away "fruit of a contradictory bringing up" (she laughs lightly and crushes the cigarette butt in the white ashtray, Martini and Rossi, on the side table with circular stains from the glasses). And the interrupted studies (for lack of economic means) are now forgotten, the dreams of greatness, the banal and disordered excess of readings, the censured films, the boyfriend. Dark entry ways, damp benches in the park, the scarcity of money, the river, wine in pubs, melancholy disguised as hope. She had acquired a certain bad reputation in the small town. "Always, of course, within propriety." She was not a whore, she was only shameless. That gave her personality, and she felt, in this way, Europeanized. She could give her opinion with sharpness, smoke in the streets (well, only the butt when leaving the local bar when it closed), let herself be easily kissed. How far away all that now, from this stupidly shameful room.

(Now the Two Old Ladies, in the city she dreamed about, offer, along with their hospitable selfishness, their modest greatness in ruins, an excessively long apartment, with rusty plumbing, cockroaches, and frozen tile floors in winter; glass enclosed balconies, urns, niches or beehives; rocking chairs, broken window panes patched together with Band Aids and scotch tape; display of articles of underwear over the courtyards, and chimneys, and water tanks where the maids celebrate their street parties on summer nights, with little paper lanterns. In the living room, a piano, out-of-tune for years, pictures painted by the former girls of the household, signed from the Sacred Heart School; ancient velvet, three-legged stands, mysterious and lying in wait in the corners; smiles of children who have disappeared, in the frieze of the extinguished chimney (with a surprising planter of modernist porcelain, there, where the fire was supposed to burn); but "it is dangerous, the butane stove is better." At the back of the drawer, a yellowing bonnet. "Ah yes, poor Sofia, you see, she never married because she did not want to abandon us. There are not any more maids like her." Little porcelain shoes with important dates on the sole, Rachel powder in the glass of the bathroom, covered with little Richelieu doilies. As it grows dark, a cat howls in the courtyard: it knows that a package with the viscera of some warm and simple animal will cross the space, from the glass-enclosed balcony, down to the red tiles; an unexpected maritime siren flees in the damp twilight: Isa remembers that the sea is near, there, behind her. Pussycats with greasy, thick hair devour intestines, hearts, livers, horrible necks. The wind has already lifted the ash from all the laurel trees, the world is now becoming bigger, like an enormous crocodile, with its open jaws; no longer floats a single speck of the dreams, the plans, of a girl who had a boyfriend, because she did not have anything better to have.)

Leaning on the handrail of the bridge, over the Ebro, a distant
Isa succumbed to the vapors of a bad tavern wine that is falsely
typical, where the decent high school girls, pretty and with boy-
friends, (on condition that they return home before the front door
closed). All of that was already five years ago. Already five years,
and all that was over with. Like five new lives, frighteningly different. The sky of this other city is enormous, red over the confines of the avenues; and it has nothing to do with the twilights in
Rey Sancho Street, nor with the Plaza de Independencia, nor with
the Parque de los Infantes. Now the sky, smooth, hard like a foreign face, scarcely strewn with stars (the sky is almost never looked
at) often turns out ironic. Other things exist under the sky of this
city. Some evenings appear to be years long, certain days, seconds. Youth is something ephemerous, bitter and intense (not a
humiliating wait). The heart, a furious weight. Fear, a religion.

Mario has fallen asleep in a scarcely sure sleep, a subtle breathing lifts his chest. "Mario is young, he will always be young."
Isa contemplates the head of dark blond curls, tawny, like a lion's,
"that twist at the roots." He could have the head of a Saint John
or a young tiger: "so thick and soft, if he did not cut it short," she
thought with sour tenderness. And even so, his touch is like that
of the little tiger of her infancy, warm, ambiguous. His eyes are
lightly slanted, his cheek bones high, his mouth sensual and awk-
ward. Mario sleeps very lightly. Isa thinks that Mario never truly
sleeps; he is always like this: alert and distrustful, incredulous,
insecure, sad and young. Irritation grows in Isa when she sees
him sleeping. Once more she rediscovers his body ("not beautiful according to standards," she smiles to herself). But all of him
is like a penetrating summons through the bed clothes. His clear
skin ("not white"), made golden by a few freckles ("like a young
leopard, but how tacky this is…")

She, too, has freckles. There, in the city of her childhood, to
be redheaded and freckled proved to be out of the ordinary. Something that set her aside for better or for worse. "What a shame, so
freckled, why don't you try some product or other?" Jacinto, on
the other hand, had confessed: "When I saw you like that, with
so many freckles, I liked you immediately." Jacinto, the boy-

friend. "Jacinto, what luck, such a good kid." "Men, you know…"
But she does not know anything, nobody knows anything, one
only knows what one really desires. "One can live, possibly, far
from here, in some place." (He said it once, that, the hideous boy
the girls from the high school laughed at; they called him the
poet, she did not know why, she had no information that he had
written a single verse, she had never seen him write anything
else than class notes; his nose grazing the paper, without glasses,
poor.) Meanwhile, Mother: "I don't want to find you again in the
entryway with your boyfriend, aren't you ashamed? Just like a
maid. Don't you have any dignity?" And later: "People already
know what happens: the man is like straw, the woman like tow,
the devil arrives and fans the fire." But that was more than a
vulgarity, it was a lie. Neither tow nor devil, nor anything else.
Jacinto had a black mustache, in order to resemble many other
men, in order to be almost like them. Since he was very virile,
and he did not like to show off, he combed his hair back, wetting
it, without looking in the mirror (that is the way he went around,
poor guy.) I used to say to him: "Jacinto, look at your hair in the
back, it stands up like a handle, you look like a pot." But he
smiled self-assured (because he was very manly): "Woman, why
would I pay attention to that, what importance does it have?" Isa
was embarrassed that their friends could see him with that tuft of
hair, stiff and curved, on top of his head. She would have willingly slapped it down: Jacinto was a little bit shorter than she.
His stature was, truly, mortifying.

Isa turns her head towards the wall. It is in those moments
that she feels the past and the present to be intertwined: and everything has a mysterious connection with Mario. All her memories are, suddenly, tied to him, even justified in him. Everything
seems to keep its recondite reason by virtue of Mario's existence. "My most distant memories are incoherent, but well-defined. I keep clearly outlined in my memory a Japanese lamp—
I suppose an imitation—hanging from the center of the ceiling,
with a pink and gold light; and I feel on my cheek someone's
breath, a feminine breath (perhaps my mother, or the nurse) that
mumbles and hisses imperceptibly, pleasantly. I inhale a deep

sensation of well-being, sensation of light sleep which, afterwards, in later years, I have longed for. For example, when in
solitude and desperation I fell ill, and someone lit a subdued light,
a lamp covered with a newspaper and, through the shining light,
a protective vapor reached me. I'm sorry to suppose that, during
many years, in the most arid stages of my life, in the most daring
also, when I felt myself to be strong and toughened, the only
thing that I really yearned for was to feel protected by someone,
or something. I had already given up my religious beliefs—never
excessively fervent to tell the truth—that brought a certain relief; like the intimate conviction that, after all, someone was
watching over my acts, good or bad. A thing which, definitely,
protected me from solitude. Because I have learned well that
human beings are not accustomed to keep each other company.
Almost no one knows what it is to feel accompanied, even though
many times one may fabricate that ephemerous shadow, the doubtful happiness of believing ourselves to be someone. Marriage
enters fully into this state of things. A woman like me, absurdly
brought up—if the case is that I was brought up in some way—
arrives too late at these conclusions. Mario often says that my
country, my world are harsh and dogmatic: fervently ignorant. It
is strange that, at times, as now, while looking at that wall, I have
the impression of being present at a slow and very cruel death-
throe. I do not love my land, but I feel tied to it in an unavoidable
way; I am part of it, of its insulating mountains, of its poor rivers, of its great names. A woman like me, in this country, has
little to do. Solitude and ignorance are its natural patrimony."

Jacinto was shorter than she. "You are going to be a little too
tall." Naturally, therefore, in a city of shorties, a girl like her "did
not have much choice." Isa contemplates her long legs, her soft
skin and (a phrase heard and read), as though powdered with
saffron. She jumps from the bed and goes toward the mirror, she
looks at her shoulders, her belt, perhaps a little too high ("especially now, when the fashion is to have it low") above bony hips
like a boy. Isa feels a childish pride in her long thighs, her knees,
her ankles ("which, like the wrists and forearms, I inherited from
the good and ancient blood of my mother.") On the other hand,

the military man left her the too closely knit eyebrows, her red
hair, her wide domineering, almost masculine mouth ("I am pretty,
but it would not matter if I were not. I would know how to appear so. I'm satisfied with my appearance.") Isa evokes other
words, already dead, balancing in a distant wind: "A little too
tall, don't you think? Well, for a woman…," her cousin Felisa
used to say, her cousin famous for her porcelain-like skin, in the
city by the river that flowed indifferently, between shady fields,
bars, houses of faded color and narrow windows, cannaries and
ears of corn in the sun. Ah, even in those days, her city did not
accept feminine youth with narrow hips, stuffed with vitamins.
And the men (the word "man" had a special echo between the
palate and the teeth of mothers) were there just as the knowing
matrons would define with acquiescence: "of middle height."
The girls, "cuties," or "darlings," or "poor thing, a horror, but
that's the way it is with a heart from here to there, and, moreover,
what a brain! A stand out, with scholarly distinctions; it's too
bad the brother did not work out this way…" "A horror." "Poor
thing." "But, to be sure, with such hands! Did you see the tablecloth set that she embroidered for the charity raffle?…" And she,
Isa, lost in a sinful world of window panes set on fire by the last
sun, lost in one more day that escaped in the waters of the Ebro,
under the bridge with its five spans, towards a distant sea. (That
only now appeared to be real on maps.) "You can't wear heels,
of course, with Jacinto as a boy friend…" There was a great,
immense dejection in her voice. Jacinto was a boy friend, and a
boy friend was the best she could do in those days, in that place
("Look, if you gain a little weight here and there, apart from that,
girl, you look very good; I find your style terrific; wish that I
were like you; listen, I'll give you what I have left over and you
will give me what I need, eh? ha, ha, ha." The pool, with its too
blue water, opened secretly, alongside a river that panted in summer like a stray dog. "Girl, you're not so skinny in a swim suit.
Look, I'll tell you what, you should always go around like that,
very sporty." "But you really have a good figure, girl, who would
have guessed it! Terrific. Only the feet a tiny bit big but, of course,
with your height, it would be unusual, wouldn't it? How well

you comb your hair, really, and you wash it at home and, go on, it's done. Gee, girl, me, on the other hand, I go every four days to the shop and there is no comparison!" "You know, the German guy said you very pretty, but really, those foreigners like them that way, really skinny, don't you believe it…" Jacinto was shivering from the cold in the entryway. (His skin, too white, his eyes, too handsome, his unforgettable mustache, black, silky, trimmed.) "Tomorrow, at four, at the usual place…or better, no, now that I remember, the dentist has given me an appointment, better when I am done, around six…but not in the bar, you know, I'm broke, better at our bench…" Everything that was ours was: the bench, the poplar tree, the bend in the river; in short, any place where something had happened there for the first time (something that in a short while had left her already as though buried, impervious). Ours, in a soft and demanding voice, falsely sweet, the voice of a future husband who is not going to agree that his wife should work, because he is more of a man than all that. ("But he wasn't, he was just a little man.") With his grey vest woven by his absent and loving mother, the wife of a county judge who sent him interminable and invariable letters: "don't do anything rash, write me if you have received the sausage, the town is very lively, really, here too we have fun, the people from the Company have come, you don't know the kind of life that we have here now, and the engineer's little girl, you don't know how cute she is." Meanwhile, the rain, in heavy drops, showed roughly on the dust, next to the wooden bench. The stationery was lined; four sides in green ink. Behind a tree, a boy with sinister, pleasurable eyes, was killing something, someone: his fingers were trembling on a yellow, plastic machine gun, his throat tightened. "Why can't one feel grief, or indignation, why does one want now only one thing: to give up, to flee?" To kill, perhaps, like what that boy is doing. "Let's kill all the desires on earth, boy, while the little man in the handwoven vest, candidate for notoriety, without eccentricity, owner of a decent and well-trimmed mustache, trembles from the cold, inside the embroidered clothes. They say: "He is good-looking"; they say: "And those eyes!" Yes, of course he has them, what is the big deal.

"He'll make a good husband." "He's serious." "He'll get ahead, that one." Yes, he'll get ahead because Uncle Edward has said that "as soon as he finishes…" Meanwhile, in the inside pocket of the jacket with leather patches on the elbows ("Listen, they look good in addition to being practical."), Mother's lined paper is outlining a madly, stupid life, obscenely insipid, inhumanly happy. "No, no. I'm leaving here…" The serious little man had (in the dark entryway where only the maids can amuse themselves) modestly lubricious moments of ecstasy. ("The man is straw, the woman, etc…") "He's short for a girl like me, he is three months younger than I, he still has two years to finish his degree. And then, who knows for how many more years he will wait for Uncle Edward's influential generosity; and, afterwards, what? To stand all this in order finally to get married? For what reason? Why? But days passed like centuries, the years, like seconds. "I don't want hanging around in the entryway: it's already time to let him come upstairs so that he can speak with your father…" And, on another day, and another: "You've already heard me: it's the last time I'm saying so, girl. If that boy has serious intentions…" It's the last time I'm saying so, the last time…!) But the truth is that no one has heard anything for the last time in this town…" That "speak with your father" was cut short by her father's death. Dad was dead, they had taken him to the Campo del Este. He was under the ground. It was raining and the wind (a horrible November wind) shook the lines of the flat roof where they hung out the clothes; they produced a vibrating noise that penetrated the bones. Dad had finally died.

Isa returns from the mirror, stretches out next to the man who appears carried away by a modest, reasonable death. His pride already beats without conviction. A faint pride of an objective that was reached too late. And moreover: "Is this the real objective?" Isa turns her eyes towards a sleeping Mario, or a Mario pretending to be asleep. He now has only one sentinel, inflexible and merciless, whose name is Isa. She is already his own guardian. Desolate, overwhelmingly alone in the middle of the room, the memory of an imitation Japanese lantern ("possibly paper") returns; on her cheek, the murmur of an old song.

Three Days of Love

It was not only from the house that I left. I left each piece of furniture, each window, each blade of grass which surrounded it. I left all that and I will always go around fleeing from there from that day. All my acts are summed up in a dreadful flight; because what truly impelled me and hurled me was fright. The fear that possessed me since an autumn morning which nothing nor anybody will erase.

I have lost my old future and I have not been granted a new one: I only float in the present moment. I maintain a rare feeling of survival, of a rescued shipwreck, wrapped up in a blanket and shivering; among drunken sailors who try to revive me, handing the bottle to one another; trying, too, to bring my swollen, bluish lips to the neck of the bottle. Who is going to revive me? A group of discontented boys, pure, unsatisfied? Perhaps desiring vague adventure only? All youth awaits the adventure of life; and some (like me at their age) managed to plan an adventure of justice, of coordination, of responsibility. To make a tabula rasa is an inborn juvenile ideal. But I am still on board, and have not brought my lips to the bottle: as if at the bottom of my consciousness a voice were calling out: "Why do they all take the trouble to make me breathe again? Let me alone, let me flee, alone, from that house, from this present door which is curiously painted pink, with plaster angels. Or aren't they angels? They are disgraceful, nude young ladies, who are trying to awaken an erotic climate, under this red light, these cleverly tilted mirrors, this side table with glass stains. There is here the echo of a sour drunkenness which begins to recede. Poor Isa, in front of the mirror. What do you expect of me? It will be better if you begin to understand it: nothing. You are now like the boys, like carnivorous puppies, thirsty for a cruel affirmation, for something more than inefficient orders and words, more than meetings, than hunger or smile strikes. Your eyes ask for, always ask for, something more. You believe that this affirmation will come from me. Bear especially. Poor Bear, timing comings and goings, looking for a refuge for your empty child's heart. Twenty years old. Only twenty. ("They are already used to me in the Club. We have gone out to the beach many times. When my uncle takes the plane for Palma, everything will be ready, agreed on...") If he is not capable of pronouncing such a long sentence, at least, by dint of short sentences, he has made himself understood. Why this thirst for blood? They have never seen blood the way I have seen it, they do not understand what my justice can become. It is iniquitous, sinister, converting into something personal, something conceptually as important as the word Justice.

I, in truth, have seen blood: exiles, biblical curses, nothing has changed for the people since the time when their sons passed, in chains, along the walls, under the cruel gaze of the conqueror, the conquistadores, the protestors, the civilizers... What do the names mean? The merchants are always the same, protected by any clothing. I have walked among those men who have cruel lips and now, only now, a curious rebellion arises in me, not recognized among so many rebellions: the rebellion to survive once more, to survive, still, once more.

Why do you look at yourself in the mirror, Isa? You are not going to be more beautiful for that, nor for all that am I going to want you again. I suppose that at some time I wanted you. But that moment is already very far away. It will not return. I'm not the man for you. There are men who do things and men who commit them, men who talk and men who denounce, men who remain silent and men who speak. (I remember that child who drew near that day; barefoot, alone, with a stick in his hand [he appeared another day on which, being very young, I believed him to be chosen for the birth of fright.] The child without shoes was nearer, I could observe that the rod was of hazelnut wood, to beat things: corners and flowers above all. The child [he was not old enough to be good or bad] laughed with his mouth closed. He was looking up, his throat trembling through laughter. Since he was a child he could punch as much as he wanted, as he pleased.

Everything that he might want: without guilt, without reason, without fear, without expecting anything after his blows. He could hit as much as he felt like it: cries of pain, evil, stupidity, tears, inhibitions. He could beat everything because he was only a little boy, with a stick in his hand. But I was mistaken. When he was alongside me I was able to realize that the child was not laughing at anything. Rather he appeared worried by something.)

The profound knowledge of a human being is not usually agreeable. Isa, if I were not pretending to be sleeping (in order not to hear your voice) I could say to you "please, get away from the mirror." Solitude, vast and varied, is not to be so disdained as you imagine. I have known people worried by going so far as to destroy, by subduing those invincible barriers. I have always contemplated with amazement those pathetic and belated efforts. For what reason, Isa? There is no reason to throw bridges from island to island, from continent to continent; there is no reason to cover the world with a sinister lattice of prison-like communications. Knowledge of a human being is not pleasant. It is not good to carry love to the extreme limits, to get suffocatingly involved in love, to convert curiosity into love, discouragement into love. Our intimate and miserable disdain, into love. It will become curiosity, discouragement, disdain. The waves will return. No one has the right to destroy or reveal certain things. To love is possible, for example (for example, why don't you try to love me this way?), from island to island; contemplating the sea that is usually beautiful (according to what I hear) even in the winter. To love is possible without going around with hooks to take the guts out of another human being; without cutting him into pieces or pulling his guts out into the light. Entrails which, on the other hand, will keep on being mixed up, horribly mysterious, before our eyes. Children who open up toys to see what's inside usually remain for a while with the face of an idiot.

Wasting Time

Now, on the eve of the so longed for occasion, after his two years experience, it would be good to say to him: "we who waste time are very grateful to you, Uncle Borja." Like a curious and indifferent, almost grateful, gladiator I could greet him and say to him: "I am grateful to you, Uncle Borja: for admitting me to your company, for taking me to you Club (a sacrosanct place, fortress of an ancient juvenile splendor); for going out together on the ocean, in your curious yacht. I am grateful to you for all that, Uncle Borja. Your correction of my mistakes in syntax when I form a sentence the wrong way. ("Cursed Indians!), your made-up companionship, your admiration because I am a good sailor, because, after all, at least you did learn that over there…" Uncle Borja, the Indians know how to navigate: in canoes, down the river; and in boats, across the great lakes." It would have been nice to speak like this sometime with Uncle Borja. Alone with him. Why alone with him? Bear smiles peacefully at his thoughts. Bear's smile comes alone (like some green and golden butterflies, during the night, in solitude, floating around a student's lamp.) Bear would have wanted to break the hard outer surface just in order to say something similar to Uncle Borja.

And many other things, too. Above all when Uncle Borja (with only a little drop of alcohol too much) lectured him, while evidently lacking conviction: "But Bear, you must realize how you are wasting your time. If you want to put the world in order, first you must finish your degree. Then, with a firmer base…"

To put the world in order. How different are these words, although they are the same ones that Grandfather Franc pronounced. To put the world in order, to change the world, they acquired a faded ascetism on the lips of the old man, who walked, between the Louvre and the Seine, in his beloved Paris; a Paris deformed by his dreams (as blows of his black cane on the stones, as a sign of enthusiasm; as in front of a peculiar and blurry engraving, only meaningful to him). In those moments Grandfather Franc was changed into the image of the most innocent, seraphic desolation. "But he can tell all," cried out an unexpected, almost strange voice inside Bear. On the contrary, Uncle Borja would turn moldy (with a little, not even dangerous, acidity) whatever he said. Except when he spoke of the sea or of the ships or of the great lakes…("And on the great lakes…") They would visit them together, in the autumn or in the spring. Chicago and the lakes were, apparently, eagerly recalled. He promised trips, he made plans: then he forgot them, he became attached to an intimate, almost painful fatigue. There was in him, in his words (and in the words which he did not utter) and unapprehended shipwreck, which Bear could not yet gauge. Nor did he speak of the war, as did his friend Fernando. (Uncle Borja had not been in the war either: "Listen, please, Bear, don't think that I'm that old…," he laughed with a totally indecipherable bitterness.)

It was a question of an old rapid launch, with two motors; adapted, repainted, transformed into an unusual and—Bear did not deny it—attractive boat. It had been of use in the Navy, in the last struggle. "You know, when the war was over (I'm talking to you about the European War, not ours, eh?), the Navy sold a lot of them, no longer useful. Generally, smugglers bought them…One of them, in Marseilles to be exact, sold me this one, at a very good price. I really took advantage of it, you see. In all, it cost me almost nothing. But next year, I am going to buy me one…" Uncle Borja spoke of the beautiful, modern, extraordinary boat that he would buy for himself in the coming year. "Of course, much better than Fernando's…" Uncle Borja did things right. But in truth—Bear listened in silence, secretly observed his tanned and refined face, his shining eyes—, Uncle Borja lived in the eternal vigil of successive and uninterrupted "years to come." The coming year (Bear discovered) was no other than the day when his old Grandmother would die. (As when he tried to follow a career in the Navy and gave up after two years. As when he tried to undertake some business deal and desisted. "I know how to wait, Bear. One has to do things right…") Bear was silent, looked out at the sea. They sailed together, often on the "Swordfish" (which, it was fair to admit, Bear was beginning to want.) White, painted and repainted by the sailor Pablo; pampered and photographed ad nauseam; continuously complimented by Uncle Borja. (On the shining waves floated a frayed ghost, it approached Bear's memory: a trivial and distracted confidence by Mother who spoke of a sailing boat which, evidently, an old madman called the "Dolphin.") Ghosts that fled, like sea fire, meandering on gunwales and rigging; strange phosphorescence, a green and legendary St. Elmo's Fire. But which, surprisingly, stood and dominated a life so frivolous and modestly cynical as Uncle Borja's, survivor of some ultimate, authentic, lost Paradise. "The Dolphin." "The Swordfish…" Bear murmured, inside his conscience, amid the shrieking of the gulls; separating himself softly from the quay, from the terrace of the Club, from uncle Fernando and his noisy anecdotes. Bear's eyebrows contracted in his struggle to understand.

As the land and the men remained behind, Uncle Borja was gaining a serenity, even a sadness, infinitely older than all the words pronounced between glasses of wine: between memories, between jokes. Suddenly, out to sea, Uncle Borja shut himself up in a silence only compatible with him: with Bear, the silent one. Forgetting the land, in a wind and a sea that already seemed to belong to them, Uncle Borja and Bear breathed the silence with relief. ("perhaps common," thinks Bear with a certain malaise).

But Bear does not want Uncle Borja's friendship, nor anybody's friendship. And in all that had to do with Uncle Borja floats a decrepit parody: of other beings, of other men, of other struggles, of another sea. (Uncle Borja, inundated by thirst, by spectres; smiling and banal, seems to advance out to sea, towards the only ocean where he could ever navigate.) Bear, in those moments, feels an unaccustomed sensation: something similar to when he saw that fly trapped in a spiderweb. He did not feel sympathy either for the fly or for the spider; only that something was not working right. And with a stick, with blows, he destroyed the fly, the spider and all vestiges of what might have existed.

That same night Uncle Borja will return to Madrid. But everything is underway, perfectly on the right track. And a petulance (consciously juvenile) envelops him, fills him like an unusual balloon; inclined to flee in this sky invaded by spring. Uncle Borja returns to Madrid (where curious emergencies always await him), but: "The same day of the holiday (a soft grunt scarcely apparent, a muzzled irritation in his voice, already well known to Bear) I will take the plane for Palma: you will meet me at the airport and you will have everything underway so that we can depart at dawn." On the terrace (lately so frequented) of the Club, Uncle Borja seems to breathe fully his indolent childhood. "The old world - Bear thinks - seems to be invaded by young-old men"; and he keeps still, looking at the transparent brightness of his orangeade (that brings on so many jokes on the part of his jocose friend Fernando). "Finally," some voice exclaims, somewhere, audible only to Bear. Uncle Borja, still without suspecting it, has entered into the game, he is already captured in the meshing. He is already a little wheel in the delicate watch that patiently, softly, young Bear develops (childish vivisection of frogs). Bear would never have believed he would feel grateful for the birthday of an old woman. And now, just now, on the edge of the great event, it would be good to tell her so: "We who waste time, we who are not grateful for what has been given as a gift by our elders (given as a gift, not earned, not earned), not earned by the sweat of our brow (even though I do not imagine your brow sweating, Uncle Borja, except in the sauna), we are not grateful for all we receive, although it may be much more, even, than the minimal and licit general comfort. (TV, frigidaires, paid vacations, Six Hundred cars, and I believe I'm not forgetting anything of this comforting lot.) Such ungratefulness is especially irritating, because we are not grateful for the most valuable inheritance either: systems and machinery (to say it in a language that is in harmony with it), nor for the words (words like race, secular values, heroism, noble ideals). We do not have a beautiful, sparkling, private ideal. We waste time, truly, faced with your mercantile ideal-society in constant competition, struggle and division. Look at yourself sometime in the mirror, uncle Borja, with honesty (although this word may be strange to you), and contemplate a solitary man crushed by internal competitions, brought down by external competitions, smashed like a nut between the hands of that giant hummer that you have paid taxes to feed; desperate and bored in equal parts, incapable of knowing where your perfect setup of stimuli and fears has taken you. Perhaps we who waste time, the sullen ones, the ungrateful ones, the privileged and discontented children; who waste courses, years (the age of youth is irrecuperable and without a solution, you said on some occasion); and we have received everything from men like you, do we want to be men like you? I am tired beforehand when you ask me: "What is it that you want?" "You are against everything that is established, like trite anarchists? Define yourselves at once!" I feel a vast yawn, perhaps discouragement. Possibly days, months, years would go by if I tried to explain to you something so simple and so evident, so absolutely devoid of myths and complications. And you would not understand it. But it had been a long time—or perhaps forever—since I spoke with people of Uncle Borja's age. In place of telling you these or similar things, in the mornings, in the Club, in the bright spring, he sharpened, outlined his temptation-plan: he would go to Palma on the "Swordfish," with Pablo, the sailor. And, on the following day (at scarcely six or five o'clock in the morning: as soon as possible, in order to calm down the bitter obedience of a poor child-old man terrified by the centenary which mocks his long impatience), Uncle Borja and he (the good Bear who loves the sea) will come back together to the Club (apparently Uncle Borja's vital center). Uncle Borja who did not go to war, who never sailed to legendary islands on a ghostly-and probably inexistent-sailboat called "The Dolphin," will be able to believe himself to be the master of some submissive kingdom, where there might have been room for the faded Paradises of a child who had heard too many romantic stories. Bear smiles, contemplates this man who becomes enthused by his idea; this man who is twice his age and seems to be an unusual little doll making fun of his orangeade while he causes the ice-cubes to make a noise in his tall, innocuous glass. Bear shudders in a sponge-like sensation of power. "A feeling—he recognizes—dangerous in every respect." It is not

necessary to hear the jubilant consent, it is not necessary to listen
to the groundless advice and warnings—preamble to this entic-
ing adventure—in order to see in the brightness of those eyes (as
if reborn from some ferocious, almost aggressive sadness) that
young Bear's watch, so patiently put together, piece by piece,
has begun to function effectively.

Bear does not need anymore to hear the words; now he can
return, in the shining morning, to the soft shade of his solitude.

Also, at the beginning, among the boys, he had the reputation
of being unsociable. Some even believed he was conceited. He
had a good deal of difficulty getting rid of this image. Suddenly
Bear feels (perhaps in his stomach) something like a tug: "The
other boys judge me this way..." "Why, the other boys? Why
this intimate self-segregation?"

The air creases the surface of the sea. Bear stretches out his
legs which, for sometime back, always turn out to be too long.
Under the sun, Uncle Borja's softly weather-beaten skin shows
the remains of an undoubtable beauty battered by use. The corners of his lips, falling lightly down. ("As is rather usual in men
of his generation.") But that is not right. "One must add, of that
generation and that social class." Bear pulled a face at some invisible audience; Gerardo—the delegate of the "non-university
boys" (he so designated intimately the boys with darkened, cal-
loused hands; with irony, where a certain unacknowledged shame
is apparent.) Gerardo is the same age as Uncle Borja, but "Gerardo
does not have the same mannerism, that's it." Gerardo's lips—a
metal worker with black eyes, dull black such as he had never
seen before—are tight lips. As if they had never smiled, as if
they had never touched a stimulating taste.

The tug in his stomach has returned. The contemplation
of Gerardo and Uncle Borja produces in him, paradoxically,
the identical attitude, identical discouragement. That the
world was not working very well, was an old thing, well
known, but..." I wanted to tell you something very simple,
and you would not understand it." (A vague suspicion flows,
like a hidden spring." The suspicion, the uncertainty always
lie around somewhere. If not, even a happy attitude would

have been possible in the morning.

The smell of the sea, dirty from the gasoline next to the boats, rises towards them.

"Raise your head," he hears Uncle Borja say. "I don't know why you always look like this, your heads always down. Of the school of Dean and Brando...How much harm those people have done to us."

The sun hits him in the eyes, he blinks quickly. A pale brilliance trembles on the brim of the glass. Uncle Borja takes a sip, leans his head sideways slightly. From the unfastened collar of his shirt slips out, in clean languor, a bow of dark silk; and, on it, unsuitably, his Adam's apple moves while he drinks. The wind carries the smell of his lotion and Bear passes his hand over the point of his chin: he has not shaved. Uncle Borja does not tell him so: he makes him notice it, in a mute, penetrating form. Bear then says:

"I have not seen any of those films. I'm only twenty."

Uncle Borja's look, on occasions such as these, is very furtive, with lightning-like rapidity, it could be said: "The hatred of the entire earth fits such a glance," Bear thinks. And, to his regret, he trembles. He had not seen such hatred even in Gerardo's eyes. "I have just called him old," he understands. He looks for a palliative phrase, but that phrase does not exist; or, he does not know it.

Uncle Borja runs a finger, very softly, between the collar of his shirt and his skin. A gesture which one could take for a remote, sharpened, beheading. Bear sees him advance, cross the terrace. Erect, his height stretched to the maximum, which (as his only defect) should have required three centimeters more. "Just the way he walks and appears, he is almost younger than I," Bear meditates, finishing off his orangeade. "Much younger than Luis and Enrique and, of course, infinitely younger than Gerardo."

But it is always stupid to come back to Gerardo. To return, like a subdued animal, to the uneasy state, where surroundings do not appear clearly outlined. To return, always, to the memory of Gerardo and the others, "those who are not university boys..."

Diary in Disorder

It seems that I lost my voice one morning. I do not know in what month, nor in what year. I only remember the sun, the light, enveloping the earth; the bare stones of the earth, like vile fangs of some invisible wrath. It seems to me that I was on a beach—there is always a beach in my memories, in my life—; and it was the light which gave back a voice, hidden, studded like a night. But it was not a beach; it was a vast plain and I was drinking a martini, at a "Luncheon"; and it was not in the morning: it was almost at night. The excess of light converted the day into a dull black. It is possible that I could recover that voice, in flashes, in minutes, or years. But I understood that the silence was not exclusively mine, that all life alongside me had grown from silence to silence.

(I have the clear recollection of finding myself seated on a terrace, above a land that was slightly terraced. I know that the wind had stopped and it was in that instant, precisely and exactly in that instant, that I thought: "something has disappeared." I could see, almost physically, an immense plundering, a total stripping; and, just as in antiquity, like certain invading hordes were accustomed to do, the world seemed sown with salt. No former grass would grow again, everything lay, as if arranged so as to become new (if something were being done).

Only now, in a few hours, I have seen again the old ivies, the gelatinous leaves of some uncertain October; the white, innocent bellflowers, renewing themselves, clinging to a stone raised up centuries before. I shall die without understanding anything.

I have thought many times—and I know that's the point—that, in reality, that my father should have dedicated himself to archeology instead of politics.)

I had never seen the maples in autumn, the scarlet leaves. Father had a profile that had grown old, in spite of skin that was tanned by sport. He was like a ghost one meets again. It pained me to think so, because what had he to do with—he had nothing to do with—the one who (raised on tiptoe, lovingly and fearfully brought close to that provincial telephone receiver) I used to hear say: shall I send you…? And never anymore could I call him father. Since then, since the first meeting again, I had to call him Franc, like everybody else. Someone had died, had dissolved into the fog. Someone that was perhaps, only, an imaginary person of a child's imaginary story. Nineteen years were a small thing, still.

I do not know what is the true age of people, their exact and true age, the moment when it can be said: I am twenty, forty. Neither the days, nor the skin nor the arteries of men and women have a great connection with these things. That autumn—I think it was two months before the seventh of December of 1941—my father, for the first time, had me with him.

I believed that she was not going to pardon me for that decision. But she said: "At least, for once, that poor Franc is fulfilling his duty." She did not pose any objection to my going away. My presence had been imposed on her but, up to that point, I had never suspected the extent of it. Only Aunt Emilia cried when she accompanied me to the airport; and I realized that, at least, she had loved me.

Father was not in Puerto Rico any more. I went and joined him in the United States. Franc had transferred to a Midwestern university whose department of Spanish was slowly beginning to flourish.

I have always thought that Bear suffers from and resents some undecipherable responsibility towards me. At times he looks at me with the same or similar preoccupation that I find in some fathers towards their sons. Why can't I order my feelings according to established norms? Nor do I feel hate, or malaise, towards the ghost of my old age, as it is usual among quite a few women of my age. I do not in any way mean that my appearance should be juvenile (after all, I think that I never had such an appearance), but that the woman I contemplate, when I close my eyes, is not temporal. Or perhaps, only ancient, remote. Perhaps everything might be reduced to an unpleasant after taste of childish petulance: we want to convince ourselves that something very important awaits us in the depth of our being, something that has not yet had its great opportunity.

Surely Bear will arrive tomorrow, he should send a telegram or a notice of some kind. But Bear does not write letters, nor does he send telegrams. (It is only in this respect that he is like me.)

It is good, this great and respectful distance between our lives, that we have laboriously built, Bear and I. Bear knows that I cannot behave like mothers usually do. (I shall not say a good mother, that definition turns out to be too compromising for me). There was a time when I believed that a mother and son should be good friends. But I remember, with horror, a girl in boarding-school whose mother was her friend.

Something exists very clearly and it is the flow of time. We will never be able to keep up with the time of our children. We will never ride at the same rhythm. Age is something undefined, but not time which molds us, as the air and the light mold the old statues in the parks. My time is not the time of my son, although my son, perhaps, might be older than I. My time is, for example, Borja's time. Although he and I consider each other as simple antagonists; loving brother and sister, cordial enemies. But, without any doubt, accomplices of the time that fell to us to live.

Why have I accepted the fact that Bear might get used to it here, in this country? I am not tied to countries, I am indifferent to origins and ties, to old concepts of land and lineage, like a fly. What are, now, most of those words? I wanted, not knowing that I wanted it, for Bear to return. It was not only because poor Franc (because of Father, I mean) longed for it from Paris, in his famous sabbatical year. Poor Franc: "My grandson," he used to say, with the expression he never had in order to say: "My daughter."

It is curious: she too, now, the great and solid indifference, has felt something special in Bear's presence. Nothing like the ordered and well-established love that she feels for Borja, but something different, a feeling that I can not yet understand completely. She has asked twice, already, during this waiting period (that begins to become transcendent): "When will your son arrive, Matia?"

All of them love Bear. At least, all of them want to have Bear around. I love Bear, with a maternal love; that is, an atrocious love, one that takes me by surprise. One should not love the children. No son is satisfied with the plans which have been woven for him. Even the least rebellious have their little parcel of dreams, individual and non transferable; even those who continue tenaciously with the mills and business complexes have their paradise of lost roses. Nobody should love their children with possessive and destructive love, with anxious desire to continue on this old and merciless earth. Love is complex; delicate, ferocious and dangerous; sad and exultant. We should ration love, as morphine is rationed to seriously ill patients. Pain is something natural, but love is acquired, like disappointment. Bear, my son, let us respect our differences and life will be more bearable.

Franc, who has dug so many distances in his life, longs for Bear. (I thought: because he does not want to die.) He would say: "I want Bear to know Europe, that he return to his homeland." But, what is Bear's homeland? Only he will know.

If my poor Partisan knew how distant his words remain for me, he would be surprised. But I will never contradict or disillusion Franc while he is alive. (As I would never have said to Mauricia that I did not believe in Saint Genevieve and Saint Margaret; that I did not believe that Saint Theresa cried when she turned over the bread.) I believe I would kill whoever would destroy this yellowish garden, covered with dust, tenacious in the sand. No one will tell him these things, as long as I can avoid it.

Bear is here; he has arrived from a distant plot of land, growing up among loving rigors of cooperation, equity, discretion and loneliness. But I say this in order to sweep away with topics, my unavoidable fall towards doubt. My doubts will not touch you, Bear. You will be free, like a thistle in the mountains. You will destroy yourself alone: I will not help you. I am a monster of goodness. ("It's not the same thing, an American degree, I want a European degree for my grandchild.") I hear poor Partisan voice,

asthmatic, angelically tyrannical. What does "I want for my grandson mean?" Who is your grandson? What have you ever done
for that grandson? In old age, she, the great enemy, the virtuous
wild animal, who can knock down conventionality, goodness,
love, ethics and escape unharmed. (Black and triumphant knight
of some Round Table of Injustice), and you, poor, gullible one,
removed from the world, determined to redeem the world, both
of you speak in the same way of someone who is as apart from
you as is Bear. "My grandson. I want to have Bear with me on
this birthday." The youngest of the family. Of what race? Of what
homeland? Of what world? Nobody knows anything about Bear.
Bear speaks very little (like me at his age). But Bear has nothing
in common with me (except silence).

Submissive, obedient, silent, I have waited for the summons
not only for me but also for Bear. One day, also, I went to look
for Bear at the frontier, we got on an old train we brought him
back.

The landscape was fleeing by in the rain, through the train
window, Bear said: "I don't like the train. It's ridiculous that you
are afraid of flying. We have lost several hours which…"

How would you have recovered them, Bear? Your words are
usually unknown signs that I no longer force myself to interpret.
I don't want to argue with Bear, I do not want to be his friend-
enemy. It is still difficult for me to escape from the foliage of
words, like a gust of wind. I myself being transformed into wind.

I smiled at Bear and said to myself: "I am smiling at a child
who plays with a puzzle. I contemplate how a child struggles
with the thousand fragments of a monstrous puzzle. I smile, hoping that he would be astute enough to know how to complete it,
piece by piece." Bear (as all mothers say when they speak about
their sons) is a child. Bear is a child who speaks with an old girl
(not dead, unfortunately for her). But ghosts do not interest Bear.

I found myself looking at the green cup. The movement of
the coach shakes, vibrates the liquid, and there is in it a minuscule and almost inaudible tinkling. (Distant children, unattain-
able, who will soon disappear, that soon will give place to unavoidable and worn out beings.)

On one day or another, without knowing how, the birds were fleeing. I remembered the ravine, the echo, the voice of Mauricia and her songs, in order that the Echo Man should repeat them. And nevertheless: "Words (she said, in her servant's tired voice) remain written in the grotto of the Echo Man who gathers them, puts them in order, so as to write fate." I was overwhelmed, and Mauricia clarified: "But child, don't tremble, come on now, look, we old women tell stories about these things. They are typical of old country women."

Without anyone collecting names, nor even numbers, in any cave, the strange scattering of the birds arrives, the scattering of life, of youth. Without knowing for what reason (without awareness of fullness or mission accomplished), on one day or another, one minute, youth takes flight.) A scattering that can not be controlled, birds that emigrate. Parodies of themselves, amorphous retinue, gratuitous procession, the fulfilled years swaying in baby-walkers, cardboard idols, among the extinguished lights.

"Let's eat, mother, it's our turn." Bear said and closed the book all of a sudden.

As always the dining car appeared packed, uncomfortable. A waiter, expert in balancing acts, held a triumphal metal tray over his head.

"Mother."

"What do you want?"

The eyes of the little bear were looking at me irritably.

"We have a language for the two of us." No, we do not have one. We had it, in time past (much more distant than the time when the maples astonished me, with their poppy colored leaves, much more distant than when, patiently and formally, Mr. Echo gathered words of shouting children and composed their future.)

The green cup projected on the table cloth its transparent shadow, almost an underwater shadow. A bit of ash fell, something weightless, puerile and transitory, like the tinkling, or the emerald green shadow. The rain fell, flattened in small drops against the window. It had become night. I heard the innumerable explosions of the rain on the windowpane, there was in each drop a tiny light, pearl-shaped; there arose the smell of damp iron and wood, the aroma of bread, the greasy and warm vapor of the kitchen (each time that the waiters came in or left, the leaf of the swinging door went back and forth on its springs, something like the breath of an animal welled up.) The noise of metal against the crockery, the green and obsessive stain on the table cloth (the splendor of a tiny aquarium). I could describe it all now, minute by minute. Nothing has been erased since that night.

Many times I have thought or dreamed that I was floating at the bottom of a sea, heavy and crystalline at the same time, skirting an almost mineral vegetation. In similar excursions I felt myself liberated and absent, marvelously set free from a thousand weights tied to my back, to my feet, to my eyes, to the audible minutes of the clocks. On that night, dining in front of Bear, I seemed to be floating in a similar dream, although strangely tense.

I closed my eyes and felt pain once more. A pain that could be said to be acid, lacerating. I moved the napkin away and clenched my teeth. On the edge of my will I pressed down on my belt. It is still a brutal pain, a thrust of the knife which slowly lessens, hot at first, burning afterwards, and it transforms itself into a tingling of sudden, sharp pain, irresistible; until the pain rises to my throat and climbs like legions of insects.

Bear placed his big, bony hand on my forearm.

Nothing. It's going away now.

The same thing as always, isn't it? I heard his usual interest, one could say customary. "It's already known. Mother has a stomach ulcer." I observed Bear, through the pain. As I observed the cup, the tablecloth. One way of contemplating beings and things (even what is closest) simultaneously, like a sleepwalker, and terribly lucid at the same time. As though the dreams were, paradoxically, the door of the rawest and coldest reality. Stripped of all feeling that was not purely visual, I contemplated Bear's face, the soft, blond hair, the dull, slightly sunburned skin, the green-gray eyes (of a little bear, with its curious edge of Asiatic shape). In times past I gave him this name: Bear. He kept on being a little bear, in any case, with his recently celebrated eighteen years of age, with the impatience of that ironic curve, somewhat cruel, in the corner of his lips. His chin, still so childish (a spoilt child who sleeps with his ears well folded against the pillow). His thin neck, the nape of his neck split by a soft furrow, covered with a golden fuzz. (The neck that I kissed so many times, under an ungodly metallic roof, where the rain resounded; in another railway car already distantly and absolutely lost.) They say that Bear very much resembles my mother. Bear's necktie bothered him, he stretched his neck in a peculiar way, he closed his right eyelid; and I felt a sudden, uncontrollable pity for his ostentatious youth.

"Don't worry. It's nothing. I'm tired, son. I'm going to go to bed."

He stretched out his hand, doubtful. An obedient gesture, it could be said, that unexpectedly pained me. "Not to think. Not even think of the tone of voices, nor of the color of objects, not of sounds, not of reflections. Do not think and only see, contemplate. Bear's face, his hand, the false green stain." Then in a sudden, childish gesture, Bear turned the glass over on the tablecloth and looked at me, with gleeful shyness. (Once, when he was five years old, he had broken a toy and had come to show it to me, smiling. I noticed that he was hoping, with a secret joy, my exclamations of regret.)

I left him there, forever. That night I abandoned him in an old railroad car with his smile of a child who likes to see older persons cry. (As on the day he said to me, I like a lot to see Beverly cry. Mother makes her cry again, as on the beach.) On the section that united the two cars the floor rattled. From one side or other came out smoke, or so it seemed to me. It certainly smelled of smoke to me. I staggered on my feet. Between the two cars the dark, swaying area gave me a dizzy feeling. A movable and diminished world shook me, disrespectfully. I stretched out my hand on the metal handrail and held myself up on the moving floor like a clown in some crepuscular little nightmare theatre. (Shaken by something, by someone, by a time retreating and fleeing at the same time: that neither reaches me nor forgot me. I wanted to seize, between the two cars, something that I was losing or that I had already definitely lost. Suspended by two invisible strings with fragile feet of ash, trembling over a trap. Suspended, between two undecipherable zones.) For a moment I wanted to move back and pat the boy on the head, on his silky hair. But I went ahead into the other car, and then to the other, I continued to the end of the corridor and arrived at my compartment with an unusual feeling of helplessness.

I was tired, nothing but tired. I could not give up the sourness, the memory of a time when nothing has meaning any longer— and therefore as if it had not happened—; to transform myself into a magnetic tape that rejects the right words (pronounced in a former time, now only a ghost of its own voice). I remembered a girl who used to say her nightly prayers in a big hurry in order to keep herself from fear, from the great punishment of the world; although she had not understood why evil had to wait for her at nightfall. Why did evil have always to return? It was a good night for committing suicide, if I had believed in suicide. If I had even wanted it. But I will never commit suicide. I will cling to life like a mollusk; like that old woman who still rules us, on the eve of the great celebration.

The door of the compartment closed, with an unpleasant bang. It was a night that had scarcely begun, I had a stomach ache, my ulcer required the medicine which tasted of chalk. But it was a night beyond sadness. (In the corridor I said, or I imagined, human couples, solitary beings, fragmented families.) I was beyond sadness, but fear was not absent. Perhaps that should comfort me. Any youthful sensation, like fear, is supposed to be good. One's forties are surprising: never reached nor left behind. One is never forty. It is one more lie, one of those numbers with which we make up for the mysterious coming and going of time, one of those cruel and useful timepieces which we patiently fabricate, in order to explain to ourselves the reason why indifference, lack of affection, the irreparable absences invade us.

I was afraid to cross the frontier, to return once more. Where I was going, catastrophe was going too; more or less apparent, more or less concealed, more or less collective. I looked at myself in the mirror: "I think I am the same, but that's not the way it is. They are not the same eyes that look at me. And, nevertheless, what is it that remains intact? That eighteen-year old girl, that woman of twenty-three or thirty, that I believed to be so definite." Unexpectedly the pain stopped. A gentle fatigue began to come over me and I thought that, at times, pain comforts monstrously. "Now, Bear is another unknown. Speaking to him, seeing him often compensates in some way for the long separation, is there any purpose in that? It is a continuous deception, painful, each time that he speaks to me, calls me. Before, at times, when he was still a child and I rarely visited him, I said to myself: He's my son. Now, unexpectedly, he is a man. Birds do not recognize their children after teaching them how to fly; nor do tigers, nor dogs, recognize their children, once they grow and are able to manage on their own. Why do we humans have to be so different? What impels us to believe that our dreams, or disappointments, can be of use to our children that we must leave them customs, memories? They love us, we love them; but love is never enough. It seems to me that I am going back to the old considerations of a time when I believed that I had discovered the world. Now the world is something grown old, a mystery that does not awaken my interest. Motherhood confers on most women a kind of kingdom, a kind of possession. For me, it seems to take everything away from me." I went to bed, put out the light, let myself be rocked in the uneven movement of the train. "But I love Bear," I thought. "How am I not going to love him? And, moreover, I love the earth, the trees. And yet, I am afraid. I fear Bear." The earth, too, the trees, the water were alive and were growing without my expecting anything from them; and even less did I require something from them.

The train braked, screeched a little. I awoke and realized that I had very peacefully fallen asleep. I drank some water, I consulted my watch and stretched out again. Through the cracks in the leather curtain the shining lights of a station which I guessed to be cold and inhospitable came through. It was no longer raining, but there was a sticky dampness everywhere. A coat hanger banged gently against the wall. The train took off again.

The mist came out from the ground and the tree trunks (they were the most beautiful I had ever seen in my life) seemed to me to be edged in black. As I used to do in the drawings and in old books: I grabbed a pencil or a little fountain pen and outlined the figures in ink.

The lawn was still green, thick, fresh. Nothing had withered. Only in the nearby disturbed Brown County did gold invade the ground, the branches, the sky. A soft and pasty gold, like laminated dust, fell from some magnetic sky. (I remembered the films of Walt Disney that I never believed and to which I suddenly gave back their integrity.)

But I was there, alone on the lawn, next to the wooden house, painted white. Near the garage rose an enormous maple. The leaves were falling, gliding slowly around me. Red, gold. I stretched out my hands to them. At six in the evening in Spain, in the month of November, the sun became detached from the sky, like an orange within reach of the hand. It was no longer burning: it was only a fruit in season, probably sweet. "In Spain (I tried to remember), the first of November, I was..., I was...?" Franc did not return until seven, he was giving night classes to students who worked. In the neighboring gardens, without fences, without bars, without visible gates—only the already known barriers, raised between one privacy and another—little bonfires announced the burning of leaves. The smoke overcame the earth, all the earth was full of smoke and fog; which was also like smoke when all is said and done.

I could read, but not speak. My high-school English was of no use for anything. Human language is something else, hard to seize and difficult, it is grasped or not grasped, beyond grammatical rules. The English in my little book was just barely useful, there, for reading the newspaper. Be silent. Smile. I had just arrived from Spain. "Really...?" asked Dad's friends. Spain was somewhat remote, a difficult country to locate on a map. What difference did it make? What did it matter? The world was wider, broader than the threats that embittered the lives of well-brought up girls (to use knives and forks with propriety and not to move their hands while talking, nor raise their eyebrows too much). Suddenly the table-rules are different. "One hand beneath the table?" The threat of the people around me turns out, finally, to

be somewhat ambiguous, almost banal, which must be accepted
without any trembling.

In the neighbors' windows the children had placed a pumpkin
with a candle inside. They poked holes in it to make eyes, nose,
mouth, and the pumpkin smiled. Perhaps it was intended to be
sinister, but it appeared terribly jocose in the middle of the fog.
The neighbor's lawn was very well cared for (not like poor Dad's
who did not have time to cut it: on weekends he gave a few
dollars to the Murphy's boy to do it. But the Murphy's boy did
not need those dollars every weekend or, more to the point, did
he have any desire to cut the lawn.) They had carefully piled up
the leaves, and the kind but distant Mrs. Murphy set fire to little
bonfires which, at six in the evening, already dominated the other
growing things or lights. The smoke came towards our garden: a
distant incense which brought me the only known feeling; the
only familiar vestige of that evening.

Witches, skeletons and pumpkins smiling or threatening,
seemed to me to wink in the windows. I did not know, no one
had warned me; a turn of childhood floated about, I felt a vague
envy. "If Dad had warned me of it…" I would have cut out black
and green dolls, I would have pasted bits of Scotch tape to the
window panes, I would have bought an empty pumpkin, I would
have poked holes in it and lit it from inside, like a lamp.

But the time of black dolls and fear had already gone by. I
was nineteen. "I don't like you to put on make-up," Dad had
said. But he did not say it the first day. He said it two days later
when he took me out to dinner at the "Hoosier." And he said it
without looking at me, as if he had contemplated me and met me
again, when I was absentminded. How had he noticed that, if he
scarcely looked at me when he spoke?

In the other land, the one which I left, the houses appeared to
be born from the ground, like a continuation of the ground, like
one more little mound of earth. Stones on stones, earth on earth.
Not here. Here, in the leafy enclosure of the University Campus,
our little houses appeared carefully placed above the lawn like
an enormous toy, on a green, yellow and pink carpet.

After the first week in the little wooden house (not very well painted) I felt a kind of alienation; as if all of that did not belong to me, as though I were another eighteen year old girl, suddenly enrolled in an unknown world, in an unknown family; the daughter of an unknown man. Upon entering my little room, which had a folding bed (where Dad had hung well intentioned pictures of the Four Seasons) I thought: "Tonight I could commit suicide, it would be easy. But, surely, I would regret it tomorrow."

A light knock on the door awoke me and a voice announced the arrival of the train, at my city, within an hour. The light was already cold, a morning light. "I had a disagreeable dream," I thought. "I don't know exactly what, but, of course, disagreeable." Magazines were strewn about on the floor. "I don't know why I buy magazines. They bore me. And the truth is that I never read them." When I went to have breakfast Bear was already finishing his. He continued being absorbed in what he was reading. He looked at me, lost in thought. "How are you? Are you better?" His book had black covers, it stood out on the pale blue of the tablecloth.

In the smoke of the station the lights exploded and trembled. How many years? How much time? Why did I remember, suddenly, a song which I liked when I was twenty?

A whitish sun broke out among the clouds.

"What luck!" said Bear. "Almost no luggage!"

Suddenly he became happy because of things like that. He emerged from his absence, from his distance, in order to become happy because his mother was without a lot of luggage, or because there was orange marmalade, or because here, at least, one could smoke.

In the park, behind the railings, the greenish shadows of the trees opened up, like clouds with branches.

"When will you leave?" asked Bear.

After having something to eat," I said. And, upon answering him, I moved up the departure an entire day, without knowing why.

I am going to tell the story of my life. No, I am going to tell the story of my story. I am not going to tell anything. Life can be changed into a series of acts without importance, a conglomerate of banalities that form a wide and unpleasant uneasiness. It may be so, I suppose. One day we are on the face of the earth; and life is apparently something unlimited and death is not expected. Death is not to be waited for, like life is. Death is here, in us, in the back of our eyes which are stupidly open to the light, to the warm wood of memory, the dark cloud of smoke, of oblivion.

There, in that street, one day I was born. There is no one in that window. It is as if it were closed off. And I have the feeling that I was never born. What strange things the newspapers say, with their want ads for rent, mechanical milling machines, pharmacies open at night, birthdays, deaths! I was never born.

Please, tell him to stop at the corner, our street is a wrong-way street, I said to Bear.

The apartment, closed up, smelled moldy. The furniture was slipcovered.

I can not tell the story of my life, nor the story of anybody. But, to be sure, I could tell the story of that door, of that empty chair, of that bed without sheets or mattress, bare as a corpse, stripped. I think of things that I have never known, I repeat them to myself as though it were an interesting and sure story, the story of my life.

Of every new city that I know there remains to me only a memory half-frivolous, half bloodcurdling: signs for drug stores, for buses. The cries, the smell, the glance of the people. I think of the Anglo-Saxon widows who travel in hygienic and compact groups. I would like to travel like that.

Wasting Time

Mother invented Bear's name, although Beverly said not, that she did. The fact is that he could not get used to his real name, Roger. And that was too bad; because, since he had arrived in this country, among these people, the nickname humiliated him in a confused manner.

Perhaps his friendship with Mario, his authentic friendship, began the day he heard the old woman call him Bambi. Mario blushed—that's sure—and cast a look at her that was falsely indifferent (as though to test his audiovisual sense). Then she closed the door and Bear thought: "I don't know why mothers do these things." Then he said something that immediately intimidated him.

"They call me Bear and when I hear a different name I don't answer. Neither to my family name nor to Roger; it doesn't not seem that they are calling me. It is ridiculous, but there are ridiculous things, so inevitable…"

(Disoriented Boy. Wasting-Time Boy.) In those days Mario was, still, only a part-time Professor. Afterwards, very much afterwards, he discovered his friend. Bear-Without-Friends would not have been able to suspect that the man who "helped himself with extra classes, while he was preparing the famous competitive examinations. (You already know, respectable people, but without money…"), he could be the first, the only friend. Mario's famous exams were the position he would never achieve (nor wanted to achieve) as Bear immediately suspected. On one occasion he asked: "Why do you do it if you are convinced of how useless it is…?" Mario said: "Because I can not give up doing it. There are things that are done for the same peremptory reason that other things are not done." It seemed to Bear a complex and rather self serving argument. But he understood that Mario was at the limit of something. Something that, in that same instant, bothered him, without yet knowing why.

Once more he walked into the entry-way of the house that, recently, he knew so well. The house which, lately, had been changed into the nucleus, the center of his existence. Even more for him than for Luis, Enrique and the others. He could not explain it, nor did he try to sound himself out ("there is not time for that, one has to abandon certain tendencies"). Bear repressed a smile of self-applause.

The house rose up on a place called (he did not know for what reason) The Extension. In the entry-way there was an unexpected marble washbasin, with a faucet in the form of a swan, always shining and polished by the sour woman concierge who looked at him severely, over her wire-framed glasses. "In the old days, they used to instal unusual things in the houses." The marble banister only went up to the second floor. An eighteenth-century splendor, a strange concept of the world, was deteriorating inside there; a kind of immovable collapse, down the walls. Two globes of opaque crystal seemed to float above columns held up by a pair of women whose skirts, knowingly whirled about their legs, originated in something similar to bowl of chantilly cream. It was not like grandmother's house where Mother was born. It was not like the house, broken down and vacant, where they told him to live, slipcovered and empty, ("on eternal vacation, for the boy without vacation who is missing courses"). Bear became aware of a slight fatigue. "Two years, let's not exaggerate the time. It's not much if one thinks how much resistance is required not to let oneself be encrusted in the mechanism, in the unblemished and delicate order". Mario's house breathed something beautiful and pathetic, "like a flower that has been stepped on." At times stupid things occurred to him like that. Bear smiled again at himself.

The concierge opened the elevator gate, with the rag she used to polish door knobs in one hand. Polite and impolite, obliging and hostile in equal parts. The buttons of the call-panel shone. ("There is one which has lost its covering, perhaps it gives off a little shock when it is pushed...") A thick humming of iron set the elevator in motion; Bear went up, as if in an unreal and somewhat grotesque holiday boat. "Mario lives on the top floor. It is not the best floor. At that height, the marble no longer exits, the edge of the steps has cracks from footsteps. The concierge with her metal polish no longer gets there."

The same old woman did not open the door for him. The same old woman (with her anxious blue eyes, as though about to cry) was dead, buried, two weeks ago now. "The woman who called Mario Bambi." An unknown maid said: "The gentleman has not yet come in, go ahead, you can wait for him."

In the silence the tick-tack of the dusty clock seemed to him unnecessarily inexorable. "I understand Mario. Whoever comes to this house can not fail to understand Mario. What he did, what he does, what he is ready to do." If one day Bear comes to be like Mario the destruction of a vast area of the world would have a considerable justification, he thought. A menacing beyond the words, the plans, the hopes (that, from day to day, became blurred). "Luis, Enrique…will they understand Mario as I understand him?"

It was already eight in the evening and they had arranged to meet at seven-thirty. Mario was almost never late. "Unless…" Bear got up and went toward the window. There, across the way, on a blue roof, between flat-roof terraces, there was, among the vast installation of TV antennas, a neon sign that had gone out. "There is nothing so ugly as a neon sign which has gone out," he thought, bored. As he knitted his brows, the antennas seemed to be crosses of some strange and iron made cemetery. A cemetery suspended over the roofs of the city. "Unless…" Of course, he will be with Isa. It's Isa's fault. Whenever she gets in the middle of things, things get twisted a bit. Perhaps Isa was the only thing that Mario could be reproached for. "Stupid and captivating woman. She is not a woman for Mario. Since the first day I met her, I thought so: she is not for him. But these things are mysterious and difficult. How am I going to bring it to his attention…? In any case, Mario will leave her. Almost after all this is ended, Mario will leave her. Also in this transition there will be a sort of self-liberation for Mario, a significant step, exemplary, of self-liberation." Bear returned to his chair whose arms were decorated with faded flowers. "And also for me." He was surprised that he was talking. In a soft voice, speaking nevertheless, after all is said and done. What was so difficult to do with his Mother, with everyone, he did it now, by himself, gratuitously, alone. The same thing happened with his smile. They said that he did not know how to smile. ("It's unusual in a boy of eighteen, twenty...") But no one thought that Mother also had a difficult time smiling. Bear looked for cigarettes.

The apartment showed a thick accumulation of dust. ("I don't feel like working," that pale woman said. "I am already tired of working...") She was heard saying so when, like this afternoon, she arrived too early. (When Mario was still only the professor. When she was barely alive.) She was one of those women who explain their domestic problems, who do not perceive other problems, sunk in their sea of the smaller sorts of problems. It's curious, the great catclysm of her life was reduced to the dust of the furniture. (On that day she returned with a feather duster. On seeing her, he got up, disconcerted: he did not understand that she wanted to clean, with her feather duster, in his presence. And when Mario came and saw her, he blushed. As on the day when, in front of him, she called him Bambi...) Everything appeared distant and recent at the same time. As on the day that Mario spoke to her in a different way, that day on which he had a glimpse into Mario's real life. It was a rainy Sunday and the day before Mario asked him what he really knew about this city, about this country. What Bear knew was not useful. It was a year ago that Beverly had given him the Dodge as a gift. He could still use it (now he had sold it, and he drove a green 600 model, dusty and dented by Mother); but on that Sunday he still had the Dodge and, for the first time, Mario drove it. They crossed the city, climbed up by a broad avenue whose buildings already appeared miserable even before time had run them down. Then, they emerged into an unaccustomed world, onto a sand and a sea that had nothing to do with Uncle Borja's sea. Could the sea offer itself like this? He was still eighteen.

A moldy reddish color seemed to dye everything throughout that area; above the little roofs and under the bridge. Down there he heard the sea continually raging against the land; the water came down through the canal and emerged on a stinking black beach. Under the bridge they had improvised rickety, unlikely houses. The rain had inundated an area which served as a narrow street. Everything—he thought—had a vague air of a minuscule lake city. Somebody had placed some boards from the doors of the shacks up to the dry areas; and across them some children arose, slowly, carefully, almost on tip toes: giving each other their hands, with calmness. The seagulls flew in groups, turning in the air, and formed unusual circles, as if they were tracing summons in the sky. ("As if they were writing in the open sky stories unsuitable for the general world.") Those two children went down to the little side-beach and stomped around with their rain boots; as if they wanted to raise up from the ground something ferocious, irate and invisible. The print of their boots broke the smoothness of the sand, almost black in that part of the beach. He was looking at them, seized by an unusual fascination, as he leaned on the railing of the bridge. At his feet were teeming people who, for the first time, he felt were caught, distrustful. The girls, the women were preparing dinner (it was growing dark); from the improvised chimneys made with waste pieces of pipe, roughly put together, a thin smoke slithered towards the bridge. Suddenly he seemed to find himself suspended above a forest of squalid and threatening arms. The smoke that emerged from those arms almost hit him in the face, the smoke which became diluted in the grey curtain of the evening. He drew away, with a sudden dizziness that he had never felt before.

A man was coming on the bridge; behind his glasses his eyes became enormous and watery; they gave him a humorously idiot appearance. Bear experienced the weight, the great and fatiguing weight of Sunday on this poverty. At the back arose three huge brick chimneys. Everything had a strange air of a cold oven, stained with soot like a red-hot-piece of city which is turning cold, slowly, in the Sunday dusk. Mario said that from the city came out people who were capable of building or pulling down. "Yes," he answered him. "This is the place from which comes the material for pulling down." And they laughed that evening.

The seagulls passed, once more, over their heads.

When they came back Bear said: "I have never come here before." "I imagined so, I brought you here for that reason," Mario answered. "He brought me," reflected Bear. They brought him, they took him away. Always, they brought him, they took him away. There were a few things, each time fewer, that he decided on his own account. The irritating uneasiness returned. From whence came that indifference, that lack of affection? The lack of affection for people was old, it did not surprise him. But the indifference towards events, actions, situations revolted him those days. He knew that he was restless.

A little later, Mario introduced him to other boys (not university students). When they returned to the car, the rain clouded over the windshield. They crossed the new stretch of the Paseo Maritimo, where houses were going up; skeletons of cement, wood, iron. A group of little gypsies, dirty and soaked by the rain, almost got under the wheels, screaming, with their hands stretched out.

They entered the city through the Barceloneta. There, too, old houses were falling down: an occasional wall showed gradations of color, siena, ochre, prints of a recently destroyed life. The city grew wider, slowly became ennobled in the rain. They stopped to let a man pushing a cart loaded with junk get through; a girl took advantage of the occasion to cross the street. It was Sunday, the girl was dressed in a long blue bathrobe and rabbit-fur slippers. On her back her braid seemed not to have been re-done. She carried in her arms, like a little child, a bottle of soft drink (those called "family size" in the TV ads.)

But now the important thing was that Uncle Borja was satisfied. Better: he was happy with the plan. He possessed a special weakness which led him to believe that in everything he assumed there was some more or less courageous maritime adventure.

Bear smiled, almost happy. But he realized that Mario was speechless. He felt like asking him if something was not going right. (It would have been a stupid thing to do. If something were wrong, he would not be ready obviously now, in front of him.

Three Days of Love

There exists an undoubted vein of madness which crosses through this earth from one side to the other. I can perceive it in all places, or almost in all. (If an accident occurs, they say it is the work of a madman. If someone is happy, if his vitality shows great pleasure: "he is a madman, he will end up badly." If someone is bent over by a gall bladder attack: "he has done too many crazy things lately…")

In the cemetery of Z., when we went to contemplate the tomb—she said our tomb—madness floated all about like a hummingbird. Sometimes, while she was praying, I glanced through my notebook and wrote. I simply wrote what I saw, in the ferocious boredom of our contemplation of death. Afterwards, going through her innumerable papers—among recipes, receipts for the gas, worn-out ribbons for bows that no one will ever tie—, there appears this sheet of paper, torn out and yellow. When did she tear it from my student notebook? I will never know. I was not able to suspect that she had it, I never thought so. The way it was, wrinkled, musty, in a calligraphy that I no longer recognize, I read: "There is a frieze of sheets of blue paper, underneath two photographs. In a same frame, boy and man, then yellow flowers, brown leaves, imitation mimosas set in a crown of metal which serves as a frame for another portrait, a woman. And an earthenware jug, with an angel painted in blue and yellow; a little angel, broken, with a torch, without legs. And a thin vase, made of crystal, with a yellow handle, like a faded cluster. And it says: I'll never forget you, ever, amen."

I thought that, away from there, from that house and those people, I would recover peace, or, at least, serenity. But peace, serenity, are completely unforeseen, unexpected things. My country was windy, my town a dry place. The window sills were filled with white dust. She was obsessed with dust. She was always looking for something with which to drag out the dust, lift it and look at it again when it fell. Now her glance is as though pasted on all the objects. It is as though her glance was not able to follow her on her way, as though it would not have been possible for her to pick up her glance, forgotten there, on top, on each piece of furniture. Especially on all the doors.

In my life there are many kinds of doors. I recall the doors of Z., of wood, unpainted, only waxed. As I recall the floor of red bricks, the tall sideboard, the side table for carving, the mirrors framed with plaster roses painted with gold. Perhaps I wrote once, on the interminable evenings, between lessons: "There was an ornamental border around the mirror. Underneath the mirror…" Why go on? It is not necessary to write anything. Things only exist in memory. If not, they become hermetic ciphers, concepts, perhaps sounds. Now, for her, there is no longer any vengeance. The word is lacking in sense for her.

I was already asleep and, unexpectedly, I woke up. The wind was grazing the fringe of the bedspread: someone had opened the balcony. It was winter, with frost on the shutters; and someone had opened wide the balcony. I discovered her in the night, sitting along side me, spying on a perhaps too good a dream. Revenge, then, was more than a word. (Perhaps, for this reason, she did not take it away herself, along with her glance.) I say to myself: the word revenge, has she ever pronounced it? I think not. I think that she never pronounced it.

Fright also arrived, wordless. Now, on the other hand, words are the only weapon. I do not know whether they could be left here this way (like objects, like glances on the furniture) when one will never return. It is possible. But when I see the eyes of Bear, of Luis, or of Gerardo, and the eyes of all the others, I believe that my words seem like the wind that moved the fringe of my bedspread (when I did not deserve sleep, when sleeping was, for me, something too good).

In Z., there was a half-dry river, but the water raged in winter and often flooded everything. That was in the past; I had not yet left Z., nor had I gone any place (not even to the county seat). Very distant times, apparently; although it does not have too old a flavor. Although I have been savoring those times for almost thirty years, minute by minute.

Once Doña Rosita saw us in the cemetery, on our tomb. She patted my hand, as when I was a child. Mother did not cry, she was stiff, stood straight up. But Rosita wanted to make us understand that she was not a bad person, that time passes, that offenses are forgotten. She said to her: "What are we going to do, may God have received him in his bosom. Poor fellow, everything on account or of his mistaken ideas." Then, the submissive, the sweet, the gentle woman turned around and spat in her face. It was in this way that I saw, physically, the face of revenge.

She never called me Bambi. It was he who called me Bambi, as a joke. She began to call me that, only when he was not there. Every time that she said it, I knew that it was like nailing my right hand to that door. Nobody can say that I was ever not fulfilling my duties. No one would have ever allowed it, either. But, often, I forgot revenge. I was fifteen or sixteen, I was coming back from high school, perhaps I felt like whistling. "How can you whistle?" It always seemed that she was coiling around me, in some way, the serpent of ingratitude. Along with revenge, ingratitude was something more than a word. The words alone were—now are, this very day, on the eve of making amends—the shadow of a very well-known reality. The word revenge is the reflection of a certainty, of a long, thick reality. It could be called in a thousand ways.

It could be called love. When I think that the root of a great calamity—calamity is another of the names that revenge uses—flows, perhaps, from love! In love, she came and went, with her feather duster in her hand, always in her horrible, grey apron—"Why don't you get rid of that apron? You don't have to wear it now"—lying in wait for the dust, in order that the dust should not cover names, dates, mysterious engravings that for her alone had a very bitter meaning. Love impelled her, night after night, to my bedroom, in order to dull the sweetness of my dreams. One can not fall asleep. One can not smile. One can not live. Love demands revenge. Always revenge. That love which makes

her remain motionless every day of her life, in the contemplation
of our tomb. When I could no longer put up with it and got her
out of there, I felt the authenticity of that expression: our tomb.
The one that belonged to the three of us.

This house, I remember well, was not impregnated either with
love or hate or with any memory. For her, for me, this house
appears empty, without footprints in the wind, without the empty
space of a body (horribly loved), making holes in space everywhere: like a space within a space.

And nothing changed. Out of my sphere, feverish, I was
startled at night: although she was not brushing against the white,
sinister, fringe of the hated nuptial bedspread with her felt slippers, the hated nuptial bedspread with which she insisted (from
that day on) in covering my bed.

She wanted the boys to come to the house, she spied on the
get-togethers, she pretended that she knew nothing; while a cruel
happiness filled her, on seeing them, on hearing them, on guess-
ing about us. She protected, happily, what she imagined was the
process, her revenge. And, nevertheless, she really did not like
the boys. Especially she did not like Bear. She hated the boys.
"They have everything, those boys. Everything, they have everything," she used to say, drowning a sigh. She looked towards
the lamp where the red and white crystals shone (just like in Z.)
"What illusion made me believe that the house was new, different? Little by little, like an invading and silent horde, her objects
arrived. One day it was a lamp, another day, a mirror, another, a
tablecloth. Who could believe that her revenge might retreat like
a conquered army? Innumerable, complex, diffuse and vast, it
lies in wait in all domestic belongings, watchful eyes, the sudden, sharp thrusts of pain of an ungrateful past. "And those boys,"
she would say, while she ran an absentminded finger over a non-
existent speck, are they very studious? Yes, they seem very studious. They love you. Isn't it true that they love you, Mario? I
think they study a lot. Too many hours."

The doors come one after the other. Glass, metal, painted
wood. Doors with chipped edges, iron doors, doors open like
mouths, absolutely abandoned. Each time I go through a door I

feel the emptiness of the other one: the one which I could not go through without being seized by fright. She impelled me. She, made me pass through that door several times a day. Apparently, without realizing it. Apparently, perhaps, like an attempt to destruct the fright. But I know what makes her push my child's shoulders towards that threshold. I know the truth of that soft, domestic, lugubrious and sweet attitude.

It is sad to think that I can not remember them together, in life. It is sad because there is no reason for it. Rather I can only remember him, alone. Isolated, with me, with other persons. And, as for her, she was not with him, in memory. They were together only in front of our tomb.

Her tomb is very different. Those civic niches, gray, uniform, produce a melancholic alienation in me.

Of what tranquility do I speak? There is no tranquility. I find it out when she remained immobile, when the death rattle stopped. "Finally. Finally," (a voice said). "There it is, the great relief." But what has ended is only the justification of an inertia. Will my only excuse not be terminated with this liberation? The attitude that is expected of me, I expect myself, year after year. Thirty years. For thirty years we have to wander, in order to discover that our great pitfall, that our great impediment, was only an excuse.

But no one can go back. The moment has already arrived, there are no evasions, no obstacles, no love. Only revenge can begin to be reduced to a simple concept. A noble, powerful and useful instrument.

It will be necessary to close the door, very carefully, on leaving.

In This City

"Of all of them," she thought, as she was finishing getting dressed, "the little blond guy is the one who doesn't like me. Not one of them likes me, but the little blond one really dislikes me." She looked towards the unmade bed. Mario was not there now; he was already another man, again. The usual silence. The silence of afterwards. What enraged her was the rush. "The hateful boys. The same old thing. The blessed political leader of youth. Yes, yes. Ok, ok." But why become bitter one more time? It was never a secret, for her, the obsession of his life, what held him in constant tension. It was that, exactly, what attracted her about him, in the past. What united them, perhaps.

In the first side street Mario got out of the taxi.

"I'm sorry, I can't go with you," a light kiss, urgent. His smile had a light and curious air of remorse. But Mario was thinking of something else, she knew it very well. What couldn't she know about him? What irritated her the most was knowing that he was in another place, while being with her. Love, she thought, was something unjustifiable, almost shameful. At times, above all at the beginning, she blushed, alone, thinking about her love. Not that she was still a prude. Well, she had gone far beyond the time of credulity, of false modesty, of inane concepts concerning decency. No, love shamed her, suddenly, in a very different way; as if, for example, they had caught her stealing in one of the department stores. So she surprised herself by loving: stealing from another being, words, thoughts, the secret beating in his arteries. Stealing, cunningly, treacherously, the solitude, the silence. But she was not able to love him in any other way. She could only love him this way, shamefully, possessively.

As she contemplated him, with his curious shyness of a serious man (of a man "who does not know how to stop," of a man "who will sweep everything away," as she had heard people say) her love was aroused as though emerging onto a luminous steppe, terrifying and triumphal, in equal parts. In those moments something opened up before her, infinitely unknown. She believed that she knew everything about him and, unexpectedly, she found herself standing up, desolate, faced with a vast region where all the years of her life would not be sufficient to travel through it. "Nobody knows anybody," she repeated to herself, one more time, "when I see him getting lost among the many other bodies that populated the street. Human beings, wandering bodies, wandering even in their concrete desire." Just as she had felt herself to be for a long time. "I am getting old," she admitted with a kind of docile fury.

The anguish of age, of the inexorable passage of the seasons struck her once more. It even continued when she climbed the stairs of her house. To grow old, at twenty-eight. How to go about it so as to alleviate the implacable, monstrously normal and daily advance? She should not make him notice it. For him she ought to be the young, strong, indestructible Isa. "Perhaps," she thought while she put the key in the lock, "I have been lying to him since the first moment? Does he really believe in a woman who does not exist?" An Isa demanding and weak, shy, inclined to annoying complaints, would not have achieved anything. A woman like that would have never held on to Mario. It was necessary to create a carefree Isa, ignorant of the time which withers the skin, the sweet and childish brilliance of twenty years old. An Isa accommodating, opportune, capable of appearing and disappearing like the natural cycles of spring, of autumn. "But can he be deceived to that point?"

From the dark corridor came the stridency of the telephone, and she felt a sudden braking in her heart. One of those strange feelings of catastrophe that, at times, left her amazed by their clairvoyancy.

The telephone had rung that day, too, in Marisol's house. They were celebrating her birthday, "just the girls." She remembered the afternoon, the table (endless banquet where country sausage and custards, pudding and boar's head alternated on the delicate laces that, with her golden hands, her grandmother had made.)

They were laughing a great deal, they had drunk champagne. Jacinto was not invited (it was not a formal thing, after all). And, moreover, men were excluded from the get-together. "Only girls. In this way, we're more at ease, chatting, laughing, aren't we?" Nonsense. There was no male on the list whom they could invite. The telephone rang, and she thought she could still hear Marinita, the judge's girl, who was crying because her sister had gotten drunk. "You always have to make a show of it, you do." The telephone was ringing, nobody seemed to hear it and she felt, suddenly, an irrepressible nausea: she looked at the aspic among pretty green parsley, and thought: "Let nobody take that telephone off the hook"; she was already terribly frightened when Marisol's mother arrived and took her aside and told her to go home and that they would be going with her: "but if nothing has happened, no, no; without getting frightened; just accept it child, just accept it, that's life..." But that was not life, it was death. Father, like an overcoat, appeared stretched out on the sofa. They had carried him back unconscious, he had fallen, just like that, on the sidewalk, in front of the Casino. "But who was going to say so. Well, then, didn't he say that he was much better? Could it be that bullet that he still has lodged in him, from the War...? Child, what things, now you see them, now you don't."

"It will be three or four days only. You know, family matters. No, don't be worried... You see, I was not expecting this. I never thought that we would have anything. It appears to be that there are some parcels of land, an orchard or something: nothing of importance. She must not have known, perhaps. You know how people are in small towns. Truly, only three or four days, No, why will I write? How dumb! Certainly not. Certainly not. Don't you worry..."

She hung up the telephone and she realized that she was still living in the first moment: when she heard the long ring, hoarse, like the buzzing of a gigantic blowfly, in Marisol's house. (That moment came back to her, and the aspic, and the custards.)

She slowly took off her jacket. It was hot, she opened the window and looked at the courtyard. On the wall across from her there were outlines of fake windows, bright yellow, lit up in the upper story. Noises of crockery, of water. Smells of meals. A kind of meowing, pitiful, hypocritical, arrived from down the hall.

"Child! Child!"

Isa lit a cigarette. Quiet, she heard the dull murmur of some steps.

"Child! Child! Are you there?"

There is no child here. There never was a child in her life. Isa was born a woman, from the first day. From the first step, from the first word.

Isa throws the cigarette away, steps on it. "Let them clean up, darn it, let them do something." A rage mixed with sadness also climbs, it appears, up the wall.

The virtuous old women do not want to know anything about Isa's life because Isa is generous. Those virtuous old women knew nothing, either, at the time of the business with Jaime. "Do you have to go out tonight, child? An urgent piece of work in the office? Of course, of course." Isa is indubitably decent, indubitably virginal." Perhaps she is not of our blood?" Isa is generous, good, unselfish. Isa deserves complete confidence. "She's hard-working, she's worth a great deal. Child, child, aren't you coming tonight? All right, I understand now."

Isa bolts the door, takes off her shoes, stretches out on the bed. A swarm of mocking lights crowds under her eyelids. "To hell with it. I don't believe in premonitions."

But things have changed lately. Isa is not given over to dreaming. ("Self-deception does not suit me.") Nevertheless, she has the feeling that Mario has subtly changed. It is not true, there is no garden for Mario, in the town of that poor old woman who, finally, has died. (There was time when, timidly, she imagined that the old woman was the only obstacle for the realization of a vague desire. At least, she was the eternal obstacle to all her plans, all her projects with Mario: "It's that my mother, being sick, alone…" How many times Mario took refuge in her.)

Now Isa opens her eyes to the darkness. She does not deceive herself, now she knows Mario. "Mario, the coward." If they had told her so at the beginning, when she admired him from a distance, she would have been scandalized. His aura of integrity, his fluent word, his lucid word..." Where was all that now? Voluntarily she had submerged herself in an alien world, absolutely at odds with her own world; but how could she interest Mario if she did not? Then, little by little, love turned, into something different, frighteningly new. Love for Mario, love with Mario, had nothing in common with the love she had known. It was as if love had grown, jumped over her barriers of self-justification; over her careful interests, over her abandoned dreams of greatness. Suddenly she found herself naked and abandoned, unarmed, before an old dream, frightfully bartered in reality. What did Mario's love have to do with everything that happened before? To the point that the outlines of a desire—categorical for the first time—appeared: finally Isa knew what she desired.

In front of the immutable mirror Isa could scrutinize that which normally is not possible by looking at other persons or landscapes. Something very hard to attain and to be attained. The only possibility, the only way out, was the total, absolute possession of the person loved. A kind of cannibalism lightly ennobled by the masochistic desire to sacrifice her life to him, her dreams, all the ingenuous vanity of everything that had been desired up to that point. "When the whole affair of the strikes and the meetings and all of that began, he walked around very cocky, very serious and efficient: like an avenging angel, among the boys. But I knew, I knew, Mario. I know you, I have cut you up into pieces, and I am poking, poking in you, all the minutes of my life; because I spy on your breathing, on your silence." The miserable woman who obstructed the most audacious acts was a pretext. "Perhaps a sublime pretext. Ha, ha!" The boys threw stones at the "security police," insulted the ruling classes, spit on the irreproachable names of mother and father. Very well, very well. Isa laughed secretly in her dark corner, between the old women and the unglued tripods. In the office she read the morning periodicals. Behind each newspaper column, each news item, wandered Mario's shadow, although she had no direct contact with him. Isa closed her eyes. (Under the bridge of the Ebro, naked children threw stones at the couples who were kissing each other

and petting clandestinely. On the outskirts of the city, in caves,
human beings imitated a grim flight of blackbirds. One day the
river overflowed, flooded the caves and dark, swollen, stinking
corpses floated down the water. Men, women, children; and a
cow, belly up, like a biblical curse, in the red water. That was
Isa's third world.) Mario was there, in the appointed house, with
his beautiful, slow voice, his plans structured like a beautiful
city. Each of Mario's words is like a stone of that harmonious,
perfect architecture. "The children have a good teacher." They
can lose classes, registrations, quarrel with the family, defend
rights which concern them or don't concern them... Mario is
there, at the back of the stage. Isa, looks in vain for his ironical
laughter; she does not love a man: she loves a complex of words,
cities, walls, woods, plains of words. For a long time they have
been boring her with their unintelligible language. But Mario,
now, is simply the man that she chose. "No one ever knows why
one loves."

In a flash she gets up and turns on the light. Her mirror is
oval, spotted and defective. But Isa has looked at herself in it and
knows all its exaggerations, its strange magnifications and magical winks. She draws her face near to its surface. A red lock of
hair twists near her ear; her eyes, very, very open, without blinking. Gently, she passes her hands over her cheeks, still cool. "I'm
fed up now, I have become tired. It's over. You don't know it,
Mario, the hunt has begun. You are not a good prey, but you are
my prey. Isa, say it once more, fearlessly, I am going to marry
Mario. Why not? Why so much fear to say so? Is there another
way to tie him down? I don't know any other which is so perfectly set up. I could not care less for your plans, I could not care
less for your marvelous ability to convince, I could care even
less for your transcendent way of passing through the world. Nor
your following of avenging angels, nor your mission, nor your
famous rights, nor your thousand and one reasons which I know
by heart. I could not care less for anything that does not have to
do with catching you, holding you." Isa smiles at her own smile.
For a moment a violent happiness seems to shake from the walls
of the room to the oval of the mirror. "In this same mirror, ro-

mantic and powdery girls peeped; but with the same intentions," she whispers. For a long time she has had only a joke left, a mocking face, a commiseration: it is called Isa. She is alone, but she has always wanted solitude, really. One achieves solitude at a very hard price. She has won it through the corridor with high ceilings, of square shadows, of musty lamps, of whispering of rosary devotions behind the half-closed doors of the study. The old women form a part of a dark, heavy, tangible solitude. The old women, the cats, the green and everlasting plants which laugh in the ceramic flower pots; the improbable ashtrays, the meowing in the glass enclosed porch, waiting for the serving of foul smelling treats; the invisible sea which invades, at times, the imagination or the breeze; everything forms a part of the solitude. Well earned, harshly achieved. (At times, she puts on a record, one of those that are in the living-room; one day she heard Mambru went to war and remembered her father.) Mother kept Father's medal, but he wore the scar. It was his, it belonged to him, he had gotten it. He was happy, with his full, overflowing, fulfilled life. He had his scar, his medal, his duty, his country, his cause, his war, his city. His memories of the front, of Victory Day. What more could he ask for?... (In reality he did not carry only the scar, they had taken everything away. In the dining room where Mother had the crazy idea of receiving everyone, the holes left by the pictures, by the sales, by the pawnshops and the pledges, were evident everywhere. She was sure that someone, somewhere, in some place, would also devour the military decoration. It was not going to be there, always, in the wardrobe, in the metal box. It did not make sense.) Probably Jacinto has already gotten married. Perhaps he now thinks he has put his foot in it, perhaps he is sorry. Or perhaps he is happy and belongs to an Association of Decent Young Men, Good Fathers, Good Husbands, Right Thinkers and Believers (and even he might do missionary work. Perhaps he has a 600, or 110), or what should I know. People, in the end, get whatever they want, what they secretly wanted. What, at times, they secretly want (poverty, opulence, the 600, marriage or the Communion of Saints. Namely...) My story seems to be the story of a poor country, beautiful but unfortunate.

Isa puts out the light and begins to get undressed. A strange thought, a sudden discouragement comes over her. "One must not let oneself be rocked by hallucinations. A premonition, pure stupidity." Before going to sleep, she again follows a diffused light which floats from the window frame to the ceiling. The noises have become muffled, the people in the house are giving themselves over, pleasurably or bored, to the task of feeding themselves.

Wasting Time

In the last weeks—he entered fully into his duty—he took a couple of quick inspection trips to the island. Both times he returned with an unusual tingling in his body. Seeing him gave Aunt Emilia great pleasure. Seeing him gave everybody great pleasure. As under a throng of innocent and curious animals who rushed to devour him in the greatest innocence, Bear detected the feminine and romantic gluttony: they did not come to the point of kissing him, they drew back on time, but the treat rested on him. "And, Bear, dear,"—Aunt Emilia reached the point of saying, "who knows whether you would like to come here, to live with us…?"

On his way back, on the plane scarcely raised above the mills, above the land bordered with white and green froth, Bear declared to himself that he would never live on an island.

He felt satisfied, if not happy, when he was silent, alone. "It is not misanthropy, it is a horror of giving explanations. He had decided never to give explanations. When he explained to the two old ladies his Bear—Uncle Borja—Swordfish project, the solemn centenarian (who spoke as sparingly as he), gave her opinion:

"I like the idea, I like it that you're such a good sailor. In this household there were always good sailors." "The sea is good," he answered, intimidated without knowing why.

Now Bear, ill at ease, reconstructs the scene. And he remembers her voice, quenched in a sudden fear. Suddenly the memory of the Great Lakes is useless, of the other sea, of other seasons. It is useless. "How can anyone celebrate a hundredth birthday? How can they get to that age without being disgusted with themselves? I'll never reach a hundred."

Four times he made the stretch from his house to the nearby city, in Uncle Borja's old Citroen, and timed the time it took.

Each time that he took out the fallen apart, almost incredible monstrosity that Uncle Borja used when he went to the island, the old gardener (called Ton or something like that) opened the garage door with trembling moderation and looked at him fearfully, he had one eye blank, obsessive. He was an old man of an incalculable age: like everything in that spot, in that place dominated by his great-grandmother. Old Ton was bent over, it seemed that he was going to cave in from one moment to the next; the sections of the garage door slowly opened under his effort. An effort of a domesticated animal, old, frightful. "How is it possible that everything here can be so spectacularly in ruins?" A controlled and invisible crumbling to pieces trembled there, wherever he looked. Surely the house was a fine construction in the past. He had seen photographs and so he believed it to be until he saw it for the first time. Now, like certain women "well preserved" for a long time, it seemed only to die, to go down, to sink in a sudden, almost immoral destruction. It seemed dragged along by a sibylline force, that was causing it to sink, millimeter by millimeter, into the ground. As if, from one moment to the other (similar to a dry and pulverizing shipwreck) it was about to disappear, swallowed up in the bowels of the island.

It had not occurred to anyone to grease the door hinges. Neither the ones in the garage. "Only Mr. Borja uses it when he comes...," the old man murmured, without anyone's asking him anything. One time he bent over, with a trembling hand: he was going to pick up a rag and clean off the dust. Bear snatched it from him, brusquely. When he saw the old man bend over, a mute irritation against the old man was born in him. "Mine is a paradoxical compassion," he thought. The sure thing is that he hated equally compassion, old age, humiliation and poverty. Was that justice? He hoped not. (When, on that occasion, upon coming out from the school, they detained him at five o'clock—him, Luis, Enrique and the other two—and they let him free almost at once, without many complications.) "One day all of this will be over with." He noticed the wind in his face: fresh, intense. The old Citroen convertible unexpectedly seemed to fly. "It's not so bad," he murmured with relief.

At times Mario said to him: "You have one good characteristic: you are quiet and you know how to dominate your emotions." Bear accelerated softly. ("How grateful I am to you, Beverly, to your patient insistence in rooting out any outer display of feelings. Pain, happiness, boredom, hunger, exposed to the look of people, results in the crudest and most abject pornography.") He timed the distance: it took forty-two, forty-three minutes. Almost three quarters of an hour, from the old house to a certain bar in the city.

It was a very modest bar, somewhat old-fashioned, with little tables, with a vague style of a musical cafe. "One of those where people (apparently) spend hours talking." People who had "habits" like that man. "The man who has the habit of coming to that bar every evening, after leaving his office. And he always sits down at the same table. His table, his corner, his newspaper, his exact hour." Men with habits. Bear thought briefly that neither he nor anyone he knew, carried his habits to that point. But the man was, therefore, a special man. In person he was somewhat different from the photograph: perhaps he was fatter; he had a heavier air, less agile. He used to come to the far end of the street, with a peaceful air. He bought the paper at the corner newsstand. Then he crossed the street (with his newspaper in his hand, folded lengthwise; and he struck his knee lightly with it). From his waist up he appeared athletic. Nevertheless he had short legs, strangely weak; the cuffs of his pants floated around his ankles like folded flags. Seated, he had a certain ease of manner. He drank draught beer, opened the newspaper, carefully folded over on the first page. He read very slowly and, at times, he rested the paper on the table and drew his face near to it, as though he were listening to it, instead of reading it. As though the newspaper were mumbling some confidence. He did not use glasses. His eyes were round, of an extraordinary light blue. Big, unusual baby eyes.

All this was already arranged, the preparations pertain to the past, to the machinery. The machinery had just begun to start. He almost perceives a minuscule tic-tac, at the bottom of the air. A count of seconds, secrely clear. "The tic-tac also vibrates on the walls of the house which is falling down. It has also begun to beat on the walls." Like the prelude to an immense and symphonic earthquake…, biblically delighted. (On Beverly's lips, the Bible gained, at times, perished accents.) Without really coming to the point, he thinks: "Perhaps I may never see Beverly again. Perhaps I will never see Franc again either." (And, almost without transition, an aggressive, unaccustomed hate against all that surrounds him, is born in him. "What am I doing here, in this house, on this island, among these old women?") But what can matter seeing or not seeing that which especially moves us? "Those things are not to be thought of. They are, after all is said and done, simple sentimental speculations." In truth there is little in his memories that aroused sentimentalism.

The quay is located to the rear of the house. Once, some time ago, Mother told him that a couple of children—Uncle Borja and she—had a boat. "That boat has grown," he says to himself, with that rare smile that he only allows to appear in solitude. That smile now comes with a certain frequency. Bear looks at the sky. Some stars, cold and diffuse, open their way through an obscure mass encircled by a halo of moon light. A peculiar, penetrating smell comes out of the ground. Perhaps the smell of the almond trees, or of the sea. Bear thinks that everyone should have a boat. That, at least, everyone should like boats.

When the "Swordfish" arrived at the little port of Villanueva in search of Mario, he realized immediately: Mario does not like the sea. For a moment he attributed his silence, his concentrated, almost sullen attitude to distrust. "Perhaps he suspects me." Then, little by little, as he moved away from the coast, a solid conviction took possession of him: Mario (who, on land, firmly held the rudder), gave into him in a total, unknown way. A rare power, a free will, without controls, took on shape in him (since the moment when Mario had stepped on board the "Swordfish" and had let himself fall—almost collapsing—on the bunk-bed of the cabin.) "He's tired," he thought. But, immediately, he noticed that he was taking possession of something. Something. Not that he had just reached it; he had just seized it. And the feeling was not fleeting, as at other times. It persisted, it grew. (A slow euphoria, a golden swarm, going up, increasing, out to sea.) "We will be lucky; a crossing without wind, without great difficulties...,") he heard himself say, somewhat without purpose. Because he could not put aside a thought. "He does not like the sea. He does not fear it, but he does not like it."

Naturally it was necessary to do without Pablo, the sailor; and Mario did not turn out to be, in truth, a good substitute. In spite of everything, they began on the right footing. He was sure.

They set sail from Villanueva around six in the morning; and at nightfall—there was still a light, a pink light scarcely blurred in a veil of foam—they made out the island, the house, the quay.

Upon stepping on land, their ears were filled with the noise of the crickets. Above, on the dark slope, floated diminutive, wandering lights. Fireflies, or butterflies of light. It seemed that the wind had abandoned the land forever.

PART TWO

Long Rooms,
Closed and Empty

Diary in Disorder

I don't know how much time has gone by since I have been asking the same things, to the point of tiring my voice. And, suddenly, it occurred to me that he had much more patience than I. Then I said to myself once more that he does not have the right to appear patient or sensibly serene when he is only asking me for something. Something that I would have never dared to request from anyone. And from him less than from anyone. Of course (I forget it frequently) that is, as they say, the mission, or the tradition (or whatever it might be) of the maternal purpose. What have I ever known about the maternal purpose? It is painful to think about it now, when I see him grown up, absolutely alien. His youth pains me, as it once pained me to see him advancing clumsily on his two-year old legs; with a handful of dry leaves in his hand. It pains me to suppose that he speaks driven by goodness or evil. Whatever comes to me from him pains me as something irremisible, and for which I feel totally guilty. Perhaps pain ressembles love a great deal.

I don't know how many times I have asked him and I do not know how many times he has answered the same:

"What has he done?"

"I can't tell you anything more."

"Can't you give me some sort of excuse?"

"No."

"Not even an excuse?"

"No, I have told you everything I could."

I have been looking at him with all the distance of which I am capable. Even better, with the distance that I will never be able to rid myself of each time I speak to him. I only know that I have heard phrases like old murmurs; and I do not want, at any price, to enter once again that world, that landscape of names, memories, facts that I renounced a long time ago. Unexpectedly, echoes that I do not want, in any way, to discover or to recover, break out and sound repeatedly.

Everything now remained in another barrier. Very far from these present days which, scarcely a few minutes ago, I decided to defend. A present time that, here, in this house on this island, was revealed to me as my only form of possible life. I am not going to regress, just at this moment.

Bear obsesses me, there, sitting down, with his arms hanging from the sides of his armchair, as is his custom. It hardly seems possible how familiar that gesture of his still is to me: his hands, limp, on his knees. That gesture turns out much more familiar to me than his eyes, or his voice (or all that he could ever tell me or remind me the time when he gathered fallen leaves, so awkwardly and threw them unsuccessfully, into the fire.) Now the only familiar thing is, perhaps, the gesture of his arms, just like damp wings; his head tilted, his eyelids turned down.

That gesture is David's. That gesture is his father in front of me. Physically sunk down in the back of the chair; but not because of what I was saying, but because it is his habitual form of sitting down. For a moment I have got to the point of suspecting that he is not really in a predicament; that, in any case, this new worry, or problem, does not add anything to his habitual worries and problems.

"Look at me," I said.

And, in spite of myself, my voice sounded authoritarian to me, and the disagreeable reflection of other voices, other orders equally useless and unfruitful came to me. "How horrible my people are," I thought. As if I were repeating something already known a long time ago.

Bear raised his head. But his look did not settle on me, but caught hold behind me, as though floating on an undetermined point. "I have nothing more to add," he repeated. I don't know how many times I have heard it from him in the last hours.

"Don't you believe it," I said, conciliatory (or, at least, meaning to be). "It is not an unhealthy curiosity, or a stupid worry of a far-sighted mother. You know that I am not an excessively jealous mother. I confess that I am afraid because of what you have done; but it is not the banal and selfish fear that this or the other might happen to you; that something disagreeable is going to happen, or something simply annoying for you or the family. I am not so ferociously tribal, you can believe me. What worries me is the gratuitousness of your actions. Contemplating you so, as I have been contemplating you since I have seen you again. Yes, son, I am not a conventionally good mother. And I know that, deep down, you must appreciate it quite a bit. I don't expect you to like me nor to be your friend: because we are not the same age. But I know that there is a good understanding between the two of us: it is the least that can be asked of two human beings that are going to live together isn't that so...? I mean, a viable trick for the two of us. Are you really mixed up in all that? Is he your best friend? Is it a particular feeling of duty...? All that, whatever commonplace thought, whatever trivial idea would be of use to me. What bothers me is your lack of motives, in the beginning. And perhaps, finally, your lack of imagination.

Bear kept on looking behind me, possibly at the wall, or at one of those luminous little points that often appear in the atmosphere. Suddenly I recognized myself in those eyes. They are not the eyes that I have today, of course, but those I had many, many years ago when grandmother spoke of sensible reasons for doing something. (The eyes that still show through that box with a mirrored top). It's sad.

I stopped walking up and down, I put out my cigarette, and sat down. And my gestures were the maximum expression of sadness. I hesitated to grasp one of those solitary, limp, and touching hands; but immediately I desisted, convinced that an infinity of human beings would repeat that gesture: from North to South, from East to West, without too much success.

"Well, then, neither do I have anything to say."

Only then did Bear blink, he looked at me with a strange violence, with a kind of growing anger (which he perhaps did not achieve putting in order within himself; at least, with the required speed.)

"Does that mean that you are not going to help us?"

Ah, finally, finally. Bitter relief. At least one thing began to be clear: there was a hidden hatred, some possibility of love. I explained.

"If I say that I refuse, that I am not willing to conceal your friends for crimes or blunders that neither concern me nor preoccupy me (crimes that I have even no interest in knowing, since it seems, in itself, not to matter to you...) well, if I say no, what's going to happen?"

Bear returned to his silence, but a subtle vengeance shone in the night, somewhere, like phosphorescent powder. I was almost tempted to refuse. (At least I would know something about you, of what drives you to all that.)

I have tried to laugh, but Bear does not find anything comic or humorous in what I can tell him. I wanted to mortify him.

"You had to be you, among all his friends, as I see it. Surely in order to make yourself stand out."

"No. It was because of the house. No one had this chance."

"At least tell me without beating around the bush: what is it that you expect from me? What role have you assigned to me in this unfortunate story?"

Bear pretended to reflect (although I know very well that he had his answer perfectly thought out.):

"You are so well situated...so protected, I mean. No one will suspect this family, nor this house. I only want you to keep him hidden for three days. Three days will be enough."

And suddenly he said something unusual:

"I have never asked you for anything."

A vague hope impelled me:

"Once, when I was a girl, I saw a man murdered because he wanted to escape by the cliff. I don't remember whether I thought of the man's guilt or not. I only know that I found repugnant the idea that they had caught him. If that's what you want to know, you know it now. I don't care about our causes; for a long time all causes have seemed good to me. Only men corrupt them, trade in them, and cheat me."

I wanted this not to be lost, that Bear should continue looking at me with his wounding steadfastness. What pained me the most, up to that moment, was his arrogance, his lack of fear and—why not?—his absolute lack of heroic feeling. I always believed that these things were done through conviction, romanticism, or stupidity. In all of these reasonings lay a depth of dubious hope, of my gelatinous hope. (Some day, in some place, someone will return something to its rightful place. If no one recognizes this restitution, even though it be unconsciously or indirectly, the generosity, the sacrifice, will be without meaning. They will not bear fruit.) Rumors, brought by Antonia, come back. Manuel Taronji's gratuitous act, for example, earned the admiration, remote and mysterious, even of his own enemies. As if one could still trust gestures like his; as if in some way they could be a kind of sentinel's call, an open wound. A wound that could not be healed easily.

I have said that I wanted to be alone, "in order to reflect," and he has not believed me (because he never believes me.) He has left and he has left me alone, simply alone, without any reflection. He knows very well that I will only return, that, I will simply devote myself to my beloved solitude. It's curious how I guess these things in Bear. It's curious that, for me, Bear is so hermetic and so transparent at the same time.

But there are no longer heroes. They died along with the gods, they disappeared from the earth. David was not a hero. Franc has lived too many years, a poor hero caught between offers and demands. Offers and demands have dried up goodness, intelligence, they could even wear out knowledge if it were capable of withering. (At least, they have degraded it.) A long and exhaustive accounting of disappearances would be useless. We know about them, we accept them, adapt ourselves to them. As if the world had lowered its head and had dedicated itself to grazing. I see before me a sheep of terrified bovine eyes; I see her threadbare and burnt wool, her lower lip softened by blows, her look, astonished and indifferent at the same time. Innumerable stolid eyes, miserly imbecile, suffering, resigned. Scarcely a few months ago, when I accompanied Franc and Bear to Europe, I traversed a long road of similar looks.

At the end of the street was the iron railing behind which the trees moved. Or, at least, so it seemed to me. The almost white trunks, in the cold spring, the yellow splendor, in bursts, between damp jumbles of leaves. At the gate, the man, in a cap and over-alls, with absent-minded eyes, next to his dog which was run-ning about, sold entry tickets. There was a poster (of coarse card-board, as though drawn by a child). There was a pipe and under-neath it said: NO. That is to say that one must crush one's ciga-rette underfoot. I felt apathetic, I do not like to see stones; he already knew it, I had told him so. "I don't like museums, nor things preserved in alcohol. I would rather see some photogra-phy." (But it did not end up being true because, that time, for example—I believe it was a town on the plateau—when the castle appeared beneath the ungodly sun, almost demolished, charred, I had to assure myself that it was not a dream; and in spite of the heat and the dust, I was climbing towards the battlements, and when I was before the open door, without anyone or anything to keep me from entering, nor without anyone puncturing little pieces of cardboard with shiny pliers, I leaned against the door frame; I was covered with sweat, in the only shade there was. Wild bushes and weeds, and the damned and dusty stones gave off a strange smell, a mixture of herds and hot wind in the nettles. That time I liked seeing stones, although I felt no admiration, nor fear, nor pride, nor what could strictly be called dream: only capturing time in some way without knowing how, conscious that it was also possible that tomorrow or yesterday, or any other moment, could have never occurred.

But there, in the Jewish cemetery, on going through the gate, the narrow path rose slightly; suddenly I felt myself immersed in something like a city beneath the sea, where water and salt had turned into a golden warm haze. A tiny city where vertigo was not born within the eyes but from the soles of the feet; and I was suspended above innumerable tombstones. Galleries of super-imposed death; stones, stones. I had to be careful not to move my feet away from the path for fear of stepping on them. I had read one too many names that were getting to me, without my knowing it, under my skin; and, there, just there, I remembered clearly some of the many names that, at random, passed by un-der my eyes. I was now reading it, in the same air, like voices in my ears: "Mire Miroslav, 24, VII...How was it possible, such precision in numbers? The mysterious numbers and signs floated, as through under the sea in the submarine and submerged world. And suddenly, I said to myself: I have not submerged myself in the city, nor in the ocean; it is time, once more, buried in time; deaf in its enigmatic signs, in its voice that does not cease, beyond the undersea world. It is the air, the light, the trees, held in some hard crystal: like the sailboat Jorge de Son had in his house..."

Antonia had told me the rumors that circulate about Manuel Taronji. I have noticed a cold wind, from some place, coming towards me. It is difficult to recapture the emotion from the facts which no longer exist. Nevertheless, I have been thinking a great deal about Manuel Taronji since yesterday. That vertigo, that wind, is not unknown to me. I was there, also, in the instant when I leaned against the lovingly wrought sepulcher.

("...you have come in order to visit a museum that is unique of its kind in the world. Happy and unhappy circumstances have created a complex where a thousand years of history are hidden...," the glossy paper said, in a vague Spanish.) The paper trembled in my hands, I let it fall among the leaves that covered that stretch of ground. (Over the sea, in the little square of the Jews, so long, so long ago, I said to myself that the island was a superimposition of corpses; that we lived above them until cut down, falling and serving as groundwork for other steps, other voices.) Leaning against the tombstone of an unknown brother, I thought of another brother, so close and so far. I felt that Manuel was there, and everything took on a body. I bent over and took up the pamphlet of the Jewish Museum, in white letters on a black background: I unfolded it and found the photograph of the same cemetery where I was.

In the photograph it had snowed, the city of the dead was covered with snow. Outside, a man was selling tickets, a dog was scratching its back against the wall, a poster, in blue, with a pipe, forbade the tourists to smoke. And I was a tourist. I could be anything. I was not taking part in anything.

We do not want heroes, we prefer victims. The strange thing

that Antonia told me, when she brought breakfast—like those stories which as a child mortified me so much, about what my mother did or did not do at my age—, is a confused story that circulated among the fishermen and people of the Port. Possibly old Es Marine told it to her, one day while he was dividing up his things, before he went to the Old Folks Home. A very strange story, an improbable legend of boys and a little boat. Now two boys have made this same route. The same trajectory, the same sea. The sea and the stories that fascinated me as a girl. The sea that El Chino (poor boy, who died in the war: The sea of the Greeks and the Phoenicians...) loved. I remember a voice. A sea, dense, blue and transparent, cloudy and submissive; like a treacherous animal. The story is not convincing, one does not know whether it is a story of heroes or victims. But nobody wants to believe it, deep down. Someone will speculate about this story. The Greeks lived beautiful and heroic adventures; and the Phoenicians gathered them and sold them at a good price.

Beverly, Franc's best friend, married a Spanish emigrant, already lost in the fog of times past. When I met her she was not married. She was one of those many women of an advanced age who are still beautiful, wealthy, fond of traveling, who populate that vast continent. Beverly had a son by that Spanish emigrant. His name was David.

Franc said that I should have someone who could help me in the early days, until I could master the language. "David," Franc said, "is going to be very valuable to you, since he is Spanish, like you and me." Whenever he said the word Spanish, he would add "like you and me." (As though he feared that someone might not know it, or forget it.)

Curiously Beverly protected her son's language with a rare mixture, of love and stubbornness, that at times, I discovered in women like her. David spoke a fairly correct Spanish (on various occasions he visited his father who lived in New Mexico). David was a tall boy, dark, with grey eyes. Big eyes, surrounded by dark eyelashes. Scarcely had I seen him, than I thought that he had the eyes of a victim.

Sycamores are beautiful trees. A black squirrel was running

about among them nervously. I contemplated his lifted tail, like
a feather-duster, among the leaves that entirely covered the
ground. A sunbeam, almost hot through the boughs, danced on
the point of David's shoe.

"It's not that I don't want to," said David, "it's that I can't do
anything else. I feel this way many times, that I don't want to do
something, but I know that I will do it. Unavoidably."

He was speaking somewhat slowly, because he had to recover
the language slowly, through the mist of childhood. A mist that
was also lost, like Halloween ghosts (like the Druids, with a costume of yellow plumage that he was talking to me about). Some
silhouettes were outlined against the trees: we heard a distant
murmur of laughs, a whisper, a struggle of laughter that wants to
be supressed. (Suddenly I remembered the king of the elfs, dancing on the meadow, and offering his daughter to the Knight: "Tomorrow I will wake up and, like him, will have died," I vaguely
remembered.) The silhouettes ran throught the fog. Upon passing through the sunbeam, they caught fire, briefly. A feather, a
red rag, a few little horns. I trembled and noticed that, on the
other hand, David had returned, for an instant, to happiness.

I, too, used to do it, it was very amusing: they do the same
thing, they are the games of autumn. They are gathered together,
there, planning where they will go afterwards...

The silhouettes became more well-defined. A little skinny body
advanced in his costume of green satin. He wore a mask of black
velvet, he was barefoot and jumped up and down among the
leaves, with his shoes in his hand. Another one, taller, followed
him, with his long and blond hair. They had stained their faces
with soot. From among the trees emerged a song, a chorus of
hoarse, little voices, unexpectedly high-pitched. I said:

"I was looking for the origin. It comes from the Druids. The
ancient Irish..."

But David was no longer listening; once more he was looking
at the point of his shoe where the sun, round and small, domestic, was shining.

Then the group surrounded us. The group extended dirty little hands, sticky from candy. The squirrel climbed up the tree, along the beautiful trunk of the nearby sycamore.

"Bring me a fistful of leaves, son."

He went almost staggering from one side to the other of the lawn, on his clumsy legs. I had piled up a big heap of leaves in a corner.

Bear held up three or four leaves in his fingers, tenaciously clutched (like golden, crunchy, treasures). The fire started, the flame shot up, red, in the morning. And suddenly, among the flames one afternoon, surrounded by golden leaves and sycamores, I found a fragment of something which showed what I meant: "The druids set fire to bonfires in order to follow the elves and the goblins. In order that the goblins might follow the road...No, it's not that exactly. It was so that the ghosts of the ancestores should find the road leading home. Just another way of indicating the road..."

But I did not say anything because he did not feel like hearing such things, he was too occupied with his thoughts.

David, was tall, thin; he looked awkwardly touching. With his fragile neck and his desolate eyes. His sweater, which was too big, made him look like a child. He began to rock his foot and the sun escaped from his shoe.

"It's cold," he said. "Let's get away from here."

David got up and put his arm around my shoulder. On the green and solitary bench, or among the trees, it seemed that we had forgotten something. It was not true and, nevertheless, I had to turn my head to make sure that it was not that: that we had not forgotten anything.

Bear, where are you...?

Three Days of Love

The succession of doors lies in waiting; they are waiting for my step, as if they were about to swallow definitely the anxiety, the fear, or simply the reason which managed to bring me here.

Off and on the moon has been hiding in a dark blue mass. Little by little it took on strange forms, and I was reminded of the white of an egg in a glass of water that, on a certain Saint John's Night, a maid had put in the window. She assured me that, just on that night, and on no other, it would form the shape of a boat. I was contemplating, with the young maid (a girl whom I now see as a girl, but who then appeared to me to be a very wise and mature creature), the glass of miracles, in the moonlight: the miracle did not happen. (But she said: Look, look, the boat is now taking shape…)

I have looked at that moon which is hidden behind the cotton-like substance, and its meaning, even now, is still undecipherable to me. It appears as if, on that night (surrounded by a constant, shaking breath; by the sea which is a terrifying warning; by this to and fro movement), a cruel force shakes me without stopping, to the beat of a colossal breathing. I have seen Bear's signal light up and go out on the cliff. I have abandoned the light vessel as my distant young maid would call it), I have climbed up through the land which is terraced, through the rocks, with the unsteadiness of those not used to nature. In this night, upon climbing with awkwardness, I feel absurdly humiliated (as when he took me to the pine grove and I felt the unsettling suspicion of being watched by animals, stones, nettles and thorns). It is curious how we men can arrive at detaching ourselves from the earth, of feeling alien to it. What slow and tenacious process of denaturalization is unfolding in men like me? Will all men be as alien and distant, so absolutely strangers to the earth as I am?

Bear alone is a silhouette, a strange, extinguished lighthouse,

pointing the road out to me. Upon pushing the door to the courtyard, I have realized that in it something was going to open and
close; something that possessed an irreversible, definitive meaning. Definitive in what way? I can not know. I only know that
from now on there is something fatal in all our gestures. As if in
every corner, in each shadow dwelt codes that still it is not possible for me to decipher. Going up the staircase, in silence, so
that the old wood does not creak; Bear's feet, with the softness
of an antelope; and that other door, the definite one, the one which
leads me to the hideout area, follow one after the other as something already very much experienced, very well-known. I perceive that Bear is barefoot. Bear has smooth, golden feet, unusually beautiful for a boy.

This is an old room, frugally furnished. I see objects shine in
the dark. ("We got lucky in everything," Bear said. "Not only an
excellent crossing, but also on nights like this when the full moon
returns, the clouds hide it.") At times, all circumstances seem to
accumulate, favorable or unfavorable. Unexpectedly you arrived,
Bear, with your baggage of favorable circumstances; this house,
this party, this boat. This family, this date. It is curious, your
circumstances suddenly amalgamated with my old plans (that
already seem to be distorted into a comfortable chimera), shake
up the foundations of this inane thinking. All opportunities unite,
the chimeras are projected towards an absolutely inexcusable
reality: that which, so long ago, was to be recorded, inescapably,
in some place. This house, this boy, this old woman who cel-
ebrates her centenary, are the natural roads, the suitable circumstances that compliment each other (along with a dead and buried woman, along with the destiny of a man recently brought
back to the island), summon and unite scattered reasons: they
already form a body, a whole, that I can not evade without be-
traying myself.

Something so light as the sudden, blinding brilliance of that
round moon, unexpectedly stripped of clouds, seems to be torn
off from the accumulation of happy circumstances, like an evil
foreboding. The darkness is broken, the underground quality is
violated, it seems. It is now that Bear opens the second door.

There are three rooms, long and continuous. They seem more like drawing rooms, rooms that await forgotten masked balls; with a special echo, a smell of salt and wind, of dust and seclusion. I have crossed the first, the second room, and I enter the third. I feel a shudder when Bear, in front of me, laboriously opens the heavy door panels, chained together by rust, trying to keep the hinges from creaking. In vain, since their groanings have resounded in the emptiness like something alive. I have not been able to avoid the impulse to look upwards, towards the hand-crafted ceilings, towards the spider webs which move back and forth, brought on by the movement of the door. Shining under Bear's lantern: miserable veils, invaded by minuscule and golden armies. Legions of insects which seem more to navigate than to fly, in this air eaten away by salt. Green and corrosive salt, there, on the doors that I discover to be carefully wrought. High and narrow doors that I now recognize as having dreamt them more than once.

My dreams are populated by doors which open and close, silently, on the passage of no one. In my dreams I anticipated the vision of those lintels that I crossed until arriving at the third room. It is furnished, crammed rather, with an infinity of old belongings. Here, everything appears devastated by the silent invisible monster, absolute master of everything. Everything crushed, eviscerated in its enormous and immaterial jaws. Only the shadows where I have sunk voluntarily-involuntarily, acquire here a real corporeality. Bear leans his hand on the bookcase that mimics the skeleton of a great, mummified animal; something falls down, with a noise that leaves us, for a moment, in suspense. But Bear has smiled: he realized (he has said so) that this house is known for its nighttime noises, for its thousand creaking noises in the darkness; for sudden falling-downs that, now, do not surprise anyone. "Because," Bear assumes, "the house will be torn apart, little by little, crumbling, sinking, with the entire family of old people that it shelters in its interior: since, here, no one appears ready to die." Bear and I have laughed; but I know that my laughter has seemed strange to him.

I have gone to the window where, through a hole in the win-

dow pane, there, —for many years now, I suppose—the coming
of the rain and the wind has penetrated and has destroyed the
wood. The sun, too, would come in here sometimes, through this
hole: as far as its long fingers of gold could reach. But perhaps it
will have barely grazed this corner of the table, this paper on
which, perhaps, remains a word, a gesture of goodness. Who
knows. Bear says that nobody comes in here, even now. Only his
mother, these days, lodged temporarily in the first of the three
rooms. Apparently, that kind of anteroom is still considered as
the first step to hell. Nobody will open another door, since it can
lead to what is still considered Grandfather's private devil. Bear
laughs quietly at this man who is probably sick; a sad man who
frightened this house and these people with his offensive extrava-
gances. No longer is anyone going to unfasten these musty bolts.
Only the mice (that I hear running about up there, above my
head; and on the floor, between the feet of the table, of the chairs,
of the bed; under the furniture that, at this moment, resembles a
curious zoo of inanimate fauna) that camp here freely. Scarcely
does a light grazing occur and something trembles and falls. It is
not dust, it is like the immaterial substance of time which,
strangely, has forgotten this corner; or there, under the curved
shelves which can no longer bear the weight of the manuscripts.

Someone brought together in this last room everything that
was to be discarded after the general clearing out of the other
shelves. There is no reason, otherwise, for the placing of this
bed, enormous and mysterious, materially covered with gold, in
the middle of the room. Bear runs his hand over the canopy which
shines like a hidden treasure. Bear understands that I am not going to be comfortable but, on the other hand, he knows that no
one, ever, will find me in this room. "If something were to happen to me and you were to die inside here, no one would ever
find out," he has said. Apparently he feels an unusual joviality
tonight. There comes over him a curiously humoristic feeling
that I am not able to achieve. If I laugh again he will think that, in
effect, something is not going right.

Why does inhuman terror, bestial terror, unconfessable and
destructive, return now, at the moment when this boy of good

faith has closed the last door on his bare feet? I have remained in fright (as only a child could have felt, his dignity helplessly knocked down, his faith stomped on and degraded). I don't want this child to return, nor that moment. Time must do with me as it did here, with this book that falls apart in my fingers, with this bed that groans under my weight, with this horrible green mold that encloses the air, the eyes and one's breathing. Let time do with me as with bookplates; let me return to ash, smoke, a gold-colored asphyxiated butterfly, behind a book or a picture.

I discover extinguished lamps; no one will illuminate this dead and long place. But terror lives throughout this decay, the cobwebs, the green cadavers of so many insects turned into crystal powder. It is useless to expose oneself to the corrosive nitrate of time when one is only an innumerable terror, in memories, in the pure and simple touch of the air which surrounds us. Time has not been able to annihilate fright and the struggle begins to wear me out. Will I go on becoming old, will I have taken the first step, will I have entered the first day of death? It is possible. Bear has left this door open: the two leaves of the door, sarcastically open, awaiting the new destruction (perhaps not even yet known) under that lintel. But I am not going to cross through that door, I am not going to arrive at that last door. Suddenly, in the shadow, these two matching rooms, long, like improbable empty platforms, turn their faces towards me; like those endless boxes, or those double mirrors where the world is repeated, obsessively in order to inform me and tell me that this is not a dream, that no one is seated next to my bed, reproaching me for a dream that arrived too peacefully.

At times something infinitely childish has the power to give our serenity back to us. The contemplation of the square bundle that Bear has left on the floor, that metal box, with provisions (canned goods, cans of beer), awakens in me an assiduous tenderness, a special smile, that could not be achieved by his humoristic-macabre intentions. (He has a curious sense of humor, Bear.) With my foot, I rub against, in a kind of playful way, the edge of the rustic box; I suddenly feel comforted; as when, after a bad dream, the frothy enjoyment of an awakening has returned.

As though I had the sudden conviction that the sun will return outside, immediately; that life, the world, is inhabited by beings that can not allow themselves the luxury of a fright, nor of nightmares, nor of very pleasant self-disdain.

Up to now he had never spoken to me of his mother. His confidence in her is curious. He is sure of a complicity that, in the best of cases, will be a form of extortion. But fate had been decided in this way and not in another. "There were not very many places to choose from, to tell the truth." (This is his exact phrase.) He does not seem to value too much the unshakable faithfulness that he assumes in his mother, in his own uncle. Why is he certain of them? But there is nothing certain, here in this world, next to the mice, the bedbugs, the butterflies and the great names. Bear does not appear to appreciate excessively that firm faithfulness that he counts on; he does not see in it any another merit than a kind of decadence, weakness or an inefficient bond of blood and mind. I never was, nor will I ever be able to be, like Bear. Everything in this life has its precise moment. Like certain pictures, the past (our past) must be looked at from a prudent and precise distance; in order not to face an enigmatic world of anarchistic brush strokes, without any apparent coordination. Bear would not have been Bear if he had been born and had lived in Z.

Diary in Disorder

After dinner I went upstairs and entered the legendary room which they have assigned me. But I already know that behind the hermetic double door, high and dark, (the door which, when we were children, frightened us and fascinated us), someone was crouching down, waiting or fearing. I turned on the light, knowing that something would move behind there (though it might be only a glance). On the other side of this door which no longer keeps its mystery—(where formerly stories of human bonfires were revived, in Borja's astonished and sweet voice: Grandfather's books, rotting on the shelves, which he described as the garden of Perversions and that I now imagine to be the sad rags, frayed bandages of some fragile mummy)—knowing that someone was spying on my footsteps. In these rooms there is no electric light and I have brought one of the many lamps with a red globe that populate the corners of this house. There is no cable here, nor light-switch, or plug: they are rooms which are completely shut off. How did Bear get the mysterious key? Echoes of child thieves are revived in me, stories of secretive, furtive and barefoot little boys, on the traitorous steps, full of creaks; feathers soaked in oil sliding between moldy hinges; children who slid keys, coins, drinks, cards into dark holes; secret, invaluable treasures. How has Bear managed to…? But I brought the lamp near and realized what an imaginative and ingenious woman I still am. There are no longer children who play at robbers and who escape like shadows or goblins (children capable of sticking their heads out over the eaves of the roof faint with triumph and vertigo: like the goblins which cry out on the weathervanes). Children like Bear (although Bear, perhaps never was a child; or, perhaps, Bear will never cease to be one; because his childhood is not one of those that are in danger, it is not vulnerable); this class of children, like Bear, wield useful and appropri-

ate instruments. The bolt of the forbidden door is carefully
smoothed with a file. Next to the lever, a little hole with blackish
edges will allow this lamp that I have just lit (which I carry in my
hand, raised up like a grotesque copy of the Statue of Liberty), to
cross, in a ray of light (like a red-hot eye) the excommunicated
rooms. (And the children's shadows do not flee on the floor. They
go in search of Mother, lead her aside, where nobody can inter-
rupt them and warn her: "I have something to tell you.") They do
not ask for, they report. Perhaps it's better this way.

I left the lamp on the table, I looked for the pills: but will I
need the pills tonight so that sleep might arrive? What better
occasion to stay up, vigilant, like a jailkeeper? Deep down, I
should be happy that Bear, after all is said and done, has given
me his first confidence. Also, why not?, in spite of everything,
his first request. Although it might appear impossible to me, I
could have been able to refuse.

If, as a girl, they would have told me that I would sleep here
for a whole week, I would have become mute with terror. At
times I think that I would like to regain the fear I had in childhood: but that, too, is forgotten. I look for it in vain; in the corners where, in the past, I spied on the devil, yearning that he
would look at me in the mirror and would want to change me
into a pretty woman. I am not concerned either about being pretty
now. When Borja comes (it will be the last day, at the last moment) I would like to witness the moment when Bear wraps him
in his noble machinations. Perhaps these boys are not heroic but,
at least, they do not have any need of it. Borja, yes: Borja asked
for heroism, greatness, evil triumphing over the earth, raised on
the tips of his feet, handsome and sweet (although a little humiliated because I always exceeded him in stature). Now Borja, within
two days, in the great false-centenary when Bear will include
you in the secret, will you stand up on your feet and cry out as
when you spoke of the colonel? It will be a happy moment for
you. Perhaps you will suppose that everything depends on you;
that you are the only one who can undo the destructive or saving
word. I do not know what crime this boy has committed who is,
perhaps now, frightened by his own audacity. But why does this

sound to me like a game that is too delicate to be trusted to the hands of two children? Why does it remind me of those pretend games of chess, on the floor, between Borja and me, while we whispered more or less provocative words, rebellious or blasphemous words, about older people, about the world, about God, or about flowers? Ah, Borja, my brother: like Cain and his ghost Abel, let us journey together, wherever we might go. Solitary, wandering; like Cain and the spectre of Abel, let us never be separated (each one on his road, both nomads, roaming around the parcel of domestic Hell or of Paradise, stripped of its leaves, that fell to our lot.)

A gust of spring is felt through the window. I close my eyes, I want to sleep while awake, to spy on that door in order that no one should cross that threshold which was entrusted to me. Strange confidence, truly. But, in any case, coming from Bear is more than what I was ever able to dream of.

I abandoned you, Bear: not when you were a blond child on the lawn; but two years ago when I brought you to this land, one night, on a night-train. Could I get you back on a night like this? No, no, I'm going to uncover again ignoble instincts disguised as love. Selfishness has many forms of being manifested: I am not going to wrap it up, again, in the illusion of love. No, Bear: no one will get you back. Puppies flee the house, they escape when they are scarcely able to keep themselves on their short paws. (Bear, Bear, little bear, where are you going?) Perhaps, in this very moment, another woman like me is fingering in her hands an old toy that no longer has any meaning. Perhaps now, in this very moment, a woman like me sleeps peacefully, assuming that the boy who is now lurking behind the Devil's Door, sleeps unsuspectingly, or studies, or drinks, or loves. But he is there: behind that door, and someone is chasing him; or wants to chase him, or do him harm; or desires his death.

I do not even know his name, nor do I want to know it: at least, this very night.

In spite of everything I opened the door and my lamp lit a stretch of damp floor, long, of a red already faded through time and dust. I felt a great emptiness and I advanced through those unsuspectedly narrow walls where the lamp awoke silhouettes (the night on which Gerda entered the Palace of the Prince and the Princess, when she believed she was embracing Kay, she was embracing a boy with a dark neck, who was sleeping on his back and the boy opened his eyes and Gerda cried out; because he was not a boy, he was not Kay; and her lamp disturbed some unknown shadows on the walls). But the silhouettes, on these walls, were nothing else than faded paintings; naked beings linked together, beautiful and remote; as though becoming transparent on the wall. I smiled internally at my sudden fright, I remembered the fondness—according to what they say—that the old man (whom they called diabolic) had for the mural paintings. And now, the diabolic old man gives me the feeling of being romantic, sensual and crazy as though I were a young maiden. There they are, in great measure, part of the evil things that they attributed to him: the not very valuable nakedness of some important frescoes which have become pale, moldy and bare; bad copies of others which, in his imagination, were desired and splendid riches, a sumptuous paradise which I am not able to tread on. I advanced through the deserted, uninhabited coldness of the red bricks, as pale young men rose up on both sides of me, young men who would have managed to be handsome in the hands of another artist. Ah, poor Grandfather, surely mistreated, homosexual, infinitely, terrifyingly alone; on this island in this world. You must have floated in these rooms, like a dead planet, longing for lights, impossible repercussions of other stars which turn in another impossible universe. Poor Grandfather, I thought, while I advanced; and I sent him a belated greeting (since, up to that moment, I had not begun to know him). I left the lamp on the floor, thinking of the unknown boy who was waiting, perhaps frightened, perhaps angered. But the light of that window, who could see it? This part of the wall looks out on the sea, to the cliff. At that hour everybody must be already sleeping. I advanced, thinking of him, into the tenuous darkness—a transparent, lucid darkness that can only be found on moonlit nights, on an island, very close to the sea.

I opened the window, something came close and fell on the

floor with a slight click; a fluttering about grazed the ceiling. But the white light, beautiful, invaded the walls weary of echoes, of immobile dancers. Something, perhaps deep respiration, seemed to rise up, coming out from the walls, like a sigh of relief. The air balanced, way up on the ceiling impossible, very rare icicles: a simultaneously dirty and phosphorescent lace.

I did not even know his name, nor what had brought him to this situation. Nor did I want to know it. One can not betray what is not known. "Betrayal there, wherever I go," whispers a bitter and well known voice, in me, or somewhere else.

I am not a happy being, I can not be so, I never was. The world is full of women like me: that is the one story of my life. Without pity for myself, or for others: selfishness, lack of understanding and solitude, are still, after all is said and done, the common and vulgar experience of women like me.

Upon seeing him I had the impression that something had changed. Something, I can not specify what, took a violent turn: what happened was not as had been foreseen, or, at least, supposed. It was different from what I had hoped, believed, or perhaps wanted. It is not possible for me to define what it is that brought me to this conclusion: but I had the clearly defined certainty that things were not as I had believed them to be.

In the last of the three rooms, the remains of a forbidden world (the inane dream of an old man) were poorly arranged; in the center of the room, among the old furniture, piled up, moth-eaten, poorly placed. I made out the boy's silhouette, sitting on the edge of a horrible bed that still shines. "What a strange layout," I thought at that moment. "What an unusual place to put a bed." Then I thought I saw myself, as if through the eyes of the boy: as if he possessed the faculty of contemplating me, in a long, narrow, hallucinating mirror; I was reflected in another mirror, then another and another. Fortunately I found the pack of cigarettes in my jacket pocket. With a certain relief I offered it to him. He got up slowly, and, to keep him from doing so, I leaned my hand upon his shoulder. At that moment, at that contact, the certainty that something was not as it should be was revived; that something happened which was the opposite of what I had hoped for or believed.

I felt better this way: standing in front of him, sensible, un-derstanding, offering a reasonable and moderately severe image. His hand turned white in the half-light, he took the cigarette, said "thanks," in a scarcely audible voice; and I felt a vague pity. Not for him, but for another woman whom I imagined in another part of the world. It seemed to me that his hand trembled. Al-though it was perhaps only a false perception (I confess that the idea that, after all, he did not appear so insolently tranquil as Bear, caused me an unhealthy satisfaction). He lit a match, and, when the flame faintly illuminated his bent head, I felt the cer-tainty of why something was not as it ought to be, or, preferably, as it ought to have been. I contemplated a part of his face, his forehead, the roots of his almost blond hair; his eyelids and light-colored eyelashes. Then, I discovered some extremely fine wrinkles in his skin, next to his eyes; starting out from the sides of his nose; in the corners of his lips. And I remained motionless, with the extinguished match between my fingers, looking towards the darkness, unusually alert. Why had I decided, beforehand, from the moment when Bear included me in his secret, that it was a question of a boy of twenty or twenty-two? The fact of being a friend or acquaintance, or perhaps an accomplice of Bear, —suddenly possibilities that I had not reflected on before are revealed—does not imply the necessity of being his age. No one told me that he was. Why this foolish belief? Arbitrarily, I have judged a youthfulness, including purity, by some facts that are absolutely unknown to me. An obscurity, much deeper than the one which surrounded me, faced me. Is it not at twenty, accord-ing to what I have heard, when men or women risk themselves in adventures and fantasies, in useless gestures, which afterwards someone cuts off and gathers, like ripe fruit, in order to sell them in the market at a good price? Isn't this what is usually done? Is not twenty the right, conventional, agreed upon, age for such excesses? All attitudes, activities, professions, sports and spiri-tual movements require a suitable age. Thus, what is it, then, that unexpectedly breaks up my chessboard?

A breach had just opened up, something cracked the solid

structure of the hopes and fears I had taken for granted. I felt heat on my forehead, on my cheeks (as when I believe myself swindled). It seemed to me that all my blood was throbbing in my face. On the other hand, in that place where everyone is assured that the heart breathes (and only appears to be a defenseless, painful, discordant point; a viscera, a part, or a satellite, totally unexplored and wandering), I felt an obviously disproportionate dizziness.

But I distrust my unjustified fears so much, I fear so much my improbable suppositions, my moments of drawing back totally deprived of any foundation: they empty into the dark street of desolation: "Thus, so he is no longer a boy. He is not of the age to take part in student revolts. So all this is more serious." But who assured me that this complicity had as justification that which, frivolously, I called, to myself, "student revolts"? Falteringly, I looked for a seat. "It can be a matter of many other things that I have not thought about even for a moment. It can be a matter of an assailant, a common criminal, a stupid thief, a maniac, an imbecile, a rogue, or a handicapped person, but who has told me? And Bear, Bear, what have you to do in this story? No one has told me, that's sure; but the truth is that I never wanted, except for tonight, and very slightly, to be informed of anything. And, moreover, why have I given him a motive, including even a social class, a priori, without anyone or anything having given me the slightest hint of it? Why did I make him studious, well brought up, young, and did not make him rude, miserable, old? Or simply a worker, a peasant, a sailor or a smuggler? How stupidly we defend our poor conscience, our brittle tranquility! I pigeonholed him in the most comfortable place (as I pigeonholed for a long time now, on high, accommodating shelves, all that which could upset the peace of my particular and incompatible island).

I have been, without looking at him, astonished by contradictory thoughts. And to think that I have even taken pity on a mother that I imagined to be similar to me. Then I have felt an irrepressible desire to laugh; a stupid, disgraceful laugh, and thoughtless from all angles. How grotesque I saw myself, what a ridiculous

image is mine, advancing through the dark and closed rooms of
the old man, a homosexual and a dreamer, that was my grandfather; I, solemn, foolish, maternal and severe; with a lamp in my
hand (as in the novels that pile up on grandmother's shelves:
heroines who advance, a torch at the ready, towards young men
who have strayed and who now cry in silence.) I can not remedy
it, an uncontrollable laugh, oppressed so that it becomes painful,
has kept me immobile for I don't know how long.

Until the tiny red circle, haloed here and there by a very subtle
shining (like the eyes of certain nocturnal animals), fell to the
floor and a heavy dull, weight crushed it.

Three Days of Love

It is an immense relief, suddenly, the orange colored slot and the button of light that punctured the door next to the bolt; those steps, the creaking of that furniture; that window which opens. A lengthened shadow comes and goes under the door. Probably he has lit an oil-lamp or a kerosene lamp. It seems that there is no electric light here. They have not touched anything in these rooms for years.

Evidently it is a great relief to know that there are human footsteps, live, on the other side of the invisible threat, of the rancor that breathes in each of these doors, cracked by borders of flowers, humiliated by mold. Now the tiny rattling, the mice that pursue each other over my head and under the furniture, lose their superstitions and their biting omen.

The door has opened and I saw her advance and look at the walls; as if, the same as me, it was the first time that she came in here. That supposition comforts me. It is like the shared unveiling of an episode that is being born and in which, perhaps, all of us have, finally, our equal shares of reason and horror. Something similar to the cowardly sensation of the more of us there are, the less we suffer, that shows solidarity in danger, against the fewer we are, the better, on distributing the booty.

Bear has scarcely spoken to me about his mother and the sure thing is that he had not imagined her. Therefore I do not understand why her dark silhouette has surprised me, when the lamp populated the walls with young ephebi, moldy and modestly pornographic. "I thought that she was different." But that is absurd; if I did not imagine her in any way she could not be different. Before she left the lamp on the floor and opened the window and came close to the other door (the last one) which opens into my hideout, I had time to say to myself: "Why is she different?" She appears very tall and very slim; or perhaps it is her shadow on the floor which lengthens it. Taller and thinner than customary, I think.

But when she has offered me a cigarette and has sat down, something unusual and embarrassing arises between us. I think that everything is planned to the millimeter; that everything has been carefully and fully thought out, except for this sudden, banal and embarrassing situation: the two of us, in the darkness, in the silence. I must be grateful to her for her (we could say) collaboration. Although it is a forced collaboration, one of being "an accomplished fact." But we can say nothing to each other, we don't know how to say anything. It has seemed to me that she was laughing. In truth something surprising, but the sure thing is that she seemed to laugh. Or, at least, hold in her laugh. It is difficult to be sure of it.

Then, she has gone to the window, to open it. "A real obsession, that of opening windows," I said to myself; I allowed myself to speak to her, to insinuate a hesitating: "Perhaps it might be better to let it be: so that no brightness be seen." (Meanwhile the weak and pink light of the other room, the lamp that she left on the floor, kept watch; the lamp which brought to life the pictures on the wall.)

"No one can see it," she has said. "These windows look out on to the sea. And, moreover, I sleep there, nearby these days. I can illuminate the rooms, on whatever night: like now, for example." I thought her voice was unusual. Perhaps the affectionate feeling was only that: something like foretelling in her voice made me think that it was different. Her voice goes down, a little hoarse. It is not a beautiful voice, a velvety voice, or a mature, serious voice. It is as though some visible resonance made a halo around each word. She spoke slowly, in a low tone; and, nevertheless, it seems to awaken an echo behind each one of her phrases; above, up there, where the raised arms are lost, the wild games of those ephebes on the murals. I never heard a voice like this one; nor do I believe that I will hear it again. "It is possible that it might be through the fault of this room, of these long, empty, closed up rooms which surround and envelop, with an audible splendor, each shade of your voice," I mediate vaguely.

I do not know what Bear must have said to her about me. I see the outline of her head and shoulders, on the window, against the lit-up night sky. I do not see her face, only her skin, apparently black, and I can make out her long, thin neck; I am aware of the oscillating movement of her shoulders. She moves almost imperceptibly, with an extremely light swaying (one could say that it is inexistent). But I noticed, as I noted many times, the sudden vibration of the walls, of the floor, of a thousand objects and landscapes; that nobody, or almost nobody, could make out. Therefore, I guess this tenuous and swaying tendency; like a challenging of the void, turning one's back, voluntarily, to the void. I feel dizzy and close my eyes.

"I don't know what Bear probably said to you...," she says. And although there is no irritation in her voice, nor even a contained or hidden bad humor, I know that her words are not friendly, not even courteous. She repeats: "I don't know what Bear probably said to you, but I hope that you don't hold me for a kind mother, nor by far a complacent one. I do not believe that it might have occurred to him to refer to the possible goodness of my heart, or plain good disposition, due to some of his innumerable manifestations of customary, juvenile revolt. In any case, I beg of you that you don't believe him: nor expect from me a goodness that, possibly, does not exist. The truth is that I still do not know what I am concealing, or whom I am helping, nor why."

Certainly nothing of what she says is agreeable, but neither did I expect that it would be: thus an unusual sense of well-being under the sound of her voice had kept on overcoming me. Even when she ends up by saying, more or less: "And, moreover, I have not yet made a decision. The fact of finding you installed here does not mean that you can count on me tomorrow. I have been, simply, taken by surprise and I have not yet put either my indignation or my decisions in order. So that, for the moment, you must abstain from being grateful to me for anything."

I believe that, effectively, I have not said anything. I saw her leave, just as she had entered; with her slow walk, lightly ungraceful, in the diffuse fatigue in which she seemed to move; as if each one of her gestures caused her too great an effort for such poor results (coming and going on this earth). I perceived, when she bent over to pick up the light, that she is a woman inundated, immersed, drenched to the bones in a very ancient laziness: a laziness that only can be transmitted, piled up, matured through several generations. A laziness, to tell the truth, that fills me with equal parts of confused admiration and envy.

Once more only shadows, outlines in the darkness, once more silence. The light has gone out behind the last door, beyond the vacant room that separates us. Once more, darkness. The double doors become white. The moon, immense, splendidly shining, projects luminous trapezoids on the floor, uncovers metals on the table previously not noted. Near it, the brightness carries a deathly paleness on the painted boys. They give the sensation of laminated, transparent beings, of awaiting something.

But the reality is not the calm moment, or the surprise, or the smile or the presence of a human being who speaks, offers a cigarette and disappears. The reality is in this: the slow ascent of terror, once more. If it were not for the fact that I know that this will not be the last time that fear will arrive, I would be able to get up, shout like one more sick person: saying that it is not possible to resist, that I have arrived at the limit of my capacity of endurance. But I know that it would not be the last time either: only one more time (and worse). It is necessary to continue, to keep on, to walk. The only medicine, the only remedy for the long stages of my journey is not to stop, to walk, walk, walk.

I would prefer to have the windows closed because, at least, I would not hear the sea. If it were not for the excessive brightness of the moon I could remain quiet, looking at the sky; discovering little by little the innumerable worlds that, as a child, attracted me and consoled me. But this brilliance blinds me, pains me.

He, too, was shut in.

In the old houses, in the towns that flood the arid, dusty earth of my country, there are always closed and empty rooms; rooms shut off that, on an ill-fated day, one that has been marked, are used for a man's hiding himself voluntarily or involuntarily. In order that he shut himself in with his crazy, chiromantic dreams, perversely or crazily scientific. Like this poor old man who flooded with dreams or visions this manuscript that, not even in the excessive light of the moon, can I decipher (each letter is the nest of a dark insect where desperate and ill defined shows of tenderness are hatching). Or like that other man of dreams: the one who was for days and nights in his narrow hideaway above the granary (which formerly was used for keeping apples and hazel nuts). Alone, with his fear, alone with his rigid, incorruptible concept of what he believed ought to be, at all costs, the world.

I still have to remain in this room two more days before returning to the light. Or, perhaps, I will never return.

That room, at that time of year, was empty of apples, of grain: there only remained, on the walls (as the ghosts of the impossible ephebes roam about here), the aroma of the fruit that was formerly stored here, of the sacks of hazelnuts and almonds, of the corn. A fine dust danced in the air. On the beams there were remains of corncobs. It was a narrow, long room, too, although smaller than this one. And backed against the wall was a false armoire, the back of which was, in reality, another door which lead to the redoubt, to the hideaway where the cot was; where he slept, wrapped up in the red blanket, which still smelled of a cedar-chest, of mothballs, of winter. Carlista wars, persecutions, crimes, fear, sounded in my ears, as a child, as something remote, already incredible: but there was the false armoire, the hole; and he remained inside there, hidden, day after day. But she used to say to me: "Never open the door." But she was referring to the door to the street. She did not know that I knew about the hideaway. At that time she was thin, with dark hair, almost black, scarcely lightened at the temples. She walked, standing straight, through the street and came home arrogant, almost ferocious, after her work, strange in that world (fresh and unforeseen for me). Or with her shopping bag from which peeped out fruit and bread. "Did you hear me? Don't open the door to anyone. Always say my father is not here. I always said: "Dad is not here, he's gone, he went away." There was a safety chain on the street door; protected behind the chain I stuck my childish face through the crack and said (to the postman, to the mysterious visitor, to the unknown women): "No, my dad is not home. My dad went away..."

He called me Bambi, because he had read a book—he liked animal stories a lot—whose central character, a deer, was called like that. "You look like Bambi," he would say to me, laughing. He was fat, good humored. And, nevertheless, when he talked he seemed to become lean, wisened. Every morning, before going to the High School, he took a walk in the pine grove. He had breakfast at six, in the wide dining room, poorly furnished and festive, with flower pots in the balcony with green shutters, among white washed walls and lithographs that represented birds, deer, horses. There was a mirror, tilted, above the sofa, two oval portraits—grandfather and grandmother— in black frames; and a very delicate indoor plant, cared for like a newborn, placed very close to the light. With infinite love, he would pull off the yellowing leaves; he would trim it with the small and curved nail scissors.

But one day, she said: "He is gone, he has left. You must tell everyone that he has left." It was not true (since one night I saw light in the dining room; I got out of bed, I went out on the tips of my toes, and I saw him; he was with his elbows on the table, his forehead leaning on his closed fists; and she caressed his arm, passively, looking at the floor). The next day, when she left for work, I climbed slowly the attic stairs. Because I said to myself: "He must be somewhere. He must be somewhere. He can not disappear like a phantom." I opened that door and the other one, and that armoire; and, miraculously, I pushed its back board, and I found him.

He took me in his arms, he kissed me, he wet my face (even though I did not see him cry). And he said: "Bambi, don't tell anyone; I am here hiding. Don't tell mother that you know it: but come to see me everyday, when she goes to work, or to the market…"

And that is what I did. When she would close the front door, I would run up the stairs. I would open one door, another door, I would push the fake back of the armoire. And he would be there. He had grown a beard, he was thinner. He was reading a book with green covers, with a variegated spine: "Bambi, sit down. Quiet, silent, Bambi". It was a secret. A great secret only for men. The woman should not find out. A secret that no one should know.

("Bambi, the story of a life in the forest", by Felix Salten. "It is truly awe inspiring how the words attributed to the creatures of the animal world animal express the real feelings proper to these creatures..."

Before the confinement he took me, at times, in summer, in the late afternoon, to the pine woods. My legs were covered with insect bites; dreadful caterpillars appeared under the rocks or on the bushes; the birds screamed out unusual warnings, in incomprehensible calls. It was cold, or it was hot. I was thirsty. There were ants and thorns everywhere. The bread filled with dirt... (Truly grandiose. Like the words attributed...) Once, I saw a dead bird, half devoured by a cloak of tiny and moving red ants. I ran away, I fell flat on my face, my knees bled. My skin had always been too white, the sun hurt me on my skin, in my eyes. The shadow of the house was waiting, at last, like still water: the luminous shadow, fresh, white, shining, of the dining room, of the mirror, or the delicate indoor-plant. Why did he take me up to the pine forest? Why was Bambi me, just me? But men like him covered creatures they imagine to be extraordinary, marvellous, with the best attributes. Men like him demanded from creatures thoughts, desires, extraordinarily high and luminous ambitions. The world was a harmonious symphony of feelings, of voices, of open and generous hands. I was Bambi, taking pleasure in the woods. (I was not—he never saw me as—a pale, frightened child who did not dare to tell him that the pine woods were repugnant to him, that he abhorred the dusty roads, that he hated the dawn over our squalid river. But he recited: "The beautiful gifts, the great treasures of the earth," in a desolate spot of sand and cliffs, of cunning lizards, of men, lurking and without brothers. He used to say: "The great family of man," and he did not have a family. He said: "The inestimable treasures of friendship," and he did not have friends. (Because when he was there, hidden, pale, with his beard that he had let grow, reading for the thousandth time: it is truly grandiose how words attributed to the creatures of the animal world..., his brothers had abandoned the place, his friends had disappeared. They no longer filled up the afternoons, the evenings in the dining room with the green blinds. ["One more bottle"], with friends, with chatting, with sayings...) "The feelings proper to those creatures," he kept on reading upstairs, under the red blanket; because the cold had arrived and in the hideaway he was not able, or ought to, light the stove. Nobody should know where he was. "And when you are grown up, I'll explain it to you; everything has its explanation. Don't think that men are evil. You will understand it later, when I explain it to you. It is only a misunderstanding," he would say. And I thought, yes, that it was true, that some day he would explain it to me and everything would be very clear, very reasonable. The important thing is, then, that Bambi should not lose faith again (like Bambi in the book), his faith in men.

(But Bambi, "don't you know how to be alone?," they ask Bambi on the day he looks for and can not find his mother. "But Bambi, is it that you don't know how to be alone?...")

He knew how to be alone, days and nights. Days. Nights. I burst into his hideaway in the morning, when the door was closed behind my mother. She did not suspect anything, on her return, when she came home tired, anxious, her nose reddened by the cold: "Son, you have not opened the door, have you? No one has knocked, have they?"

No, nobody had come. I had not opened the door to anyone.

But I do not know how to be alone. I do not know how to be and, for that reason, Isa entered into my life, she took possession of me, she stuck to me, like a voracious crustacean. I have her nailed to my flesh, wounding, annoying, inevitable. Because I do not know how to be alone, the boys get together around me; I feel the glance of their eyes. They believe me and I believe in myself. I felt myself grow this way, in the silence of the nights, in the inaudible buzzing of the afternoons, with the boys. When I engaged each and everyone of them in the extraordinary system of a precise and valuable watch; in a savage, delicate machinery, suitable for moving a world where men are they themselves the only misunderstanding, where creatures (animals, all of them) "express the real feelings proper to these creatures..."

In This City

_____

Even without waking up she heard the rain against the window panes. The outrageous, hateful alarm clock shrieked in her ears and she stretched out her hand to silence it. "Boring rain," she yawned. Scarcely had she seen her long and rosy feet, her polished nails, against the flowered mat, her heartbeat like a warning, returned to her the ingratitude of the past night. The oblivion of sleep ceased; she found again the awareness of a sharp, implacable edge, sinking into some very painful area. Isa heard herself, in a low voice, almost whispering: "Mario."

It was not a day like every day, a tedious reflection about other people's business, other people's affairs, other people's interests; about the typewriter keyboard, about papers and manila folders, about file indexes and telephone calls; in the hateful passing of hours, in the infamous torture of suppressed insults, in an abominable effort of smiles, of interest; even illusion she heard the voice of Ortiz, the head of the proof readers' section on the other side of the pane of glass. "If one does not work with enthusiasm, it is not possible to work well. One must have enthusiasm even for the simplest task..." She heard that voice almost clerical, hypocritically cordial voice, in the morning and in the afternoon (indistinct in the eternal neon light, because no other light was possible, the sun never entered there.) It was not a day like every day, it was worse.

Isa noticed herself feeling faint, helpless at the beginning of the day, of these inevitably repeated hours. The jokes, the pranks, the slovenly stimulating pattern of coffee, of cigarettes; Pelayo's obvious ironies, Margarita's complaints, the participation (with feigned enthusiasm) in the collective soccer lotto... On this day not one of these hours would be bearable, compensated for by the single reason that could maintain her, still, in a lively and honest attitude in the face of the world: "Mario is not here. I won't see Mario today."

She ate breakfast in a hurry, without looking at the old woman who advised her to put on her galoshes; in order not to see her dull-colored hair, tumultuously entangled under the blue hair net ("Why would she wear that hair net? Goodness knows where she probably got that from..."); in order not to notice her bare gums, still free from the dentures, not to see her bathrobe; or her shoes, or her hands, spotted with pink and white, nor hear her falsely maternal bits of advice. ("Where would this kindness end, if the familiar little envelop would not arrive, or the familiar presents, or the familiar "extras." We would see how so much love would stop, if they would not take half, or more, of all that has been possible, and is possible, for me to scrape together in this filthy world." Her passive, customary, bovine hatred, so fully practiced in the office, flowed at home. "They were not so kind five years ago," she remembered as she went downstairs. "They were not so kind, of course, the first years." When she arrived at the big, new city with her baggage of dreams, poor, stupid girl; when she still nourished the crazy pretension of resuming her studies, at the cost of night hours stolen from her sleep. "Burning desires of work and perfection..." Where did the unhinged innocence stop, the goodness replete with ignorance?"

Crammed together in a compact group of people, anxiously crushed together against the door of the bus, Isa dealt discreet blows of her umbrella, with an inexpressive glance. She climbed over the human mass, she set out, in the humid and hot atmosphere; submissive and absent, in a tiny world, crowded with discussions that transformed themselves into an irate screech, absolutely dramatic, the changing of a hundred peseta note into small change. The rain whipped against the windows. On the other side of the trampling, laughter, resignation, and boredom.

Jacinto, as usual, had left for the town right after the exams had finished. In summer he rejoined his family: mother, sisters, the honorable judge. In that period of country rest between bushes of thyme, poplars and mountain air, he recovered from the excesses and the scarcities of student life. He returned around the middle of September. Isa saw him getting off the bus, more tanned, heavier. She thought that, in his absence, she had gotten a more stylized idea of him. She had already spent three Septembers, waiting for the bus from the mountains, in the new and splendid station of "Benitez Buses"; three Septembers going to meet, with a vaguely mystical smile, the boyfriend who was returning to his books, to the arguments in the boardinghouse (according to him, he had been robbed of the invaluable sausages carried in his suitcase); to the evening walks; hand in hand, the kisses in the forbidden entry-way.

The fourth summer was already ending. Dad had died. Isa was still wearing mourning. The faded skirt stuck too much to her hips (it always seemed damp), she wore for the first time the blouse with tiny little white dots, black background, a sign of conventional end of formal mourning which did not correspond with reality.

But in that fourth summer he got himself "engaged" to a girl, daughter of a wealthy landowner, a pretty, tall, blond girl who possessed an endless amount of good qualities that the Anchorena sisters (who knew everything about every family or regional happening) slipped patiently and like Sybils into the ears of her mother (and in her own). Isa and her mother, in the dining room, vital center of the apartment, in front of the glassed-in gallery, attempted to put together a banal conversation. But they fell again into silence, interspersed only by poorly disguised moans and sighs of her mother. One by one the minutes became more intolerable. Everyday someone arrived (a girl friend, a simple acquaintance) who added news of Jacinto. "What a pity, what a pity: a creature so young and so good…" Isa felt herself becoming more angry, a slow and deaf anger. It seemed that all of them wanted to bury her. As if, at her recently attained twenty years of age, she had just died: or that they wanted her dead already, already gone, already in another time.

She began to go out alone in the evenings. She would go to the Ebro, fled from her friends, from their futile compassion or their false compliance. (Except Maruchina, who said to her, very clearly: "Girl, you should know, that the way the boys are here, the worst possible thing is that Jacinto has ditched you. If you

don't leave here, with the bad reputation that you already had…"
That was saying to her, more or less: "Either you leave or you
devote yourself to charities."

"Then I'm leaving," she repeated to herself with a secret rage,
that afternoon. In front of the river which, on many afternoons,
had witnessed their languid embraces, their repeated kisses, their
family plans, modest, discreetly happy. On the opposite shore,
two little gypsies, half naked, were running about between piles
of garbage; on a thin and soft green grass, inconceivably clean
among the filth. "I am twenty-two years old and I have a store of
knowledge which not all the girls here have; some courses, although interrupted, that can help me to get ahead…" Why not
complete those courses? Leave here, escape from the miserable
city, from its narrow streets, from the arcades, from the bridge;
from the walks and the teas; from its saints of incalculable worth.
To leave, to abandon all of this forever. On that evening Isa discovered the force of her will, obediently suffocated during twenty-
years. ("Because a girl must appear submissive and sweet, although she is not sweet, but caustic; not submissive, but iras-
cible.") Unexpectedly, she surprised herself laughing. She had
found a full laugh, jocose, in the middle of the afternoon, next to
the poplar trees; uprooting tufts of emerald color, in front of a
river that flowed without worrying about the world, nor girls
covered with kisses, nor the shores invaded by rusty cans and
mismatched, rotting shoes, among the dung. Upon seeing her
laugh alone, seated on the grass, the two little gypsies began to
shout things at her (unintelligible names), between fits of laughter. She left them there, shameless with their dark navels uncov-
ered, rolling about on the grass, when she was already drawing
away, drying her cheeks; because never, never, had she laughed
so, to the point of tears, as on that afternoon. Mother, the conventional customs, the money…? Yes, she was merciless. Mother
was going to remain alone? "What a bad daughter!" Yes, a bad
daughter. "But, where will you go, you little wretch, where? What
are you looking for that you don't have here?" The Two Old
Women arose from the photograph albums, from the old family
stories, the tribal anecdotes: Father's ineffable, dignified, lady-

like and ruined cousins (who loved him so much when he was a boy, when he remained an orphan: "Because one can say that they acted like mothers, real mothers, for me, until I got on the right track...," she heard Father's voice, remembered the wetness of his eyes). Thus, she then took out two beribboned ghosts from the dusty closets of the family past, shook the dust from them, placed them upright on the dining room table and argued: "I will go to my aunts' house and I will pay for my stay; it will be much cheaper for me and I'll help them a little." "Oh, oh, these daughters of today." Mother, doña Dolores, the Anchorenas, sighed with pleasure, looked at her out of the corner of their eyes; with premonitions, forecasting a logically ill-fated end for the rebellious girl who did not have the good taste to let herself be buried alive.

The two Old Ladies received her with the exhilaration of supposing that she was the bearer of goodies typical of the small town; filled with possessions and gifts with which to gladden the sordid dignity which lay there, which agonized in a veiled misery. Isa's glance ran over walls, ceilings; contemplated the last note of attention to the house, the desperate message of the furniture, of the pictures, consoles, mirrors. As if each chair, each vase, hung on with invisible fingernails and teeth, to the walls, the floor, to the air impregnated with camphor, saffron and "Roses d'amour"; silent things, painfully obstinate and tenacious, unwilling to disappear in the cold entrails of the Pawn Shop. The surprise of the two old ladies was rather dry, when Isa made clear—she had not done so before, knowingly; she did so when she was installed in her room, still surrounded by welcome, damp kisses and pinches in the cheeks—that she had to go to work if she wanted to pay the costs of her studies. "But your mother...," they stammered, their features suddenly resembling cardboard (transformed, already, into pure and fleshless, almost voracious, dentures). "But your mother...she's not going to send you anything?" No, mother did not even send regards.

Isa burnt her first bridge: on entering ("as a little gift") she deposited half of her savings in their avid, stretched out hands (palms of striped dirty porcelain). "And don't worry. I really have everything well organized; everything is really well planned, well taken care of…"

On the way from the office Isa still felt the harshness, the sordid coldness of the money counted out, cent by cent. "I'll eat away from home because my work does not allow me to waste time…," she said.

She did not eat out, nor in, nor anyplace. She gnawed a roll, in little chunks, to make it last; she sipped slowly an undecipherable infusion, in the unappetizing suburban cafeteria. She deprived her hunger of two pesetas in order to buy a newspaper, like a sacred and untouchable treasure: and she read, between sips of a bitter and dark liquid, between mouthfuls of a soft and exquisite bread (she never thought in that easy and stupid town, that a bite of bread could be something so extraordinarily good), the want-ad column: she was looking for some reality, something that was not just a vain hope, a subtle fraud disguised with generous rewards; a complicated business labyrinth which asked for alluring services and ended up, as a last link, in the simple stomping of one's feet around the city (in order to offer, from apartment to apartment, an unknown brand of detergent). She still did not have a job, she still did not have anything. The last withdrawals of her laughable fortune in her savings deposit book, begun the day she was born, increased by the modest efforts of her father and the more substantial ones of her godfather Fernando (until he died), by the special gifts at Christmas, Twelfth Night and Saint Isabel's day…. Why remember now, in the morning's cold rain, the cruel word of negatives, of closed doors, of corrosive hunger, intolerable, that returned her, half-drunk from extreme weakness from lack of food, to her aunts' apartment where she offered, dauntless, an impeccable smile of work satisfactorily accomplished? But the Two Old Ladies did not live on honorable and painful smiles; the Old Ladies frowned, stretched out their china-doll hands, expressed the opinion that "special gifts," signs of respect, "should be arriving. ("Ah, old maids, weakly denied to death, old girls spoiled and cruelly kept up, like disjointed angels, in a world that no longer accepts caresses, children, signs of respect or any tenderness.") Because you must understand my dear: after all, we have you in the house for much less than what you would pay in any boarding house…"

Isa's office formed part of a new building, built in a section of town still in the planning stage; a section that, apparently, only exists in some imagination, in some plan. As she continues on from the bus stop, Isa contemplates the enigmatically glassed-in facade of a building where the sun has been exiled.

The proofreaders' Department is her department. A small cog, a tiny cooperator of the great machine which produces Dictionaries, Medical Handbooks, volumes of some indecipherable scientific publication, comic books, novels for young people, and a whole range of other things that Isa is totally incapable of grasping. Upon entering her office, the disagreeable impression of having absorbed in her body the smell of damp clothes, of unfriendly umbrellas accompanies her; the sweat, the breath and the working-day bad humor, of the bus. She puts her time card in the control clock (the "informer"), she presses the button, hears the jingling, smiles vaguely at no one. She hangs up her raincoat, leaves her umbrella in the plastic pail—totally unsuitable within the functional harmony of the furniture—and submerged herself in the keyboard, the neon light, the scarcely audible noise of moderately secret conversations. On passing by, Pelayo says to her that she looks ill, with a lewd irony. To look ill, for Pelayo, (Isa contemplated coldly the loose, grey sweater, the idiotic mustache) implies mad and unrestrained nights of love. ("Candid and filthy is your imagination," Isa says to herself, imitating distant strophes of the many which float, lost, in her memory. "Dirty and optimist…")

Isa hates this office where she met Jaime and loves it because she saw Mario here for the first time. For various and different reasons, on each keyboard, on each piece of furniture, in each face, Isa reconstitutes, each morning, her story of contempt and her story of love. On the wall the clock offers its white face to her; troubling, like the face of an old accomplice.

Before arriving at this office, she worked (different and enthusiastic, easily deceived and timid), first in a shoe store, then in a household appliance store (Accounting Office); then, in another office. Until she arrived here and remained anchored, already engulfed in a net of Social Security, end-of-year stocks, double payments, special editions, pay-slips, personnel lists, etc… Isa now remains distant, the Isa "of the future," without protection, without excuses, without "insurance," without "Bonuses," Isa walks across the brown carpeting with a slightly possessive air, a little sedentary. Nomadic Isa is over and done with, the dangerous independence (on the edge of Benefits, Sickness Insurance, Other Perks). Isa smiles wanly at her pencils, her manila folders, her ashtray (still spotless). There is a subtle, imperceptible fatigue in all that her glance embraces. Isa's studies, who remembers them now? She only went to a few night classes in English, in the modest Academy installed in the same apartment house where she lived. A disappointed laziness, a sad awareness of it's already too late, moves her further away, more and more, from a world that, in the past, she thought feasible; even beautiful.

It was Jaime who awakened her old desires to appear different "from other women" (not from all others, but from other women). Jaime was a robust man, with black curly hair, who used glasses with black frames., When she met him he was probably around forty-five, big, black eyes, a little bulging behind the glasses. Some woman in the office commented that he was a guy "with charm." Isa looked at him on the sly, when, at times, they met by chance in the elevator. He did not seem to her to be handsome, or ugly, or especially attractive. Only on that day, when he called her to his office and put her in charge of "an assignment with more responsibility," she felt, surprisingly, that a forgotten and stimulating vanity was reborn in her. Now, with her eyes fixed on the page which she does not succeed even in spelling out, Isa reconstructs the glance of the black eyes, popping out from behind the glasses. On that day, she thought they were strange eyes; they looked like two fish behind the glass side of an aquarium. "A purely optical effect," she said to herself, with a stupid smugness, on leaving the feared and admired office. "Because of the glasses making things bigger." Days later, Jaime thought that Isa was a girl with great aptitudes; that she merited a more responsible job; an opportunity. "Yes, he's got hold of a good job and really takes advantage of opportunities," Pelayo laughed, bitingly. "That guy is here with a salary that you can't dream of, dear. He is the one who resolves all the tricky issues, censorship and all that. A tremendous guy. Of course, with his other job, anyone could do it. The world belongs to them."

Isa remembers the transition to the Top Departments (where there is more heat, where heels become silent in the carpeting, where the machines, the desks, are convenient, modern, useful). Isa reconstructs the "movement upward"; the kind of faint vertigo of the first day: when she had her desk, her machine, her individual kit; not shared, not confused, not mixed up with others'. Isa, tidy, proud, entered, finally, her own little territory (small and modest, but still her own, finally). Of the world which she believed belonged to her.

Now, these things do not have merit, stimulus, or any interest whatever. The morning passes, the rain keeps on. Outside, the street waits: invaded, once more, by groups that are waiting for the bus, who are returning home; who will come back, within an hour, two hours, to the same protests, with the same complaints, the same jokes; in the same rain. A slow bitterness slows her down, she remains the last one in the office, looks for her umbrella, her raincoat. Now only the concierge remains, waiting, with the keys in his hand.

"If Mario does not return, I'll go looking for him," she suddenly decides. At least, don't let anger abandon her, don't let the only thing that propelled her, up to this moment in which the rain dampens her face, abandon her. Isa lets those cold drops slip on her cheeks, frail, with a diffusely rebellious pleasure.

Mario appeared in her life by pure and fortuitous chance. Among her duties was included waiting on Mario. That was the first time that she experienced what she heard people call "premonitions." The day on which Mario came up to her, sat down next to her desk and listened to her voice. The day on which she became aware of his distant and somewhat disdainful air. "What do they see in that guy?" Pelayo commented. "He seems like a hungry greyhound. Some woman, messed up by him, walks around here." The day when she saw for the first time his copper gold hair, his blue eyes, his prominent cheekbones, those hands with long fingers, that picked up, smoothly, the end of the paper and pointed out something that Isa was not able to see, completely immersed in an unknown feeling. For the first time in many years, she felt admiration, respect towards a human being. She contemplated, with a childish fascination the peculiar tone of his skin, oddly covered with something (she recognized that she had recently been reading too many banal stories) that seemed "sprinkled with golden dust." For the first time in her life she had the certainty that that man and no other, would be inscribed in her life. A certainty joined to a vague fear. Something painful, friendly, sour or sweet. Bad or good, but impossible to avoid.

The bus appeared, finally, among the murmurs of protest of the group in wait. (Isa remembered vaguely a documentary film: savage men, half-naked, on the alert for the passing of some animal which emerges walking in the bushes); Isa moves away to the corner and contemplates a woman who is running and who protects, with her apron, a girl in a school uniform. A man is locking up his grocery store. Isa crosses the street, moves away without heading anywhere, aimlessly. "And on that day ill omens entered my life: disorder, fear, jealousy, desperation…" A modest bar announces, painted on its windows, in the rain, hot appetizers, sandwiches, coffee. It seems empty and dark, like a hideaway. Isa closes her umbrella and enters. As if she were treading on a distant earth, foreign, suitable for oblivion.

Three Days of Love

I awoke abruptly, as if this time sleep were really a crime, a forbidden luxury. I don't remember when I fell asleep. I have looked for my last memory among those half-devoured books; something that could isolate me in a state of unconsciousness. The books that speak to me of ancient and refined systems of torture. Whoever took refuge here from the world, in the past, felt an excessive liking for crematoria, crucifixions and massive exterminations. Perhaps for that reason there is something like the sticky track of greasy smoke incrusted on the walls and furniture. A smoke which must have filled the sky, at times, with scrawls above definite points of this island. ("A greasy smoke, black, arrived: proceeding from human torches...the devil dissolved, escaped, humiliated, converted into a black and greasy smoke...," someone wrote here in this room.)

I intended to decipher the manuscripts, those delirious dreams, a mixture of witchcraft and scientific arrogance. It is strange that none of all this turns out to be alien to me. Not one single thing, in this fallen-apart and dirty private paradise, refuge of a man already dead for many years, turns out to be unknown to me. I have known that man. I have read those books, those manuscripts, in innumerable corners of this country where I was born. I have come across, an infinite number of times, identical insane structures, beautifully drawn, identical and crazy dreams of austerity and lust. I know these desperate jumps backwards, this search after a reason which can be used as an excuse, or standard, or shelter, for a great and forsaken fear of this world, of death, of pain, in the end. This pathetic backward movement after crumbs of eternity, this unfortunate zeal to out-last forgetfulness. "I do not want to die, I do not want to die," scream all the objects: the piled up furniture, the shelves bent over by a weight made up now of only dust and humidity. The torture of the flesh, knowl-

edge, solitude, negligence, the sweet and vague love for the impossible: these naked, discus throwing little boys, crowned with
grapevine leaves, who lift up their arms towards inexistent heav-
enly birds… Everything cries out, moans, invents a small token
of eternity, a hope of eternity. "I do not want to die," I hear in
creakings, in the sudden shrill cries of the mice, in the silent and
implacable descent of dust upon dust. Nothing is strange to me
in this room. Rooms like this abound. In whatever town, in whatever region; between mountain chains, alongside rivers, more or
less dry; in the distance or behind rows of black and white poplars, there always exists a narrow room, long, empty which awaits
in vain the return of a ghostly kingdom, of some faded carnival,
perhaps never celebrated. Empty and closed up rooms. Empty
and closed up men. Walls, papers, bundles of papers: calligraphy
that is unique, with ornamental borders, arabesques, solemnity.
Calligraphy. The words have changed, under the dust, into simple,
now outdated, calligraphy. Still—and I think that my country is
not only one city, nor two or three cities, more or less advanced—
we find ourselves overflowing, infested with narrow, high, closed
up rooms, where it is always possible to hide a fugitive. Invaded
by rooms where the light of the sun no longer arrives. Where
doors are closed off and the bolts become musty. Big rooms in
reserve. Great reserves. My country is not two or three beautiful
cities, my compatriots are not only my friends. My friends close
doors, nail down windows, jealously guard the dust, the rotten
paper, in order that the rats feed on the beautiful, graven, unique
calligraphy. ("They no longer write in such good handwriting.")
What great contempt can be harvested still in the great reserves.
Mines of contempt, still unexplored, of profound, solid, unbrib-
able ignorance. Long and narrow rooms of dancing without dancing, ghosts of masks showing through the walls; infinite reserves
of solitude. Any man surrounded by questions, can say that, certainly, now he remembers it: he, too, has a completely crazy uncle,
closed up in a country house, and who was the laughing stock
of…almost all my compatriots enjoy the kinship, the friendship,
the memory of men completely insane and very amusing, voluntarily shut up among telescopes, compasses, theories and oro-

graphic or maritime maps. Great reserves. Calligraphy.

I awoke with the imprecise shock of having committed an error: to sleep, to rest, to forget. Life can not be abandoned this way, so softly, without losing it. To live life, carefully, in order that it may not fall, or break, right there, alongside, next to the clothes, shoes, watch, glasses. And to pick up life tomorrow, when the sun returns: brush it, shake possible specks from it, and use it again. It is a mockery of life, I imagine, to abandon it in such a trivial form, since life is not easy, nor easily accessible, nor agreeable. It is an unconsciousness, a frivolity, to fall asleep the way I have. My eyes hurt, there is an excessive light in the sky, even now, when the moon has faded like a petal and the dawn is only a golden liquid, transparent. There is something excessive in the smoothness of this daily birth of light, for me. It wounds my eyes. I have the vague suspicion that the sun hates me.

The astonishment coming from her new visit still lasts with me, when she has already left. That she sat down and that she has spoken with me. I did not hope to see more of her and less even without the tapestry of the night, without the easy ignorance of the dark, where one can not make out a gesture of danger, or of fear, or of simple confusion. It is strange that she has returned and I imagine, or better said, I am convinced that for her this return is also inexplicable. Here, on the other side of her door where, apparently, they have accumulated all that which, in the past, could make her suffer or dream. It is strange that insecure and sad desire that impels her too (as it does everything that breathes on this soil). From the summit of her present moment, so painfully acquired, year after year, she runs desperately backwards, she searches for some loose end that surely must find its balance in vain; in order to grasp it, perhaps, and to go back to a country or a reason more convenient than this land and this reason. I guess that she hates these walls, that this dust repels her, this rotten wood, this floor whitened by time and salt. But she comes here, returns to this place where I am and which, definitely, has been imposed upon her; she might be able to hate, or scorn, or ignore someone who was from here. Always, the burden of circumstances, the dispersed particles which float in the air that, unexpectedly, a strange wind reunites, brings together, gives form and meaning. It is strange, but it does not completely amaze me. Because, since everything began (and it began from the moment in which I closed the eyes of that woman and contemplated her nude lips forever, and hid her finally with her longing and mute revenge in the narrow hole of the urban dead), there lies, in all that surrounds me, a renewal, an insistent re-encounter.

The most insignificant details gain a special meaning. She has seen the box with the provisions that Bear left here last night, and she has realized that I have not even opened it. Everything, up to the most banal, acquires a precise, exact emphasis, if one is locked up; in hope of the great, the unique justification. The enormous and crushing opportunity for revenge.

Locked up. As he was, together with Bambi's less and less meaningful—I imagine—wanderings, of a Bambi who drew away, definitely in the last remnant of his faith. I believe that the color of objects, as the light increased or went out, turned out decisive for him too; the glow of the sun creeping up the wall, the last vestige of night on his eyelids, or on the paper, where it could be read, still (the eyes, finally, become accustomed to the absence of light): "But Bambi, don't you know how to be alone?"

She has been a good person. She has brought a tray where coffee was steaming; a smell, as they say, comforting and stimulating. I have taken, and take each day, so much coffee that I no longer know whether it is a stimulant or not. She has sat down here, next to the table, in that armchair of elephantine configuration, where she seemed to be lost. She has been a good person: we spoke of nothing transcendent, of nothing sour, or festive, or allusive. We spoke like well-brought up and circumstantial visitors: about the island, about Bear, about the sea. I pretended that anecdotes about the island, the vague references to Bear's studies, mattered to me; and I agreed with her opinion about the beauty of the sea. But I have the absolute conviction that she knew perfectly well that the anecdotes, either of the island or of Bear, do not matter to me, nor that I like the island . I knew so. I read it in her eyes, in her hands, in all of her figure, only strangely rejuvenated, sunk in the bottom of that unimaginable chair—it is only possible to create or design a similar piece of furniture in a similar place—; as if she were going back to a time that was very tender, very young, very sad and loved. More than rejuvenated, timeless (like the ephebes, on the wall that has lost its plaster, in their immobile dance). It is curious; I contemplated her, lost in that kind of animal-furniture; behind her opened the door, and at the back, I could still make out a boy, imbecile and naked, with his arms in the air. I have not been able to separate her two images, nor stop thinking that there was something natural (known and recognized formerly by me) the vision of that woman and that idiotic mural as a background.

She does not seem older than I. It is strange that we are almost the same age. I assumed that there was a total distance between the two of us, and, nevertheless, how very rarely have I seen her, suddenly, near, when the light has been the most violent—that light I don't like and suddenly I welcomed and desired—, when I made out, clearly, her features, the color of her skin, of her eyes, of her clothes. Her hair was, in short, black, shining, smooth. I have lost the content of her words—not of her voice, which has surrounded me again, as last night—, but her skin lightly sunburnt, especially soft to the glance, was revealed to me. It is not a smooth girl's skin, a blooming young skin, sweet and fresh. It is a softness that is appreciated, simply by contemplating it, a skin where resided, undoubtedly, an infinity of hours, of minutes, of a time that has nothing to do with the timed emptiness that we use in our comings and goings, in our efforts, and in our business dealings. A secret time, reserved, uniquely perhaps for solitude; gently remote, pleasantly sad. It is interesting, she never smiles. There is a grin of seriousness that I imagine was, in other far-off moments, a precocious seriousness. Like that of some adolescents from whom, suddenly, one requires a mature attitude. That unusual seriousness has not abandoned her countenance. Without knowing why, it seemed to me to be invaded by an unknown, inexplicable and subdued beauty. A curious feeling, to know that beauty is not formed there by the outline of her face, nor the curve of her eyes, or the color of her skin. An old-fashioned beauty, scarcely known. As though torn off from some mysterious region, that beauty comes down and invades her, just like rain or radiance. Her face, light brown, her eyes, her thin body (inexplicably saved from an aggressive angularity), her delicateness, seemed to me, unexpectedly, most beautiful, even though they might not be so.

Isa is much younger, much more beautiful, surely more attractive. Even though her beauty might be now, for me, something commonplace and obvious like her words, her gestures, or her love. I do not understand for what reason one has to prolong weariness, when love, or desire, or the simple enjoyment of the unforeseen, are impossible to be prolonged. I believe that, similar to possessions, we must program a more equitable and just distribution of our feelings.

I do not know what her name is, nor does she know my name. Never as today, on this strange and special day—a day that appears suspended and without hours, within the darkness of two nights which must give shape to the time of vengeance—, did her words appear to me so ornamentally useless. Like the calligraphy of the old man who invented the tortures and the delights, absolutely inane, now, on the paper. Perhaps a smile can supply a complex and organized system of words: also a disparaging or mocking gesture, lips doubled by pride or a quiet, warm hand on another hand. Although, in truth, she has not smiled at me, nor has she shown to me a behavior that was not totally conventional. In spite of everything, something has emerged (emerges still and keeps growing in the day, in the air, in the atmosphere) which assumes the words, the names, even the passage of time. This coming together is not frequent, this unusual approximation, like water becoming wider, down the slope, filling up furrows, great and dry holes; like water that tears out stone stones and converts dry dust into mud, and returns, finally, to a life in the ocean, green, still inexplicable. I feel as if that sea which I vaguely fear, which is like the image of a terror that grips me, would turn into an imaginary and improbable beach; a soft and inoffensive coming close of the sea, lacking in terror; a sea that moistens this dry sand that surrounds me and turns me into an

island, and submerges me, at the end, into an abyss where the
light is different, and the light has a new and unknown dimen-
sion. Where words can not be heard, nor another language exists
but the flowing of life, displacing itself, uniting itself, separating
itself; I imagine myself as floating, just like certain fishes that I
watched on occasion, with a certain uneasiness, in aquariums.

There are many classes of life, of beauty, of faithfulness; and
there are days like this one, in which I deliberately exist, oppressed by some kind of submarine law. Oppressed and liberated. For example, liberated—although it might be for a short
time—from sharp and decisive gestures to which I feel that I am
irrevocably bound. Am I? Or have they forced me? Doubt is my
only possession. Great doubt, finally, that, on this day, floats
slowly towards a frequently hermetic surface. Doubt is my only
wealth. How strange, when she has returned—and her return did
not seem improbable any more—it seemed to us (I already possess a new sense which permits me to link her thoughts and mine)
that she had never been absent. Or, at least, that during her absence, we had known each other better; that we had explained to
one another small, meaningful, buried things or publicly known
things, but infinitely ours: hers and mine. (At times, a painter
friend used to say to me: "I stop painting for a few months and it
seems to me that when I take up my brushes again I discover that
I know much more, that I have learned much in that apparent
leisure.") In that invisible school, ghostly and wise, someone,
during her absence, instructed us in the difficult science which
consists of the inapprehensible, irrational, difficult proximity of
two beings. Two beings who desire to express, understand, hear
or destroy, jointly, any doubt. The doubt that I discover also in
that other body: not in her words. I do not know how—at times—
the physical reality, the body, the skin, the touch, which form a
human being, can free themselves from its thoughts or its words,
from its spiritual essence. That thin body (which could be almost
wounding or unpleasant, if it did not appear held in her special
boundary of fragility, of intensified sweetness) revealed to me
her great doubt, also, with much more clarity than any word or
manifestation ("...proper to creatures of her kind"). Each move-

ment of her head, of her knees—almost a girl's knees—seem to
me so revealing; the curve of her cheekbones, her mouth of tired
and serious lips, without a smile. Fleetingly, at some moment,
she seems to be a boy. In other moments, a remote sphinx, an
intrinsically female idol, implacable and blood thirsty: only re-
deemed by its remote cruelty through the centuries, in the ero-
sion of the stone beneath the wind or the whip in the arena. Without knowing why, I have realized that her eyes are not black.
They are only darkened, sombre eyes: but if the sun enters them,
they light up like grape seeds. I think, looking at her, that she is
like the embodiment of a great uncertainty, of some unfinished,
infantile question; of a pathetic incomprehension of the world.

Only when she was no longer speaking, when the silence remained floating, coming after my words—of her words, too—I
surprised myself and was startled by all that I had said to her.
Now I understand, in opposition to what I thought before—that
everything happens at once, so dizzyingly and so slowly; everything turns out so contradictory and consistent—the value of the
words, of the single weapon that a man wields laboriously through
a jungle of blows, blood, cruelty, ignorance, stupidity and ambition. Desperate words in constant struggle against brutality,
against guttural sounds; against the cries of savage pleasure, or
the roar of the obscure belly of the world. Contradictorily, I have
reconstructed, through the fragile and feathery calligraphy, word
by word, a long pilgrimage of terror and hate.

Only when silence has returned have I perceived that the sun
was sinking, that we were definitely losing daylight; that one
more day, with its light, its wind, its solitude or its hidden, recondite happiness, would be submerged in the great well from which
there is no coming back. How have I told her what can not be
told? How do I know about that which is not easy to understand?
I do not understand, now, in this silence, that unites us, so strangely
brought together, so much so that our knees touch each other and
I feel the brush of her hand. I do not understand, I say to myself,
people who relate the story of their lives, in an orderly fashion,
severely, consciously, chronologically. No one has a history, I
think, in this silence that is pressing upon us in a form that is

more and more unbearable. The only thing that can be done is this: to speak about a child, a landscape, a tree, a great fear. The only story I can relate is that of a subdued and childish faith. We were able to speak together and reconstruct, or re-encounter. Together, in linked and pasted together stories, the roots of uncertainty; the incapacity to understand; the great amazement. Now, in this sudden silence (which is only, in reality, absence of words) I met again, buried under a thousand coverings and self-justifications, an unfathomable and almost sweet disappointment. "I was not so reasonable nor so lucid, nor so admirable...," an obscure voice, dispassionate, recites.

I am a vulgar merchant. I have sold myself, bit by bit, little by little, in order to speculate, progressively, about my own truth. I began to buy for myself little bits of my own truth the day on which I said to myself: I can not do this, or that; there is a great impediment in my life, the great responsibility that it means...I continued buying for myself parcels of self-truth when there was revealed to me the force, the innocent wisdom, the disarmed indignation of some boys who have not learned how to speculate, nor have they wanted to engage themselves in the system of self-consummation in which I caught myself. I kept on selling myself my own truth even among those boys who do not need, in order to rebel, neither hate or stupidity or hunger. But they are young boys and I have lost the boy I was. Or, perhaps, I never had him, I was never that boy. It is a strange sensation, that one, as though I was contemplating myself from an angle, apart and clearly; young as they were, a grotesque imitation of Gore Gorinskoe (carrying on his shoulders an old woman who beats his sides with her heels, who whips him and forces him to walk, with amorous phrases: dear little boy, walk, walk, walk, pretty little boy...). It is as if, suddenly, I saw them, in front of me, turning the corner, getting lost. And I saw myself running after them, with the old woman on my back, feeling her blows and her sweet names: and I screamed at those boys that they wait for me, that I don't want to lose them. Poor and humiliating truth, a boy grown old, vacation time teacher for boys who missed a course; obscure editor of pages which speak of petroleum, of the future of aluminum, of girls who kiss mature men in the last chapter, of dreadfully uttered translations: irreconcilable languages in a merciless struggle against the dirty, disgraceful and miserable man who drags along the corpse of an old woman; heir to a single possession: revenge. But I have followed, and I follow, I am even at the very limit at which the unbridled running appears suspended. I am still buying myself and selling myself. Each time I sold myself at a higher price, each time I bought myself at a better price. I have made splendid deals with myself. My truth on sale has been well self-priced. I remember that once, being a child, I met a man who told lies and he believed them. If he had not believed them I would have held him as a joker or a liar. But, since he believed them he only appeared an innocent madman.

I think of the mysterious reason of this mutual and irrepressible search, in the reason for this inevitable meeting that keeps us prisoners. Yes, truthfully, we have nothing in common except doubt.

In This City

Three long days without any call, or a line, or any news. Mario always says: "I'm not going to write you, it's not worth while." He said it so many times, when he travelled to anyone of those places from which she remains excluded, with mute rage, in a held-in resentment that she has to muzzle very carefully, if she does not want to lose the last bit of that which represents, now, her only reason for living. But at other times she knew perfectly where he had gone, with whom, why. Not this puerile and clumsy lie, this badly presented stupidity. "It is as though I did not matter to him, as though it made no difference whether I believe him or do not believe him," insinuates a perverse and internal voice, drop by drop. She never received a letter of his, that is for sure, and very few—only the most necessary—telephone calls. She was always the one to settle meetings and appointments; the one entrusted with fixing days, hours, places. Mario limited himself to saying yes, to accepting. At the beginning, with a hesitating pleasure. Now, with a total surrender to boredom, to habit, to an easy assent: because he perceives and fears, perhaps, that refusal would be more inconvenient.

"He does not know me as I know him," she thinks now, sitting at the table, between the two old women who pour, equitably, in the dishes a steaming and insipid soup; who chat between themselves in curious monosyllables, a kind of signs picked up in the air; like messages in a climate already gone by, already lived in before, only intelligible to them. Isa has arrived at the conclusion that they speak between themselves like birds, in an old code, a half-language made of repetitions and echoes of other conversations which had already happened, had been already known, year after year. A language that permits them to insinuate, or scarcely pronounce, half a syllable in order to understand each other. To hear their strange chatting is like listening to an infinite symphony of short, guttural sounds and prolonged final "s" sounds. For a moment Isa wonders if happiness will consist, after all, in this: old age lulled in the simple fact of not having to get rid of the silver sugar bowl with the initials of Mother and Father; in pouring trickles of steaming soup on those plates with blue arabesque flowers which, "fortunately it was possible to keep." With a bitter smile Isa takes her memory back to the time when contentment (poor contentment, based on a pathetic "things not getting worse, not having to get rid of that which, up to now, we have considered our entire world").

Those were the days when she began her brief and vulgar story with Jaime; when the monotonous, anodyne, absolutely desolate life of the young Isa ("then, yes; then she was truly young") breathed, grew, rested finally in a world of tranquillity. "Tranquillity, not to have to recount, think, distribute. To live life decently—she thinks, immobile before her plate—with the minimum dignity necessary not to cross through it like a bandit, or a beggar, or a wretch, is much more difficult than she can imagine from a provincial corner, on the edge of a river, next to little gypsies who laugh at life among rubbish, rusty tin-cans and decay. "To live, with a minimum of comfort, without pressing end-of-the-month ghosts, bills, shoes that can not longer be worn decently, is much more difficult than what a poor girl born in a small, family oriented, merciless town may think. Isa begins to eat in silence her weak plate of soup; determined to forget, to let herself be rocked (for a few moments at least), outside of all hope, of all malaise; of all omen, good or bad.

"But it is difficult not to think. We believe that it is possible to say: I'm going to lie down for a little while, close my eyes, rest. And it is not sure that I am going to rest. No one can rest if he is awake: thoughts fly and lead to that zone where we do not want to return, and return, and return. That horrible area that brings us a different time, the one we might have wanted to bring to a standstill in the clocks, in the calendar; and the other, the one we want to scare off, to erase from the world.

To think, to think; and to remember Mario, Jaime. To remember the story by bits, by intervals; the time of Jaime and the time of Mario. "Jaime was not evil. He was never evil with me," she thinks suddenly in order to scare off the burning fear, the diffuse pain the very name of Mario nails in her consciousness. ("He will not return. I have lost him. He will not return.") Jaime, then ("such absurd things happen in the monotonous course of our days"), acquired, in her imagination, the attributes of evil. The good and evil of children's stories and innocent films, become linked together in Isa's mind like an idiotic toy; a grotesque wheel of beings taken by the hand, that invent good, evil, sin, virtue, honor, perversion. "How much bad reading, how much imbecility, how much poison," she says to herself, with a soft rage, incapable of awakening her, or impelling her. "How much idiocy disguised as wisdom."

Now, in this moment, ridiculously seated before a ridiculous plate of soup, Isa remembers the "evil" man, the "seducer," the "self-seeking man," and recognizes, floating in a diluted despair, (while the plate displays twisted wreathes of a lovely and gone-by grandeur), that "he was not so evil." As far as the good, the just, the fair, the loving...Isa experiences some old-fashioned desire to cry. "I never cry," she tries to convince herself. Something iron-like, merciless, tightens around her neck like an intolerable threat.

Isa gets up and wants to say: "I don't have an appetite, my head aches, excuse me, I'm going to rest for a bit..." But she can not even say it. It is disappointing, too, to know that, now, her brusqueness would be welcomed with benevolence. Now, they will let her go, with a tender and understanding glance; they will say: "Poor girl, she works too much." "Just like then," she thinks ironically and pushes her chair, which creaks rudely. She seeks her dark room, falls flat on the bed, leans her head on the too soft shape of the pillow. The rough surface of the bedspread scratches her cheek. She pushes it aside, uncovers the top part of the bedsheet, looks for the coolness of the sheet. This is it; now, a sudden dampness, warm and desperate, dampens the tiny piece of linen, next to her temple. This tiny piece of linen, which smells softly of a distant room where there was a Japanese lamp and an extraordinary, inconceivable comfort, filled the air, the world;

an impossible sensation of luxurious and defensive shelter. "Jaime, too, then, gave back to me a similar sensation." It was no longer the remote and lost heat, the impossible shelter. But, to be sure, a related and desired relief, a great repose. Something almost forgotten: the notion of what could be the world without fear of malevolence, without fear of the evil that surrounds her, without mattering too much to her the sad and mean defenses of those who—like she herself—had to strike, bite, dig, trample, in order not to sink definitely into the dust that buries everything. "He was not too evil." What more could she ask, in a world where the closest thing to human relationship was envy? What more could she ask, then? Isa closes her eyes. Her tears are now the thread of a ball of wool, of a desolately interminable skein? "Why will folks say that crying consoles," she thinks. "Who said that crying is the beginning of being consoled?" Some stupid person that has only cried at the dentist. But she can not even smile at her own jokes, like other times, when she sought a funny commentary with which to paliate intimate—and now too frequent—disillusions. "It's not wrong to give back to a girl a taste for life, a desire to look at herself in the mirror, to try on a dress, to have dinner in a decent restaurant, to be able to have a good time, to dance…"

Once, many years ago—perhaps she was thirteen or fourteen—in an illustrated magazine that Patricia, the maid, received every week in exchange for a modest bit of money, Isa read a detailed scene of seduction. In the kitchen, while Patricia was engrossed in the reading of those pages, Isa observed that she was whispering, in front of a table smelling of bleach and stews under the makeshift-gypsy-domestic tent which seemed, on a rainy afternoon, a laundry rapidly rescued from the covered balcony. Patricia was not paying attention to the request of a girl, hungry and chilly, who returns from the unpleasant High School. "Patricia, please, give me something to snack on; because I won't have dinner, because I have an exam tomorrow and I'll stay up studying until I don't know when." Patricia mumbled, got up reluctantly, abandoned on the table the pages colored with pictures—as she said—and went to prepare a sandwich. Isa observed

her while she divided a roll in half: Patricia seemed taken by a
diffuse, half-idiotic, half-angelic dreaming; lost in a distant world,
no doubt beautiful. A world that now lay abandoned on the kitchen
table, from the parenthesis where could be read, in italics, (continued) up to the parenthesis where it said, in the same characters
(to be continued). In the colored, square picture a blond girl was
giving away, in a horrified and gentle way, (as at the mercy of
some barbaric but unavoidable invasion) to the unexpected force
of a strange fellow who showed off black, curly hair and a plaid
jacket. Distractedly, Isa eyed the magazine. "Why do you read
these things, Patricia?..." Patricia gave her the sandwich, and,
without answering her question, snatched the papers from her, to
become lost once again in the adventures and arguments of that
curious pair. Isa remembered the days on which, patiently, she
taught Patricia how to read. Poor Patricia, then recently arrived
from the country town, an orphan, because the wheels of a wagon
of alfalfa had cut in half, without any consideration, Father's
body. Above Patricia's wretched bed in the inside room where
the sun never entered, stuck to the wall with thumbtacks, was
still the picture of Father, in a beret, with a halo of blurred shadows that tore him away from his original place in the family
group—from which he was separated, enlarged and retouched—
in order to relegate him definitely and palpably to the kingdom
of the dead. "Why do you read that, Patricia?," she repeated later
obsessed by mysterious questions that linked, without apparent
logic, the scene of the girl being subdued with Father's photograph nailed to the wall. Patricia was already washing the dishes,
in the steam of hot water and bad humor that characterized that
time of day. Isa nibbled, with apparent disinterest, an apple.
Patricia said: "Don't you have to study? Get to your books and
leave me alone!" There were the pages, already pawed over, piled
up, destined for the kitchen shelves or the bottom of the garbage
can. Without being able to avoid it, in an unexplainable impulse,
Isa picked up, furtively, the jumble of already wrinkled papers.
She carried them off, changed into a shapeless ball, dirty with oil
and impregnated with the smell of onions; she smoothed them
out, put them in order and inserted between the pages of the cold

and reasoned out Chemistry. In fear of being seen by Patricia and the slight terror of the exams of the following day, she devoured, at once the sweetly truculent story, the spectacular and exemplary loss of a woman's purity.

That scene of seduction was not erased from Isa's memory. To judge by what was read, seduction was constituted by rigid norms and circumstances—still within the most varied range of erotic fantasies—; to wit: a wealthy, older man wanted—with a fury beyond all reasonable explanation—to possess, come hell or high water, the young, soft, virginal body, economically weak of an ignorant young woman, intrinsically good, but doomed to be sacrificed for the sake of the well-being (or health) of another more unfortunate being: be it father, mother, grandfather, little brother, or whatever similar class of people. The consequences of this sacrifice were likely: the insane lack of scruples, cruelty, of men with inordinate appetites and with a full purse come to bloodcurdling extremes. Although, in order to watch out for good practices, the seduction took place in a form that repelled the delicate feelings of the women readers. Everything was dyed with fatalism: everything happened because there was no other choice. Even when the years deprived Isa of similar credulities, this scene persisted, although vague and distant, in the mists of the misfortunes of Adam and Eve and of their expulsion from Paradise; along with the image of the Guardian Angel, face turned to the wall, weeping for the first mortal sin of his charge: a sin which, of course, committed a crime against the sixth commandment. Isa experienced a rude shock, then, that Sunday morning, shining and warm, on which Jaime, one more time, requested her "extra services," given the need to resolve office affairs that could not wait until Monday. The good secretary, the impeccable, efficient and punctual Isa, ardently anxious of fulfilling satisfactorily her new responsibility, the satisfied Isa, recently promoted and well thought of, in the sunny Sunday morning, went towards a Jaime—a respected Mr. Jaime still—serious, proper, incapable of the slightest frivolity—neither during office hours or during "extra" hours—. It was not the first time she responded to similar requests, to alleviate the excess of work of the busy and kind

Mr. Jaime. Until that day the work was carried out without any hitch, without a single phrase or look that might differ from the precise and impersonal orders or dictations: without the slightest vestige of apparent humaneness. On the appointed morning Jaime seemed once more to be spotless and as sober as his shirt, his cuffs or his tie (nothing further, Mr. Jaime, from a certain plaid vest and certain black, curly hair that embodies still the image of a libertine and a somewhat stupid seducer). Isa's fright that morning was not due to the discovery of Jaime's intimate desires, the fright was due only—how clearly this defines itself now, in her memory!—To the old-fashioned nature of the event. Something similar to an insipid protest "but, man, it's not that way...," shook only her stupor before the erroneous belief that it was a question of honest and efficient work, when Mr. Jaime—suddenly just Jaime—bent over her and, instead of explaining a problem totally about work, suggested to her that she go with him to his studio. Without any apparent excitement or the supposed—and so well described in the magazines—erotic excitement in his reddened eyes, Jaime, with a calm glance, enlarged by the magnifying lenses, manifested, with a precision not exempt from homage, how much he appreciated the turn of her legs, her lips and some other things. Then he insinuated the possibility of making happier the annoying life of a girl so poor, so badly dressed and so beautiful, with the attributes and accessories to which, without any doubt, she had the well-deserved right.

Beginning with that clear and succinct explanation, her fright increased, faced with the intimate ascertainment that, although the scene of seduction did not correspond exactly to those others in which blindly, dreamingly, and outrageously Patricia informed herself, in spite of everything, it was a question of a real seduction: and, nevertheless, it was received with (recently discovered and hidden) joy on the part of Isa.

Without even a single kiss, in the radiant morning, Isa followed Jaime: she got in his car, sat beside him, advanced through the streets of a city suddenly new and luminous; they left behind sidewalks populated by people who were coming from Mass, carrying little packages of baked goods; they climbed towards an area even more luminous and sunny: among trees which seemed to retain an ancient and very longed for silence—a childish, sweet and pleasant silence—towards the so-called studio (and she only thought, serenely, that Jaime was truly a person not very fond of wasting time superfluously).

Nor was the first step towards dishonesty too cruel; she did not feel herself to be different from the people they just saw: those with the little packages of Sunday desserts. On the contrary, although with stupor, she could state that, suddenly, she felt much closer to them: at least, in her outward aspect, Isa resembled more those girls who were not dragging about the same coat for four winters, nor who tried to hide the heels which had been mended too many times by the corner shoemaker. "Before now I was much more distant from them; before, to be sure, I felt myself to be of another, inferior race, humiliated, deprived of hope, empty...," she said to herself, with the uneasiness that the discovery of intimate truth apparently produces. A truth that, until that moment, she had taken for cynicism. Jaime's first kiss was not worse, not by far, than Jacinto's first kiss, or that of any other young man, (and these equipped—it was clear—with more dubious intentions.) She would not go to wait for Jaime on a hypothetical bus, carrying hypothetical intentions of marriage. Jaime was almost fifty; he had a wife, children; a house, a profession and activities that had nothing to do with Isa's life (nor was it necessary for her). At times she remembered the atrocious phrases of Margarita, the shorthand secretary, aimed at the bastardly nature of the masculine race. Sadism, acts of meanness, endless brutalities, etc., were not too compatible with the hours of healthy relaxation, in the tiny and scarcely extravagant studio—closer to a second-class hotel room than to a properly called studio: or, at least, Isa imagined so—of a man who knew how to appreciate the value of youth and beauty; a man young enough, also, to appreciate her with pleasure; but, undoubtedly, at an age not given to excesses (that neither his schedules nor his work advised him to perform). Jaime's first kiss (standing, he scarcely helped her to take off her despised coat—and, on taking it off and its worn-out blue lining she had the feeling that she was getting rid or all

her miserable circumstances—) was a sweet, warm kiss and (if it
were possible to clear away any reference to incest) almost paternal. Without his glasses, which he carefully left on the little
table, Jaime turned out to be younger than his day-to-day look
could offer. His eyes, suitably, got smaller in his face, softened,
discretely sensual; and Isa discovered in his dark green iris a
tender and attractive myopic disorientation; a return, almost, to
his not completely lost youth. When she embraced his broad body,
his robust back, she thought it was a pleasant, almost delicious,
feeling: something like embracing, for the first time, the most
comfortable, just and undoubtedly decent aspect of life. "Indecent," she said to herself on more than one occasion after the
good-bye kiss lovingly placed on her cheek, "it is indecent to
cross the world like those poor dogs which, among the whistles
and throwing of stones, chased a chewed bone across the open
ground." Decent, on the other hand, was to wake up to a day
clear of the end-of-month anguish, from unpaid bills, from humiliating mending which were now reprehensible. Decent was
the smile of the old women who, from night to morning, seemed
flattered, softly gagged by a modest comfort.

Jaime's hands were not rough claws (described by Margarita),
nor his caresses the sbylline and astute snares of the devil (which
she read with enjoyment in Patricia's kitchen). Jaime's hands,
big, dark, with powerful and salient knuckles, that even today
she remembers with a diluted pleasure. "And, perhaps, that was
also love," Isa says to herself with something similar to a thirst
on dry lips, among the held-back tears of difficult classification.
Then, if not, how to explain to herself, now, in the thoughtful
recovery of time that has fled, in the ordering of facts which,
thus, can be classified, serenely, and even filed away, as if it
were a question of one more aspect of the office? How to justify,
if it were not a question of some kind or some aspect of love, the
circumstances which happened, absolutely unlike those which
the amorous-narrative magazines of Patricia foretold trough the
studied seductions? In place of the cruel and merciless desertion
(on a cold January night), in place of the sarcastic laugh of the
libertine with curly hair, in place of the solitude and the aban-

donment which invariably followed the consent of defenseless heroines in novels, her relations with Jaime, after that Sunday morning, were increased in intensity and frequency. In place of the "weariness which is the sequel to desire satisfied in the caprice of a moment," what happened and happened frequently, were their meetings; and, even, the signs of affection (or love, or whatever they wanted to call them). It was no longer the appointments in the studio: they increased in nocturnal, daily, evening dates of all kinds. On more than one occasion they took advantage of a short weekend trip: two comfortable days, in places and countryside where she never before had hoped to visit. Jaime was not the congested, frantic person that Patricia learned to hate, nor the vicious reptile that Margarita despised; nor even the imbecile and self-seeking, representative of a kind that, personally, Isa found the opportunity to know. Jaime offered the aspect of a clean, agreeable, well-brought up, and in no way exempt (Isa relives an itching feeling, sadly fleeing, in her arteries) from the mysterious magnet, capable of awakening in a young and unconcerned body, warmth, thirst, gentleness and the excitement which make up, obviously, the love of life.

So, after all (Isa sums with the disheartened resignation of someone who has trampled on something very useful), when her relations with Jaime arrived at what, in Patricia's novels, would have been described as its zenith, Mario appeared and, from night to morning, she kicked out, accurately, the only reasonable stage of so untidy a life.

Suddenly Isa feels a cruel sensation of poverty, of depression. "To dance, to have a good time…Who is this girl capable of having a good time, of becoming happy over a pair of shoes, or a purse, or dancing? Where is this girl? She no longer exists. It is as though she had died. And for this death, Mario alone is responsible." A passive rancor overcomes her. "Mario, awakening the illusion, once more, of my believing myself to be a superior woman, of not being a poor girl like the others. The stupid, ignorant vanity of believing myself to be "European" along the poplars of the Ebro, because of kissing a poor devil, with a mustache, chubby, imbecile, selfish. Awakening, once more, that Isa who could look over her shoulder to Maruchita and all the others (who knew perfectly well what they wanted and expected from this world). Talking nonsense, once more, becoming upset. And, on meeting him, feeling again that she had recently arrived from another much more sordid city. Poor Isa disappeared, buried by Mario. For what?"

Jaime behaved well. He was not brutal, nor demanding, nor did his story seem like those stories that, sometimes Margarita told with an air of sufficient experience; a story that summarized "the indecent, the bestial, the filthy things men are." No, Jaime was not like that. And, nevertheless, since Mario, starting out with Mario, she turned him into the great swine, the representative of that rottenness which ought to be exiled, without pity, from the earth. From the moment when Mario entered her life, Jaime took on, by himself, everything detestable, execrable, venal in this world. Isa sits up slowly, brings her fingers to her cheeks, wipes away those tears, humiliating and devastating. "But whose fault was it? Only mine." In the half-light, she again follows, with her glance, the edge of the bedcover, the edge of the carpet, the shape of her hands which stand out almost white. "It was me, only me. Not Mario. I must not be unjust. I have always struggled—that is not to be doubted, it is the least uncertain thing of my story—against hypocrisy. I hate hypocrisy. And if something good remains of that young and rebellious Isa, is it not perhaps the faculty of knowing, is it not perhaps the ability to analyze my acts, my feelings, the sufficient serenity to begin again, every day of my life? No, it was not him, it was me, Isa, Mario's blind admirer, the one dazzled by Mario." Although I had never said so clearly to myself, I have always known it: "only if I enter his world with him will I be able to have him." It was she who slipped in, between smiles of false bitterness, of false disappointment, an exuberant story of seduction, of exploitation, of poverty, solitude and desertion. Jaime ("who was, in his day, the great and desirable big first prize, the lucky lotto ticket) was changed, on Isa's lips, through Mario's hatred, into a bastard, into the ugly bad guy of innocent films. It was not Mario's fault. It was she, only she (because there was no other way, I did not know any other way, I could not undertake any other way in order to obtain the only thing I wanted to possess in this world").

Isa, startled, looks at her watch. "I must hurry, or I'll arrive late…" Going down the stairs, she thinks: "How strange: I have not been able to regain the anger, or the despair, sufficient to get up and say to myself that everything will continue, and that everything will be recovered. On the other hand, the movement of the hands on the watch, the routine, the passing of the hours, the docile submissiveness to what is customary…"

Life, she reflects, is perhaps much more simple or much more perverse than that we suppose.

PART THREE

The Story of the
Mistake is Simple

Diary in Disorder

On several occasions I said to myself that dusk—like alcohol—is an easy and useful accomplice for human beings thirsty for love or for a long, placid, although painful, self-confession. For the recovery, for example, of a vast forgetfulness.

They are, thus, in truth, what people call apparitions, ghosts. Undoubtedly, when we forget, when we lose some memory, it is as though we have never lived it; the things that no longer have room in memory have not happened. For that reason, if (outside of all logic) a solitary and amazing memory arises it is like seeing the ghost of a being, who has disappeared already from the earth, float.

This old and well-known battle of complicity and challenge, of pleasure and malaise; this renewed, self-evaluation and self-disappointment, this love, and undoubted reality, physical and beautiful, is, on this night, torn away from the dusk like a curtain, once more, a cause of stupor and incomprehension. I am not used to deceiving myself in these things. I can not say that the end of this smooth incline through which I began to slide from the moment when I opened the last door (closed at the far end of the narrow, empty room, daubed with paint, which Bear so kindly unbolted). How is something so old and so recurrent going to surprise me? How can the statement deceive—nor has it ever deceived me—of something so visible, audible and recognizable as is the early, almost immediate conviction that a skin will cling to my skin, that (sooner or later) those lips will be kissing my lips, that body will be a continuation of my body? It will be a useless relationship of so many images more or less sincere, more or less made into myths that can free themselves form that mysterious, simple and daily event: a woman and a man who, perhaps for only an instant, or an hour, or a few years, can turn out to be irreplaceable by another woman or another man. What I did no know (nor I know now, perhaps, in this moment when darkness returns, beautiful and warm, and shelters our embrace), what I did not know ever, before now, is the why of an embrace, of a skin against my skin. I believed that these things can not be reasoned out. And, nevertheless, I can reason them out, now, quietly, in the darkness, with my eyes open; while my neck brushes the harsh touch of his hair, and I feel on my shoulder the soft dampness of his forehead. It is something similar to the possession of a great, although discouraging enigma. A long and uselessly pursued revelation. Solutions to great enigmas are not, generally, so intricate, nor so beautiful, nor so malevolent as the mystery that made us look forward to them. But now I know and feel, in a physical way, in our embraced bodies (in this half-sleep that leaves his head on my shoulders, in his closed eyes, in the almost inaudible respiration that causes his chest to rise). I glimpse the weight of an expanded, innumerable betrayal.

Always, for years and years, betrayal gravitated over all my acts. Already it has rubbed against me, I have felt separate itself from some invisible vault. Just as the night falls down from the sky. Over me and over him float wandering and blind, many other small and big betrayals, other infinite and incessant acts of cowardice. Every day a child sells his best friend. Every day a man sells his brother, or a son betrays his father, or a father ridicules the dignity, the innocence or the worth of a son. All of us want to survive (even though it were better to die violently; even though it were better to die gratuitously, and remain in the memory of people as an improbable legend, fit for those ears without malice that can believe, admire, admit everything as possible and beautiful: even the most unreasonable story of love, or generosity).

But we want to survive, to avail ourselves of our noble and stolid condition of propitiatory victims, of scapegoats, of creatures which, not guilty of having been born, are obliged to bear, with protest, the weight of years, disappointments and calamities. We want to subsist, weeping without cause, triumphant executioners, engendering and giving birth to men and women; covering the crust of the world with men-women-victims-executioners.

Nothing has changed in her, between the first day I met her and her last letter; or the letter that she can write me within a year. Beverly has an enviable faithfulness to herself. I suppose her to be desperate without David, without Bear, without Franc. But she will keep on writing, unchanging, staggered and regular missives. I can recite her next letter even without receiving it. She will say: "Thanks for telling me your new address. I have very fond memories of that city. Now I am spending the last days of vacation in V. I return to M. on the eighteenth of this month. What wonderful days, here, with the conventions! The Chicago one shocked me a great deal...but, at the same time, I believe that the explanation of the two points of view about X. turned out to be useful. I believe that, for the first time, our university students begin to participate in the politics of the country, with all the extremes of attitude. Tell Bear that. Tell Bear that in F. there is a free expression of ideas. Until now we have not had "riots." Ah, it is possible that I might visit you. Ah, Spain keeps on being attractive to me. A very strong attraction! Truly that city exhausts me. With its houses by Gaudi and the excellent museums. I hope to return. Is Bear still studying? Everything that has to do with Bear interests me..." That's the way her next letter will be, and all letters, past and to come.

Beverly. You are exactly the same in that letter of last September, of a future autumn, that day when I saw you for the first time. Your words and the blue of your limpid eyes, overflowing with practical wisdom. Sure and punctual, like the sending of "alimony." Beverly, you and your letters, are a great discovery. Even then, at that time, I did not know how to understand it.

I always felt an abstract desire to protect David from something. The first day I saw Beverly's son (arriving from an Eastern university) it surprised me that, being her son, he was not strong, sure, decisively important. For that reason, when she appeared in our house with that boy (I believe that the first time was during Thanksgiving vacation) fragile and dark, with his nose surrounded by freckles, and his astonishing, big grey eyes, he awoke in me an inexplicable compassion. Franc used to say

he appreciated David very much. Franc has always believed tenaciously what his good intentions tell him to. But a very different thing is that his intentions might coincide with reality. Franc
felt towards David the same way as he did towards me. I mean:
he knew as little about David as about me. He imagined us to
be—I suppose—good, beautiful, well brought up and intelligent.
And, moreover, we were Spanish (David entered into the game,
since among other less solid inheritances, he manifested such an
unquestionable surname as Diaz.) "Spanish, like you and me."
Thus, then, who could doubt, not even for a minute, that David
was a fine boy?

The curious friendship of Beverly and Franc was maintained—
and I imagine that it keeps on being maintained—in an indescribable zone of appointments, greetings, conversations about
their work or business, opinions about the temperature and saying good-byes (until the next appointment, punctual and set up
by telephone before; until the following day, or the following
fortnight, or until the return from vacation). It is possible that
both might have wanted for themselves, vacillating and unconsciously, what they were ready to verify without any kind of
doubts, in the two of us. It was not strange nor difficult, that
David should remain in F., and be enrolled in some University
where I began my courses in comparative literature (which even
today I try to apply to some aspect of my life, without an osten-
sible effect). It was not strange that David should be congenial to
me, among other reasons, because in those days he constituted
the only living being, under thirty, with whom I could exchange
a handful of intelligible words. "It will be very good for David to
practice his Spanish with Matia, "Beverly used to say. I suppose
that David's English was good for me too.

But what was not good is what happened unexpectedly
to this friendship, to this vague love and fear that united
us. It was not good? Perhaps it was not so bad. Now, at this
distance, I do not know for what reason things had to happen the way they did. What difference does it make! In one
form or another, the road has to be traversed. Whatever
form, in short, is good, if one does not die on the road.

(Even though, at times, one can remain crippled.)

"Too late," David said.

It was irremediably late. He could not get rid of the devouring present; his feet were well planted on the ground (on that square of ground, precisely, and no other); with sycamores and maples and squirrels and beings in the fog, with his face blackened by soot, with his shoes in his hand. And I thought, in the confusion: "It is because the Druids..."

"Don't cry mother," David said. "Don't cry. It is late for crying."

But the woman cried, and held him in her arms, clinging to her, pressing as if she would never be able to let go of him ever. I felt uneasiness (perhaps because that did not move me as it would be desired; as if I believed that scenes like these ought to move me. At least they have taught me so.) "If one day I have a son, I will not do this to him," I thought only and vaguely. But it was absurd to devote one's life to thinking of these things. Plans could not be made, yet.

A certain unhealthy satisfaction opened up; and that was perhaps the cleanest, noblest, the most restful of all that was happening in the last twenty-four hours: plans could not be made anymore. The fact is that she had been living (for too many years) as a victim of innumerable plans. Plans and plans and planning for the future, arose from here and there, from all possible corners, like mushrooms. And here you have, suddenly, everyone being frustrated, being broken and disappearing against something so unforeseen and brutal as a war.

"You are a little bit the evil witch," said Franc in the morning. "You leave the war and enter the war. Let's see if you bring good luck sometime."

Halloween was far off, with its human little puppets disguised as elves, glazed with fog, barefoot. But David and I had, all of a sudden, done with the plans, and he appeared happy, satisfied, relieved. Because, suddenly, his doubts were resolved; he already knew that there was no other choice than: going to war.

I always thought that Beverly would never be able to surprise me in a too evident manner. I was mistaken. Only on the day when I saw her, hugging David desperately, calling him in a guttural and unintelligible voice. The day on which David stopped, finally, the whole world of danger, of going under, of doubts and choices, did I understand how much patience, how much firmness, how much endeavor and iron will that refused imagination, she must possess in order to offer, every morning of her life, a fresh and pink face (although over fifty), a perfectly blue shine in her eyes, an absolutely indifferent nuance in her voice. Commenting, in the same tone, how the roses were doing, the tornados, the racial problems and the breakdown in the plumbing, Beverly always was, for me, a living and unforgettable example.

From that moment on, innumerable couples whose men had been called up decided to get married. David and I got married, too, one cold morning, without any ceremony.

That waiting, that enormous time that seemed to me to be deprived of all meaning now comes back to me only in fragments. As if it had been a short time, a bitter minute; although then I found out that boredom (the useless passing of hours) never took over a human being as it had taken over me. On the contrary, the rapid succession of the facts that developed after waiting, are still weighing over me; now in this very moment in which the head of a man about whom I know nothing (nor the reason why he must hide, nor the crime he has committed and can commit), his weight on my shoulder, is revealed to me, in this kind of sweet half-sleep, half-awake, relieved of rancor, passion or indifference (simply resting on me), like the only possibility of total comprehension between two living creatures. Supporting one another, as I have seen trees and plants in some forest; only like this, resting in the darkness.

The moon has run away now, like a fugitive, behind the tumultuous and changing clouds. Only like this, in the certitude that he has closed his eyes, with the smell of his skin near me— a blond, unmistakable smell—can I, without fear, without rancor, reconstruct the nausea, the stupor, the degrading sensation of having been a witness and a part of this infinite human condition.

"And what became of them? What happened next?"

"Wait until I finish setting the table; in a moment I'll come back and I'll tell you, dear," said Mauricia.

"But, first, tell me one thing, only one thing…"

"Wait, honey, I'll come back in a jiffy."

But then they sent her a message, she went out, leaving the door open, and I remained next to the warm ashes, swinging my legs and without knowing the ending of that story of the town; of many years ago, when not even Mauricia—or anyone I might have known—was alive.

"It's a bad dream," I thought. "For some nights I have been dreaming of strange things."

I got up and went out to get a drink of water. Just as it had not happened for many, many years. Only in the distant days of childhood, of adolescence, I got out of bed in one jump and went, barefoot, to get a drink of water, with an irresistible thirst.

I turned on the tap and filled the glass I used to rinse my teeth. I was mistaken, it was the hot-water tap. I was always mistaken. I looked at myself stealthily in the mirror. Helpless eyes; like the eyes of little dogs that I saw once, so pathetic in their cages, on the day when David lost Doff and the dogcatchers got him. I pulled a face in the mirror, and it returned it to me with a magic punctuality.

David was as fragile as a poppy. I had picked, not too many years before, a poppy; I remember my eager hand, closing, because I had caught it; then I ran away to show it to someone. I opened my hand and that uncertain mass appeared.

Or perhaps not. Perhaps it was a butterfly. But now that I remember, I had not even asphyxiated the poppy: it was there so alone, cut between my fingers, dismembered and dead. All trace of a flower had disappeared and, in its place, a limp and red petal, more dead than any decay, surrounded a hairy stem, long, black unctuous, like a caterpillar. Something sinisterly soft, ephemerous, banal; treacherous in its softness, like a line of ants. I cleaned the palm of my hand on my bare child's legs, I ran away. But I could not forget that dirty cadaver, blood-curdlingly wretched.

David! I called, knowing that he was not at my side, that he was far away. I called him in order to hear myself calling him: or at least wanting to do so. And, nevertheless, that name sounded hollow, false, as though it did not belong to anyone known. Anyone could be called David, at that moment. It's all the same, one or the other name. Everything was so absent to me, so strange. How could he withdraw from life, like that? Moreover: how can feelings disappear, if the object of those feelings was absent? I tried to imagine that it was a brief absence, that, in reality David would return on the following day, at the latest. It was useless: David was only a word.

In the darkness, on the little night stand, the alarm clock indicated a phosphorescent hour. I turned on the lamp, it was three in the morning. I felt that three o'clock was a magical hour, I could almost say it was definitive for me. The same thing with the number three. I feared it, and—many times—like that time—a terrible warning repeated in the depth of my consciousness its solemn message of ill-omen; and I did not want to hear it. In those moments the confused cry—it was an opaque cry, without stridency—remained smothered by big cushions of clouds and damp words that limply hid any meaning of ill-omen. Nevertheless, afterwards, when misfortune happened unexpectedly, the cry raised up, horrendous, triumphal, as a malevolent sybil among floating rags—my poor reasons—; and it turned towards me, and pointed at me with a long and hard white arm, of white stone, stretched out, shining with evil; and the cry turned into a screeching whip (shaking a distant and not forgotten cane field).

There was nothing strange that early morning, even though the number three tried hard to appear like a warning and I would like it to be the promise of some good omen. Although I knew it was the instigator of very close evils.

When I returned to bed, sleep had totally disappeared from me. I did not like to get up at that hour. Through pure routine I wrapped myself up again in the sheets, closed my eyes stubbornly, tried to scare off any thought that was not sleep, sleep. But it was useless and I knew it.

The sun was shining, slowly, through the curtain, that early morning. It was a green curtain, with faint designs of branches.

A pink light mixed with the green appeared gradually and it made me long for the maritime gardens of a certain little mermaid of my infancy.

It was the fifteenth of November. Generally I did not know on what date I was living. But that date was a living, distinct number. And I remember I said to myself, while I was looking at the dawn: it is the fifteenth of November.

A little later, the first bright light and the noise of the day arrived. (When there was a big wind, the whole apartment seemed to shake. The wind crashed against the walls of the house and I heard something similar to distant detonations, as when they set up charges in order to break up the rock in the quarries. At the beginning I thought it was a mysterious and nocturnal din, but then, little by little, I realized that it was only the wind.)

The day went by without change. Nothing new had happened. I was studying all morning, and around twelve I put on my coat— it was clearly very cold and snow was predicted—and went out to eat. There was a coffee shop at an intersection, not far from the building. The window panes were steamed up by the steam, by the high heat. I hung my coat from a hanger, and while I was doing so, I noticed the persistent steadiness of someone's eyes. It was something impalpable, but sure. I scarcely dared to raise my eyes. Lately I had that feeling. When it happened to me, an invincible fear fluttered next to me. I did not dare to lift my glance and find that other glance, invisible, as if in this way I could scare off some possibility, escape to some purpose or event that it still seemed possible to avoid. As if for a few seconds, I had in my hands the possibility of straightening out the curve of destiny. Even though, rationally, I did not believe in these things.

I looked for a table next to a window, framed by yellow-ish curtains, which turned bright from the light of the sun. In that enormous flat plain it was frequent that in the cold-est days, there was a round and brilliant sun in the middle of the sky. On the table shone the sugar bowl, the saltshaker, the bottle of catsup and the mustard. I took the menu and pretended to look avidly for something, seized by a subtle spying. And this scene, and this day, were repeated, like a stupid nightmare, once, twenty, a hundred times.

A little later Bear was born.

Nobody would have recognized him when he returned except me. If the first time that I saw him I thought his eyes were those a victim, when he returned I understood that he had made of it a kind of profession. Stories of exemplary punishment, of unheard of harshness and humiliation came with him, as all the baggage he had. Bouts of delirium, trembling, nightmares and fits of weeping, were the daily mark of that return.

At times, we ate in a kind of "snack-bar," which was located in the suburbs. I contemplated his face, his freckled nose, his head bent over the plate, and I said to myself: it is not possible that they have hurt him to that point. It was difficult to start again (I vaguely began to suspect so) something that perhaps never existed, or arrived with too much delay.

Boys and girls, like him and like me, were chewing pensively alongside us; lost in days which were already pure absence, years used in something that was outside their plans (from the wildest to the most modest). Even then, the David of the orangeade and grapefruit juice had turned into the David who was inseparable from whisky. But those were only tokens, vague signs, or indications (warning signs that give life to someone blind man, deaf to all that which is not what he intimately longs to save or make up.)

I supposed that it was Beverly who harmed him. Beverly, her monthly checks, her eternal watching over David. Our house, our city, our surroundings. We always found a person, an occurrence, a moment suitable on whom to unload our long complaint of guiltless victims. It is possible that Beverly was not a stranger to that submission, to that mean and sad spectacle. At times, beautiful strong and sensible women can absorb, like a tornado, weak trees, modest, little wooden houses. David always appeared overwhelmed, confused, by Beverly's great common sense. I said to him: "Let's go away from here, escape from this dependency, from this horrible and suffocating garden, where everything is taken care of beforehand, where everything evil, ugly, sad, must be avoided, where every human manifestation must be packaged

in a perfumed and knowing way." It was a time when I still believed in humanity, the way some children believe in their books,
in the stories that narrate and resolve, satisfactorily, good or bad
actions, the ugly or beautiful things of life, and keep a last chapter for the right solution of each case. "Let's go away from here,"
I used to say to him; and I remember (and I know that nobody, or
almost nobody, probably spoke with greater conviction about
something that he does not understand; with greater faith in something he never knew). "Let's give up this dependency, this submission, this absolute giving in to her decisions, her money, her
good sense..."

I did not hate Beverly. I never hated her. And, nevertheless, at
that moment, she appeared to David (to us) like the compendium
of all the evils that could have chosen him. She was the cause
that David had collapsed; that he had been shipwrecked in a reality, in a cruel reality that others could bear, and even forget.
Beverly, the strong and courageous Beverly, had protected David
to the point of leaving him completely empty before the past, the
present, the future, I thought, full of rancor, "Let us give up this
place, let us go and build our own life, without anyone's help."

Trembling, I still hear my voice. For David, with the same
fear that I would feel if I were to see him on the edge of an abyss,
without the strength to remove himself from the vertigo, the void.
"The Veteran's Act—and I made use of magazines, papers, announcements which, at that time, still interested me, even filled
me with curiosity or worry about the world (ugly or beautiful,
good or bad) which surrounded me—takes care of veterans who
have lost valuable years, like you...They grant scholarships to
carry out whatever kind of studies. Everything is on easy terms,
David; we can not fail to take advantage of this opportunity..."

David assented weakly, with his face of a child lost in the
world (the child who spoke of druids and of a certain Halloween
that can no longer return).

At nightfall, we arrived at a kind of city, or town, or metallic
jungle, made up of an infinite number of trailers where a multi-
tude of boys, of young couples, began the recovery (or, at least,
tried to) of the years of desolation, of death, of dirty cruelty from

which they arrived. In that boxcar-housing (half circus, half bus), the feeling of irreality, of beginning a dream, with a metallic shudder—perhaps that wind which causes to vibrate those unknown plates of zinc, I don't know where—began also our hoped for and credulous stage of independence, self-made stability and, perhaps, love. "It's a marvel," I said to him installing my few belongings along with my stupid hopes, in the interior of that long and grounded dwelling—; "it's something really good." "Yes," he repeated, "really good." It was difficult, impossible, to ask him for an opinion, the least personal observation. I peeked through the window and made out there at the end, comforted by a distant taste of tears, the outline of some trees beaten by the wind. I recognized the smell of earth and grass, like a very intimate friendship.

Bear was still a baby, he was beginning to walk on his short legs, to raise his hands towards objects, to emit sounds (strange to everyone, except to me). Bear would look at me, even though he did not speak and, nevertheless, in his eyes there was a mute intelligence, a smiling intelligence that went from him to me; and held me astonished and moved.

It is not easy to understand, without having experienced it, how atrocious narrow-mindedness, privation, can turn out for someone like David, what an idea of poverty—even more or less honorable—can represent in a palace where wealth is the natural order of things. The frightful misery that can be—as it was for David and even for myself—the simple "not having anything" where "everything is possible and ought to be had." Whoever is not immersed in that kind of misery, in anyone of its facets—can not come to appreciate the infinite range of edges, angles, and motives that can present (from the misery that keeps one from entering in a place because of the color of one's skin, to the stupid privation of a fancy desire, common to everyone except ourselves). It's laughable, now, to state to what extent he did not know any other harsher or more merciless misery: but very late the knowledge reached me and I could not be consoled then.

Poverty was (this, to be sure, I can remember clearly) the nights of insomnia; waiting for the arrival of a vaguely human being; a being overwhelmed by his own ineptness, alcohol, and delirium. I remember my hands clutching the window sill, forcing myself not to look out, not to look there where he could appear, in the night; and towards where he could appear, after an absence of two, three or more days.

At times, if it rained, the roof of the boxcar resounded with a special rattling; hollow, cold and tortuous. The rain beat, without stopping, on the roof of our house-boxcar, as the next storm of cries and monotonous, insane weeping drew near. Monstrously infantile.

And on that night, a call, an inhuman lament crossed the air, the walls. Outside, fallen flat on his face in the puddles formed on the mud after the recent rain; in the middle of the paradoxical and immense solitude of a jumbled town (or city, or unreal country formed by innumerable metallic, closed, boxcars, in the silence of the doors and hermetic windows, of the deaf ears that transformed each object, each body, into a mirage of false humanity, his horrible and already well-known scream emerged and wounded.

He was at my feet, and in the great solitariness only the distant silhouette of the trees, black in the night, gave me back a little of the courage that I was losing, minute by minute. There he was, fallen on his face, in the puddles, with the convulsive and well-known trembling: "I will not do it again. I promise you, I will not make that mistake again." I heard, like one more joke, behind that scream, interrupted at intervals by the horrible chattering of teeth, cutting off words and voice like an atrocious knife. Then, slowly, the light of the moon appeared; some clouds moved away; and it seemed to me that the scattered and ramshackle world of the metal appeared recently washed, shining. At my feet, an enormous rat shook itself—I saw, many years ago, a sticky rat, swollen, wet, drown itself in a wash basin. Suddenly, something exiled from me any pity, any puerile and useless patience, the ingenuous conviction that in the last chapter the solution is the right one. Mine was a malign and poisonous innocence; mine was a criminal faith, useless belief, absolutely dead all of a sudden, in "all is going to change, all is going to be taken care of, this will pass…" The easygoing, thirsty justification for any act that was not a fine or worthy act: "wars are cruel, wars destroy good, sensitive, fragile boys, whom we ought to protect, not only from war, but from all harm, all evil…" Against what ought we to protect that enormous rat, convulsing, wet, its gut on the ground, that offers a scream absolutely lacking in humanity? That long and dirty rat was not larger than anything, it was nobody. Nothing remained to be saved, since no war would be able to destroy it, it was its own war.

I remember that I dragged him as far as the trailer, taking him under his arms, as I had done so many times. But that night (upon invading me once more the well-known vapor, the intolerable vapor of the alcohol coming through like sweat in a sick body, a body knocked down and shapeless), on that night, for the first time, I refused to hold him up. I let go of him, I heard his head against the ground; and he stayed on the ground with his stultified groan. I ran to the end of the trailer, without being able to repress the great nausea (which came from far away, from many and many other suppressed desires of flight). It seemed to me that my whole body expelled some repugnant, shapeless love, that was no longer of any use, to anybody, for anything.

But only I was guilty. It was nobody's fault but mine, mine alone; I had believed an infinite number of phrases, that I had read and believed, that the world was full of goodness.

I don't know what this man's name is, nor how old he is, nor what kind of life he has; his past, his present, or the possibility of his hopes. Nevertheless I had arrived at the conviction that none of these things can weigh on us now, when the early morning arrives, at this absurd old house, alien and familiar in equal parts. A landscape at one time loathsome and unconsciously beautiful.

This early morning is strange, this peace, beneath the light that reconstructs, before my eyes, his body already indelibly inscribed in my memories, recognized since the first instant as something that breathes in my very being, in my very appearance; something that rests on my own silence, like a common language, without words.

Contrarily, another man, whom I know, or thought I knew,

with whom I built, jointly, a language, a present, a future, with
whom I had a son, was able to coexist with me and disappear
from my side, absolutely unknown, alien.

Detached from my being, as though made from a substance
that has nothing in common with the substance of my body.

Bear existed, grew, at a time when something similar could
signify a kind of evil and good combined. At least Beverly thought
so.

I have always admired Beverly, but now even more. Some
day, I hope, I will achieve her control or her voluntary ignorance
of the least fortunate of the world. The memory of Beverly in
those days is based on a certain old song which irritated me in
my infancy: some girls from the school Nuestra Señora de los
Angeles played and sung it, with a peaceful air, without any ag-
gressiveness, to what other girls said: "the watch tower, the watch
tower, I came to destroy it"; and serenely lined up, facing each
other, the other girls responded, unperturbed and singing: "the
watch tower, the watch tower, you will not destroy it." The puerile wrath it caused me, at that time, the stolid and melodious
battle of both groups, is what most resembles, in spite of its
incongruency, Beverly's attitude towards me in those days. I see
her advancing, serene, almost sing-song, almost melodious: "the
watch tower,—I heard it, in spite of myself, at the bottom of her
sensible reasons—I come to destroy it."

Although, in truth, poor Beverly came solely to raise up, brick
by brick, if not a tower, at the very least a despicable hut among
the ruins of a false city hoped for, drunk and absolutely barren.
"You ought to separate, dear. It's the only way to do it. Because
life, really, can only be put on the right track at the cost of formulas, of recipes more or less simple or complicated; but recipes
that knead that enormous and monstrous cake called the world.
Without any doubt."

I was mistaken: the world is not conquered at the cost of distrust, rebellion, hope or desire for love. All that is fine to begin
with. But if you are already involved in it, sunk up to the waist in
the viscous dough of the cake, it is necessary to restore each
thing to its place. It was true what Beverly said: men and women

who—suddenly—seemed to belong to an unknown and atrocious
fauna, ready to devour each other, to cover themselves with mud,
to tear each other apart, slowly and with an almost Biblical pleasure, eye for an eye, tooth for a tooth. (Oh, no, atrocious ideas of
disoriented boys; the Bible is something else: the idea of the prodi-
gal son, the manna in the desert. That is the real Bible)—men
and women and their problems could be something simple as
well as explainable. Because men and women (once separated
and chosen from among the horrible fauna which it is better to
forget), can find a good and reasonable solution to all the stupid
complications. How could she doubt it?

Now, still, I manage to retain an infinite fatigue from that
conversation which, suddenly, gives way, deteriorates. Seated in
front of Beverly (who, for sure, had put the finishing touches,
with an extraordinary hat of blue and yellow flowers, on the
golden arrangement of her hair), while, finally, my silent tears
broke out, and I let them run down my cheeks without any shame,
like a puzzle putting itself in order, adequately. With a simplicity
of a woman getting on in years, who can understand it (even the
world and men, since she never let herself be bowled over by
any one of those two things).

"I knew that she was wealthy but not to that extent...," was
the only and stupid thought that filled me, while she explained
and developed before my eyes, like a beautiful and well drawn
map, the advantages that the situation of a divorced woman can
offer; the infinite range of possibilities that such a situation presents; the great invention of alimony. (She herself—she would
say—who was already well situated, she had managed to speculate very satisfactorily with her own alimony—since David's father was a man of great means—; and, as her financial sense was
very sharp, she had increased, in very convenient numbers, an
amount of money that...) Beverly unfolded and smoothed with
her chubby and well-cared for hands a vast range of absolutely
honorable projects, overflowing with common sense. An unsus-
pected, flat plain began to stretch out before my vision; a long
steppe of peace, rest, almost dazzling in the cold morning; comforted and kept warm in the soft warmth of the Restaurant, whose

sign, through the window pane "Luncheon, cocktails," blinked off and on in pink. Comforted by the martinis, the soft music, the sight of Beverly's hat, covered by an indestructible and very beautiful flowered spring. A hat that filled the entire room, that presided over our conversation like a symbol. A hat absolutely honorable and Saxon, (I thought, idiotically), whose antecedent was possible to scrutinize in the heroic and disappeared chests of the "Mayflower."

Immersed in a calm over which pink clouds flew, Beverly talked about the rest I deserved, of a well deserved and long period of vacation ("For example, dear, it's a suggestion, take it as such..."), or of re-encounter with the old country. Perhaps a trip, like those she was accustomed to take through Europe, so pleasant, so agreeable and interesting; and I remembered her photos; the group friends, decorated with flowers, softly guttural Daughters of Republic. In the middle of this plain of peace, limitless, without even horizons, I saw myself, floating. A weightless body, one more cloud. "I no longer have to worry economically. Now everything is taken care of. There are laws. Everything is perfectly well taken care of..." In a well-organized world where absurdly uncivilized acts could be avoided, Beverly and I were the most decent and honorable allies, I heard her dispassionate praise of cities (Venice, Rome, Paris or Amsterdam, without too much order). As if it were a question of homemade prescriptions, but efficacious, against all pain. Beverly, after all, was that afternoon the greatest expression of human wisdom.

I saw Beverly's album many times. The beautiful album of her selected, numbered and graphic memories. The photos where she appeared in a print dress and comfortable, buttoned up, white shoes. And she was smiling. (Although, suddenly, her smile was that of a clown, an old clown, drunk, sorrowful). But Beverly enjoyed her vacations. Beverly smiled in Venice, in the middle of a compact group of friends. Beverly, and all these women, knew well the ground which fell to them to step on: they swept, cleaned and put in order that crappy and ramshackle kitchen which is called the world. Although Beverly's figure, cut out on a background of spires and towers, on the complicated architectonic lace that a wise and ferocious fauna, now remotely built, Beverly, suddenly, appeared like the image of the cruelest and most fearful solitude.)

"Each one in his appropriate place: resting, and beginning again..." Therefore, of course, Bear would remain in Beverly's house, with Beverly. And David in his perfect and extraordinary Sanatorium.

Final point. Whatever thing Beverly might have been able to say that morning would be blindly accepted, appreciated. Because no one would have been able to infringe her extraordinary, blessed peace and wisdom. And less than anyone the dirty bundle of pain, of withered hopes, seated in front of her, assenting, without being ashamed even of weeping, or of docility. A force turns off, goes out, precisely at the end of the line; in the mysterious frontier when, still, even yesterday, we thought we were standing. She can thus quench pride, the will to overcome disdain; and the teetering edifice that we produce so laboriously, between long waits, shouts held in, falls down and cover us with ruins. "Momentarily, Bear, with me..."

To return, to go back to the world which she should never have left. ("Each thing in its place.") To go back to this world, where an unknown man leans his head on my shoulder (he should be a boy with golden hair, curly and thick, which surely humiliated him). To go back to the world where people do not appear excessively inclined towards happiness; to the place where children can leave school and begin work at eleven years of age; where children can drink, in public, red, heavy, wine, often of an unknown brand; where children can still be slapped, beaten, without infringing the law, without too much fear of their disappointment or possible inhibitions. Where there are still children who know how to laugh after each blow, and are getting ready to rob us of our ultimate vestige of credulity.

I returned, I left Bear with Beverly. "Every year you will come to see him, dear. Now you need to rest." I left David in his admirable sanatorium for alcoholism. "Where it seems to be, they have had positive and rather notable experiments..."

"Momentarily" is a very large space of time. An uncontrolled time, falsely provisional, treacherously elastic. How could I lose Bear this way? How did I manage to lose him this way, stupidly, pathetically, unsuspectingly? Momentarily is a long time where stupid women travel without direction, try jobs, lives, love, without a precise aim or conviction; where stupid women float, wanderingly and provisionally, and go and return and kiss cheeks of a child that is no longer a child; who looks at us like at a forgotten photograph. Where, from kiss to kiss, the distance increases more—"Now he is in W. Look at his picture..."

Bear is no longer there. No one can see Bear any longer. The distance is already not to be saved. And he can no longer return the glance of eyes that learned to talk before his lips did; the innocent and mute complicity of a child, under a metallic roof, or on a green lawn, with dry leaves in his hands.

I lost Bear, and I never recovered him. Neither in Franc's sad illusions, nor in travels through Europe, nor in this land where, perhaps, I ought not to have returned or ought not to have abandoned. It was not in a humid and nocturnal train that I lost Bear, but in another train compartment, far away and metallic; there where a child, who had not yet learned to speak, wove a subtle string—golden, tiny—of his glance to my glance. Without supposing that I myself would cut it, perhaps forever.

Three Days of Love

I can not have dealings with myself any longer. I have to admit it, I have to say it. I have to explain—to myself, to someone, not only to her and to these doors that will open or that I will close forever—the day on which I opened a forbidden door, and the great terror was born.

I would like to open my eyes now and say: I have deceived you. I have deceived everyone. I deceive myself everyday. It is not true, I do not hide, no one is still pursuing me, and this hiding place still does not have meaning. Even at this moment, if I were to leave here, no one would pursue me or be able to cause me harm. Everything has yet to happen. Today, tonight (look at the map so well drawn by Bear's hand), is when what we slowly planned must occur. I developed it many years ago. Better said, I wanted it, I have been desiring it, and only now have the decisive coincidences, or fates combined, as it customarily happens, quite often in life. Since the day when I met Bear, since I heard talk about this house for the first time, my plan began to hatch, desire began to goad me. When I met Bear he had just informed me: the object, the single motive that had guided me for years, the one source of all my energy for years, he, the valuable and inestimable object of my revenge, had been transferred—men like him do not travel, do not emigrate, do not change domicile: they are transferred, moved, like apparatus, instruments or peasants—to this island. Everything seemed to merge, to coincide: everything arrived from disparate regions, and, at the same point. The body of revenge was being born, finally, and the great excuse alone detained me; there was an old woman, who had climbed on my back, to whom an unpayable debt united me: someone I could not abandon, even leave more alone, because of the simple luxury of explaining my life, my future, or just my present.

Life is something more sordid than an unhappy marriage, more cruel than abandoning children to the hands of others, sadder than wandering through the world in search of a moment of love, or of enthusiasm, or of peace. You, poor woman who now embrace me, will never know it. Life is made up of such vulgar things as a salary, a market basket, medicines, shoes. Life is even worse: it is a disgrace, a continual humiliation, a vast oppression, hour after hour, of requests, waiting, applications, smiles, empty serious words. One day, scarcely two weeks ago, the great apology ceased to exist. It no longer exists. The old woman has died, with all her memories, with her faint and sharp sting.

Only when I saw her dead did I comprehend that what had already begun to change into a poorly disguised cowardice could not be delayed any longer. Valuable elements were offered within my reach; someone (perhaps the breath of the great revenge, subtly audible in the earth or the wind, or of poverty: a motionless beating in the air, over the scraps of waste material, over the detritus of the factories; over the barren and dirty countryside; this blind and irate beating which, at times, shakes the windows in winter, when a terrified boy studies, or hates or weeps) had accumulated, in front of me, the extraordinary circumstances which had the name of Bear, of this house, of this untouchable and irreproachable family. The plan, from being so simple, could be perfect: the possibility of entering the island, of leaving it, without anyone (except Bear, you, me and Borja) knowing it. Neither you nor Borja would ever say anything, ever: I hope that Bear would be too valuable to you. And, still, perhaps more than Bear, a name, a world, a class, however you wanted to call it. But you have not refused. Bear knows those who surround him, he is an intelligent boy. At times I thought that Bear ought to have had another family. But then he would no longer be Bear and would be of no use on this occasion.

Here are the firm lines, his map, simple and perfect, like a sketch or the eyes of a child. Bear has been instructed in the idea that the man, the one who has been transferred, is the keyman. The one who is on the way to destroy the complicated net which we have so laboriously woven during these two years. Bear believed that that man holds in his hands the signs that will lead him to the safe way, the way that leads to the destruction of our patient labor during the past two years; that scents the air around us. Unexpectedly he is "transferred"; the wheel of coincidences signals the ultimate and definite part. The occasion can not be disdained and this map of Bear's copied, faithfully and conscientiously, the house where the man-object lives. Do you see this little back gate, opening on to the garden? The beautiful garden with the narrow and solitary street, where Bear will wait, in Borja's car. Bear has lived, step by step, all the habits of this solitary and methodical man. It is only necessary to wait, the man will arrive home, will close the door. I will wait in the garden: he will have entered somewhere around there. You can finish a man with noise: everything can be clean, tidied up, rapid. A man can die without noise, I know it very well. One has only to go out into the garden, jump over the fence, get into Bear's car and come back. Nobody will miss the man-object until the next day. And, on the following day, Bear, Borja and I will already be on the sea. No one has news of me on this island, no one has seen me, no one knows anything about me, in this house, in this family. Bear is a boy outside of any doubt. You are all people outside of any doubt. As simple as this boy's sketch.

That is what I want to tell you. But how am I going to say it to you? I am the man who pretends to be sleeping, when he is alert. So, with my forehead leaning on your shoulder, in the warmth of your skin, I close my eyes and pretend that I am sleeping or dreaming. I always lied or pretended. Nor can I say anything other than that to you: that now, in a premonition of dawn, through my eyelids, something begins to fall apart, it seems that something is becoming undone around me. As if the innumerable, accidental particles that make up the great body of revenge were disintegrating. I cannot tell you that, suddenly, I have the feeling of giving Bear away of doing with him the same thing they did with me, in the past. That, suddenly, Bear seems to me, along with his map, a child who plays with a weapon that he has not learned how to handle. And that I, on whom he relies, do not exist. I feel the anguish of having disappeared with the shadows of this night which begins to abandon us. Bear, the man-reason, has become dissolved, as the last shadows of these walls flee little by little; as if, with the light, my shadow were to return to what it has always been.

I have sold Bear, and a vast world of people who believed in my principle; because he supposed me to be a destroyer of idols and altars, destroyer of myths. They have backed me because they imagined they were following a destroyer of falsehoods, or rotting structures. Perhaps only in the bright morning hour, like this one, when I caress this black and smooth head, when I kiss these lips and embrace that body that I love in vain, I perceive, in all clarity, the trace of infinite moments of being untrue to my principles. I desire this body next to mine because I see it tired, furrowed, sunk down by rivers of disappointment, melancholy, doubt. Perhaps only in early mornings such as these is it possible to get to the bottom of the great lie, the atrocious farce.

How brief a life can be and how slow and long a death. I have lied, I have deceived; during a long period, which begins on that day, I have been only a dead man, a ghost, who was hatching (not the desire for justice, not the implacable means which will destroy the great shop of the merchants), who was only hatching my small, particular and obscure revenge. I have lied: that man, he is not the keyman. I have lied to you Bear, treacherously, looking you in the eyes. That man is not our man; he knows nothing, no thread of our net has been caught in his hands, he can do nothing against us. That man whom I decided to eliminate has grown old, perhaps has forgotten, probably is already tired, or sad, or full of peace. He is not our man, he is only my man, the object of my most personal and private revenge, of my personal and mean right to hate: private, enclosed, possessive. Of my own untransferable myth. I have deceived all of you, I have deceived myself time after time, always.

The ogre in Tom Thumb cuts the thread of his daughters while they sleep, the wolf devours neatly a gullible girl, a king, jovial and covered with amethysts, wants to marry his little fifteen year old girl. Stories for children are simple and ferocious. The history of error is as simple as a tale for children.

The error began one morning, in the cold and the sun, on the still vacant marble cafe tables under the arcade. A waiter was sweeping rubbish from under the chairs, and the flagstones of the square were shining because a luminous rain had fallen. The stall of the roast chestnut man had just lit up. In the hideout it was very cold: neither fire, nor light, nor heat should give away the hiding man, Bambi's secret. But a proper cone of chestnuts, burning in the brown paper, warmed his hands, numb with cold. "He will be able to warm his hands." In the exciting secret of the morning, when the wife went to work and would be late in returning, the minute that kept a shared, intimate and amusing secret (much more amusing than playing at cops and robbers under the porticos) was coming back. He was going along with the paper squeezed in his hands, feeling the heat on his chest, when someone said; "Bambi." He did not say: "Mario." He said: "Bambi." The wisdom of the betrayal has the subtlety of lace, in the most rough hands.

I remember it with total clarity. Moreover, I believe his recollection has a more real emphasis than all the realities among which I move. Nothing since then has had the materiality, the color, of that recollection. He was seated next to one of the columns of the portico, under the half-torn off bullfight poster. He was leaning against the back of the wicker chair. He was drinking beer, foaming and intensely golden. His newspaper was folded over, on the marble table, next to the glass. No one had called me Bambi except for the man who was in hiding. For that reason, I stopped, looked at him, obeyed his gesture that I should come close. He stroked my head and I thought (only now do I know I was a victim of self-deception, upon hearing the softness of his voice) that he was whispering (only those who were like us in those days whispered) while contemplating in his eyes, enormous and sincere blue eyes, the same distrust that I knew in the eyes of the woman who ordered me not to open the door.

The snare of one word: "Bambi," which belonged uniquely to the secret world, to the hideaway, made me say to myself confusedly: "I know him, I saw him before, at times, with Dad." One by one, without the slightest forgetfulness, I can reconstruct all his words. Even the softness of his hand, too small, too soft, of an almost obsessive whiteness, is still on my cheek. He said: "Bambi, pretend, son, act as if I were speaking to you of something else: I really do know, I really do know that no one is supposed to know where your father is. Don't worry, Bambi. Now we must hurry. Here—and his hand was placed inside his jacket, next to his heart,—I have something important for him, I must give it to him immediately, in order that nothing bad might happen to him. Pretend, son, I will accompany you, as though taking a walk. We can't lose time, so that nothing bad might happen to him." I remained calm, looking at him. I thought: "One mustn't delay, the chestnuts will get cold and they won't be useful to warm his hands." (It is absolutely inconceivable, now, to know that I only thought of that.)

I took him with me, I said to him: "Get the key, I have it in my pocket." He, with a paternal gesture, took out the key and opened the door. He followed me up the stairs, and I remember that I went up running, and that I only thought: "They are still warm." Upon reaching the top, in the already forbidden granary, I squeezed the brown paper package with my left hand and with my right hand I opened the closet and called, "Dad, Dad."

But he did not answer as was his custom. So I put out my right hand, pushed the trapdoor, and only then, from some unknown sky, an intense cold came down, I loosened my hand on my chest, and all the chestnuts rolled on the floor. He was stuck against the wall, white, breathing, panting, his eyes too wide-open in his unshaven face, looking at me as never a man or animal has looked at me in my life.

It is not possible to make tabula rasa, to cut out by the root, memory or hate. One can not begin again, one can not reconstruct a reflexive serenity, a severe and aseptic posture, without flooded pools of love, desperation, settling of scores, if one is not like Bear, Enrique, Luis, or any of the boys. Bear carries in his memory only a friendly lawn, intensely green, from which it is perhaps possible to forget, destroy, build. He will be a good architect, with his plain lines, absolutely devoid of excess. Just as he has exiled useless ornaments from his words. Bear ignores florid and unique calligraphy.

No one has repeated to Bear, one by one all the days of his life, the word revenge. No one has awakened him at night, without any other reproach than a suffocated sigh and an intense look, cold, devastating, disguised as gentleness. No woman in grey slippers (now her fascinating slippers have already been changed into two enormous rats that run about prying into empty attics) has remained, during his entire lifetime, always awake and dressed before he was; shaking, removing and contemplating the dust, with an avid look; mindful, deliriously thirsty for revenge. Revenge, in the encouragement and sacrifices so that I attain a place in the miserable wheel of cash, drinking in chipped cups, at one time beautiful, leaning on decrepit furniture, on falsely new floors. (Our tomb, every day of our lives, in front of our eyes). No one has brought Bear before a tomb that, at the end, can seem to him to be dug by his own hands. And in those hours of unbearable silence, to guess at insults, blows; to feel hated for having taken from a being the only thing that gives meaning and life to her existence. No one has done that with you, Bear.

You, yes, you can begin it all, you can finish with everything. I can't. I can't deceive myself again, begin anew, with formulas of collective claims, that which is only an intimate and untransferable private claim: private as only hate can be.

I will not do it. I will not kill that man, a ghost can not be murdered. I will never confuse again my dishonest and lustful personal revenge with a pompous concept of common justice. I will not sell myself parcels of justice, of truth, of human rights that I do not possess. You will have to elaborate your own plan, Bear. You will have your own plan, Bear, uncontaminated by me. All of you will have to begin, you alone, that which I lost some time ago.

Perhaps, a new species will merge gradually or it will hatch from amid the dry earth, or the sad rivers; some sort of courage, totally unknown. In some place, he will be looking at you. In a great abyss, like the one towards whose stars I looked, stretched out on the ground, being still a child. When I told myself that there, in remote and flickering systems, would exist, perhaps, a concept of order, of peace, of love, absolutely unknown by men.

In This City

At seven o'clock in the evening, in the month of June, there was a lukewarm sun on the leaves of the plane trees. In the new sections of town, among the vacant lots, the sun seems to her to be closer, more real, as in the city of her adolescence. Isa abandons the office, seized by a single idea: "Mario has returned, Mario is here." She is not going to wait for, patiently, that call that will not arrive. She has already called him several times: she still hears, with tense anxiety, the ring of the telephone, modulated by distance: monotonous, boring, cruelly impassive. Nobody has answered that ring. "But Mario has returned, Mario is here, and I am going to look for him," she repeats to herself, insistently.

Many hours ago—more than a day she gave herself over, vanquished, to her famous premonitions, to omens, to fatalism. "I am not going to struggle anymore. I can't stand it any more." She knows herself to be within an inkling of despair, down which she will slip, without fail. "The inkling that began with him, since the first day." Even when she thought him different; when she thought him untameable and all-powerful, when she even did not want him as she wanted him afterwards, as now: upon knowing him to be cowardly, weak and terrified, absolutely incapable of living. She did not love him then, as in this moment; beyond disdain, horror, or admiration that can awaken a human being. In spite of his faults, of his virtues, of his simplest and most inane acts. Simply just because; through an obscure force, which emerges in spite of will and reason, of egoism or the desire for happiness. Just because, for that unusual dreadful, nameless energy which impels him, which is his only reason for existing. Something similar to a diffuse and very old appetite, a voraciousness without limits, a kind of ferocious and cannibalistic religion. "Certain tribes devour their enemies when they were brave," she remembers having read, and modified, in this kind of delirium which invades her memory, which obliges her to advance towards that street, that house, that are fixed in her mind, like the only landscape, the only horizon, the only living object. "They devoured the heart in order to take possession of their valor…" Memories, fears, uncertain phrases float around her forehead, like nocturnal insects, in the evening which is gradually fading out on the asphalt, on the passing of the cars, on the lights, red, green, yellow, which begin to be turned on, scribbled on her eyes. Isa advances, in a sort of tense dream, towards that street she knows too well. She walks slowly, but inexorably, towards that place that is still distant, that it still slow in appearing. "There's no hurry," asserts a voice, subtly malevolent. "There's no hurry; in any case, you will get there."

When she finds herself in front of the building, as well-known as her own room, her personal objects or as her most hidden thoughts, it is already very dark. The woman caretaker draws near, with the key in her hand, she is going to lock the entry door. Isa comes forward, pale and smiling, and her own voice sounds harsh, strange:

"Good evening. He hasn't arrived…?"

The end of the sentence becomes faint. She sees the shine of glasses of the woman who says no, a little rudely. Isa, with her forsaken agony, looks at that stairway whose marble handrail reaches only to the second floor. On those stairs which, on account of the woman-nuisance, the woman-screen, of the woman-apology, she has never stepped on. That stairway which, a long time ago, she had wanted to explore, climb: to enter that apartment, those rooms. But this other laconic, impatient woman, says no. "He has not arrived. No, there is no message. No, no, nothing, nothing."

Isa recedes to an enclosed and strange world, absolutely alien, peopled by beings who hurry up, in front of her, next to her, behind her; beings left behind, who even run, like that girl, towards the entry way which is about to be closed. "She is a maid," Isa says to herself, contemplating the rapid kiss of the boyfriend, a young boy, with strange shoes and tangled hair. "She is a maid.

The entry way. Don't stop in the entry-way like a maid," she remembers confusedly. This is a different entry-way, pretentious and old, with a woman caretaker imbued with a strange authority, with a conscientious and grave commitment which, suddenly, she imagines to be stupidly useless. ("I don't want to see you in the entry-way, like a maidservant."). Once more she feels the discouraging wetness of her tears. "I'm crying in the street," she says to herself faintly. "I'm wandering in the street, I go into entry-ways, I beg for news. I loiter in the entry-ways. Like a maidservant. Like the beggar on the bridge, with his hand outstretched and his watery eyes."

It was then, shortly after her incipient friendship had begun, after the first dates, which made her drunk with happiness, when they arrested him for the first time, because of the affair of the leaflets, and they took him off to the Modelo Prison. The news reached her from other mouths, from other sources: not from him, of course. He would never have made her know it. It was then, still in the thrilling beginning, in the high excitement of her admiration.

Now Isa knows that Mario's motives do not matter to her or the faction in which his extraordinary idea of the world moves (or that in which he wishes to convert the world). Wherever his ideas might have been, they were only Mario's ideas, Mario's convictions, Mario's activities. For the first time she implored, searched, inquired; and when she saw him, finally, like a noble and beautiful animal through the thick grating which suddenly filled her with hate, the delirious and passionate desires to sacrifice herself for him were born. She felt herself ready to devastate the world, to ensure that he (he, not his ideas, not his objectives) should achieve what he wanted. "As the boy spoiled by his mother, who has to have the toy or whim he desires." That was the alienated, hot-headed, climate which carried her to a wild search in order to take him away from those bars. To shorten those twenty days—she remembers them with the precision that was habitual in her—. It was that which made her gather her savings, look for a lawyer—Jaime's friend—and become involved, because of his cause, in a murky area of re-encounters, of shady and wise ruses, of the utilization of some resources that she thought already displaced from her life. "Everything is allowed in order to get the only thing that matters in the world." Mario would have everything that he wanted, Mario would have all that Isa could give him.

That morning, when Mario left, finally, awaiting the trial, she will never be able to forget. She was wearing the print dress that looked so well on her. She was waiting for him in front, in the bar, in the uproar that she knew well already. ("What number is being called?" "The third person has already been entered." "They're calling for the second..." The line, the women, the children running about in their holiday clothes; she said to herself that, after all, it was a Sunday morning. The unforgettable courtyard. The dark green color, the grey doors, the pair of policemen, the corridor, the covered balcony. "They're calling for the third one!" The waiting was still a sweet and acid feeling of a recently discovered world. A world which, for the first time, she felt was her own, which belonged to her in a categorical, incompatible form. Now she feels the rebellious sadness of having lost the world; or that they have seized it from her hands; or that the world was never hers.

Isa closes her eyes, she does not want to go back in memory; she does not desire to peep, once more, through the hole that opened up that day (much later, on the eve of the trial, when she once more went in search of Jaime.) "Jaime was not bad, either, at that moment. Only a little sarcastic. But the least sarcastic that is possible in a similar situation..." It was not humiliating, since everything, everything, was allowed, acceptable, so long as Mario got everything that he wanted, what he deserved, what he desired. The big pothole was something else: the one which opened up on the day when she began to guess, to understand, to know that Mario was not unaware of her intrigues, that Mario accepted and perhaps approved. It did not matter to Mario that she sought out Jaime: that Jaime had used all his "influence"—that obscure and talked over "influence" that they, half-envious, half-fearful, attributed to Jaime in the office. Isa does not want to evoke the first surprise, the first knock of the door; warning and beginning of a mordantly revealing comprehension. But what did matter to Isa, the admiration, the distant virtue with which she might decorate the passage of an impossible Mario, an inexistent and—now she understood—stupid Mario? "The important thing is that Mario should have what he wants." What Isa fears rebuilding is something else: the verification that her love emerged there, when she discovered him vulnerable, weak and nearby, and she felt him to be truly hers, attainable, favorable. Mario, the weak, Mario, the one who is afraid; the one who lived under a thick, profound and devastating fear, whose origin he could not or would not want to know. It was thus, little by little, that the first dazzling moment disappeared and that this possessive, feasible love arrived. Much more violent and obscure. An aimless love, without reason, without false illusions, without hypocritical self-idealization, "I was not born for dreams," she thinks. "I was born to struggle, to attain concrete realities." Unfortunately or marvelously—she does not know clearly—in order to take possession of all things, she treads on the world, with the sole objective of clinging to and proudly defending a love, without mystery, without the least vestige, now, of curiosity or of candor.

The street has become deserted. It is an unsure hour. "A stupid hour," she thinks, within the distance, and the absence in which she now floats. An hour when nobody arrives, and nobody leaves; not even the night-watchman's staff is heard on the sidewalks. A lost hour, hanging, empty of any meaning.

"Mario, Mario." She listens to her weak voice; it seems a doll's voice. Like that of those puppets, behind the screen, in the park of her childhood. The ones they called the "curritos." Their voice was the same, a nasal voice, an imbecile voice that made the girls laugh, except her. They seemed to her to be contemptible, dirty, ugly, without any interest. Because Isa stood out in that city, she was always different from the "other girls."

Mario, she repeats to herself, with a sudden terror, now, just to hear herself. And it is finally, in the hands of terror, of that indescribable terror of hearing that voice, when, finally, anger breaks out. She recovers her anger, embraces it, greets it with a furious joy. She feels it burning her throat, as when one suppresses any desire to insult, or to laugh at, the world. Anger, bubbling, friendly, invigorating, breaks, explodes like a spout.

A cool wind shakes some papers, trash that now absent multitudes dropped on the edge of the street, in the wells about the trees. "Mario," she says, with a clear, calm voice. "Go to hell…" She breathes slowly, deeply. Once, twice. "Soon I'll hunt you down." She recovers, little by little. She is adding words to her thoughts: anger, courage, strength. "I'll hunt you down, don't worry. Although you are not man enough to stir up a life, or a country."

She breathes, breathes, breathes, until something gives, and she restores, little by little, her scattered emotions, her scattered and agonizing final bits of desperation, to her region of hope, of endurance. "But don't worry. I'll soon get you hunted down."

At the far end of the street a little green light lights up and comes close. "A taxi," she thinks with the same fright that another day before resuscitated her from her apathy to check the advance of the little hands of her watch. That was yesterday afternoon, or a thousand years ago, she no longer knows when. "If I don't catch that taxi, I will not find another at this damn hour…"

She is tired, she is not in the habit of walking so much, her feet are aching, she can't go on walking as far as the house. She must rest, she does not want to feel this way tomorrow, without direction, limp like a rag doll. Or like one of those disgusting Curritos that were funny to the rest of the girls, but not to her.

Wasting Time

He awoke around nine in the morning. The sun came in through the blinds, in strips. There were three wide windows, open to the cliff. Blinking, he contemplated the rays of light on the floor. "The rooms that Uncle Borja reconstructed." To tell the truth, he thought, Uncle Borja had ruined half the house. He had had partitions taken down and had installed, inside there, a curious heap of more or less valuable knick-knacks; strange objects proceeding from different countries. "All the big clearing out of Son Major," Mother had told him, because that house had always intrigued him since he was a child.

Son Major, above the cliff; adored by Uncle Borja. Why would he adore that place, lugubrious, abandoned, empty? It was slowly being demolished. Nobody looked after Son Major. The rock roses and the nettles invaded what was once, according to what he has heard, a beautiful garden. Bear saw the wooden handrail of his balcony (which had lost its paint) fall, physically, in pieces. But all about that house seemed to obsess Uncle Borja. Now, the remains of that vanished world lay in that kind of studio that Uncle Borja had constructed for himself. For what reason? What kind of work or study was carried out there, if it were not to gather together friends, drink, or be alone hours on end, amidst the desolate vestiges of what a child adored, and which, perhaps, he did not even like anymore? "Because this happens to everyone." Also to Bear, certain things (which years previously had attracted him), had stopped filling him with enthusiasm. He did not understand how people were determined to delve from inside, towards the past; as if things which no longer exist, which have died, were not better forgotten, left there where surely it is natural that they should be. On the other hand, Uncle Borja had accumulated marine maps, a dusty sailboat inside a bottle, clocks, compasses, primitive statuettes, jade figurines, African sculptures of questionable origin… And all of this for what reason? "If he almost never comes here. If he almost never comes to the island? If he spends his life in Madrid, in Barcelona, or on the Riviera. Although he might say that in the summer or in the spring we all go to the Great Lakes, I know that that's not true. He does not feel like going. Uncle Borja's world is clearly stated in detail, one can go across it blindly in a map. I believe that he is always deceiving himself when he says that he likes to travel, that he likes to read, that he even likes this decayed house of Son Major (which, finally, because of one of those serious testamentary provisos which say more or less '…to my beloved son Manuel, and in his demise…'; and in this case, Manuel's demise, it reverted to Uncle Borja. When Mother told me, I saw her smiling and sad. She probably knows why. Whenever she speaks about those things, it seems that she is smiling at her own sadness; but neither her laugh nor her sadness are the truth. At bottom Mother is a good person; the fairest Mother one could wish for. She does not go around sticking her nose where she shouldn't, as does, for example, Luis's unbearable mother."

He jumped out of bed and thought that, after all, although Uncle Borja criticized and made fun of him, Uncle Borja had not done anything other than imitate his mad grandfather, the one of the upstairs rooms. While he was taking a shower (in the miserable but only acceptable bathroom in the house) under the cold and comforting water, Bear repeated to himself once more that Mario was always right. "The human factor," he remembered, "the machines, because they are accurate, are used to fulfill their duty with precision: but do not put your trust blindly in machines for the success of a plan, because they are utilized by human beings and the human element is unforeseeable: it sneezes, it trips, it says one word, the one inopportune word which provokes the cataclysm." If Uncle Borja had not seized for himself half the house (taking with him, among other things, that which was Mother's former furniture), they would not have lodged Mother, against all that was previously considered, up there, in one of the shut-off rooms. They would not have had to convert Mother into Mario's accomplice and guardian. But, he thought, the one person that they would never have been able to do without was Uncle Borja. "And, perhaps, Mother is involved in this, even more closely for the simple reason of being my mother. It will be easier to convince him."

Through the open windows arrived the noise and the murmuring of a great bustling about. "The great day has begun." But not even the great day of those who carefully used the hundredth birthday party. The old woman did not know that this extraordinary day had truly arrived.

Those in the house had explained their program of festivities with some insistence. Family mass, said especially in the private chapel (which was simply grandmother's study, arranged for this purpose, since the old woman could no longer make it to the church, as he was able to verify). It did not turn out to be very bearable, of course, but on that day Bear does not want to express even a single discordant note in the great family commotion. No one must stare at him with special interest or disagreement. It is necessary to act inside the comedy, to remain at the service of the ceremony, as one more element of it. Like a vase, a chair, or a stuffed suckling pig.

At ten Uncle Borja would arrive and Bear had to go to the airport in the old Citroen to wait for him. At twelve, according to the announcements, the great to-do would begin. After Mass, the long cocktail hour—with the bigwigs, old women and old men of the surrounding area, and the misty and complicated relatives from the island—. The lunch only for the family. The family had come up from everywhere: fallen apart female cousins, unglued male cousins, distant nieces and nephews, bald and insane, who had their unchangeable place in the hierarchy at the table and in the solemnity of the day. A solemnity that, definitely, was embodied in the enormous platform for dining, which had been set down there. The night before he saw the platform, still bare of tablecloths and dishes. It looked like the frame of a gallows; it reminded him of that drawing in the closed rooms, the one which reproduced the preparations for an exemplary, collective penance.

Antonia knocked softly at the door and entered with

the breakfast tray.

Uncle Borja appeared happy. Not with the day that was waiting for them, of course. The day that, evidently, made his blood
boil (Uncle Borja's textual phrase). But he was happy, almost
exultant, because of the return of the "Swordfish." As soon as he
got in the car, he began to talk about that. "Everything was going
along alright?" They had a great crossing, of course. Magnificent. Bear, of course, a real sea-dog. Yes, a great fellow. He gave
him a little slap on the shoulder.

Bear observed him from the corner of his eye. One should not
have confidence in such jovialities. "The moment has not yet
arrived to speak to him." He always favored, along with everyone, that which had been carried out already. From Grandfather
Franc, to Beverly, herself, to Mother. With all the people he
stumbled upon along the way, each time that he needed someone, in general, nothing gave such good results as the act that
had been carried out already. "I believe that we ought to leave
tomorrow around six...," he declared in the meantime.

Now Uncle Borja was driving. The breeze ruffled his hair a
little, so carefully cut, smoothed down with lotion. The profile,
sharp and suddenly sympathetic of Uncle Borja agreed. "Great,
great." "Naturally," Bear repeated to himself; and once again the
unusual smile, that only arrived in solitude, came down to him.
"The sooner we escape from here, the better it is. He wants this
horrible day to pass, that six in the morning should arrive, he
wants to forget the old woman who is keeping an inheritance,
already squandered several times, for him, he wants to spin out a
little more his humiliating patience, and, finally, out!"

Bear also wanted it. A mute groan of relief arose in his chest.
He already desired it to be six in the morning, that another day
should return again. That everything should be over with: the
centenary, the lurking about, the death, the flight. Life is something too important to be wasted stupidly. Poor Uncle Borja. Bear
felt a certain, unaccustomed, weak tenderness towards his Uncle
("a nasty compassion, to tell the truth") towards him. "Uncle
Borja will never ruin Mother. He can't. If he did so he would not
be himself." Suddenly he possessed a great assurance.

Now the spring wind arose far from the words of Uncle Borja. Now it did not matter what Uncle Borja was saying: "Uncle Borja is dreaming again about the sea. The sea is the element where Uncle Borja seems suddenly to emerge from himself; to live like a man that is not he; a life that is not his own." When they returned to the sea, everything would be over with, no one would ever be able to go back. "Perhaps, why not? Uncle Borja will be grateful to me. One day, personally." Perhaps on that hypothetical day, that something so simple that Bear does not know how to explain to him, must have an answer; that which he asked him at times, and that he can not answer. Uncle Borja, floating in his confused and transcendent concepts of honor, family, race; between the clicking sound of fraternal kisses, even with a childish gesture, made him uneasy. Mother and he, their jokes of grown children, reviving childhood quarrels with an abundant smile; quarrels that they strive uselessly to revive. Uncle Borja will say to Mother once more: "How awful that hairdo looks on you!" "Just like them; you always have to tell me the same. As if I had ever used a hairdo!" Mother will say, proud of her apparent simplicity, of her hair and dress so apparently simple (Beverly alone knew the exact number of dollars that Mother's simplicity cost.) Uncle Borja will give her a kiss (these people kiss everybody). Uncle Borja calls Aunt Emilia "my poor mother." Why is Aunt Emilia always called "poor," said with a peculiar raising of his eyebrows? Poor in what way? Uncle Borja goes towards the house that he hates with all his heart, but that he does not dare challenge. The house that shelters the perversity of a hundred years, greedy and tyrannical, seated like a ferocious cerberus over the Great Chest of the Treasure.

Ah, Uncle Borja, how well you revealed yourself to Bear, immediately, in the morning when the outline of the house appeared against the innocent sky; how clearly Bear saw you, against the remains of your honesty, caught somewhere, "like a pennant of something caught on a nail, honor, love, memories, family pride, have caught, somewhere in you and in the house…" Everything, Bear thinks, floats in this pennant that is now only a faded little flag when there is no wind that makes it trail out like

a flame. "But very timely now." Uncle Borja will accept the deal
in his way. Never will he ruin Mother. Uncle Borja will never get
Mother mixed up in a dirty story of illegality and terrorism: in a
dirty story where also converge circumstances (favorable) of nocturnal coexistence, in the lofty and shut-off rooms. (But still respectable.) In this irreproachable world, the sins of the flesh and
the spirit only can appear so: painted on the walls by an unskill-
ful artist, almost innocent from being stupid. "And Mother, in
spite of everything, is already involved in this story. Perhaps…"

But in all the plans, in all the structures, exists the possibility
of the "perhaps." If not, they would be legends, stories. "Perhaps, the man with the eyes of a baby, suddenly may disturb this
night (at the exact hour when the clocks signal exactly the exact
habits of orderly, silent and methodical men), perhaps, at the
awaited hour, the clocked hour, the stated hour, the baby eyed
man might suddenly break his diehard habits. Perhaps, the invariable solitude of a man alone, who likes to live alone, might
shatter tonight in an alien presence, untimely and absolutely gratuitous presence. Perhaps, for the first time in his life, someone
will wait for this man that no one ever waits for, in the garden of
well looked after pink gladioli, geraniums and a small shed where,
in a very neat arrangement, the gloves, the shovels, the rake,
used by the methodical man with the methodical hobbies of a
solitary gardener are piled up. Perhaps the motor of this old piece
of junk that Uncle Borja is now driving might arrive at its last
performance, on the other side of the garden wall, and not get
started. Perhaps a dog might bark inopportunely, or Mario might
stumble… The human element is not precise or accurate."

But he who stops in the perhaps will never achieve anything,
anywhere. Bear hears the gravel crunch under the tires, and the
car stops. The unbelievable old man comes forward, clumsy, slow
in his rheumatism; he opens the door of the garage which appears more like a stable. "He who gets bogged down in the perhaps will never take the little or big step that can change life, or
the world."

Upon climbing the staircase, he is aware of the purring of
"poor Mother," who goes down the steps towards the sick boy,

who never lets himself be seen. Tomorrow, at six, at dawn, the sea will appear beautiful, vast, a newborn world. Tomorrow, when the sea will carry off from the island Mario, Bear, Borja, as if they had never been on the island, the man with the little eyes like a baby will still be lying on the floor, or in his armchair; still mute, still immobile, still incapable of undoing what he had gained over almost two years, with so much patience, so much ardor, so much sacrifice. Everything will follow its normal course. Nothing will hinder the inevitable course of what must be, and can not stop being.

Upon climbing the stairs, after Uncle Borja's hug, and one from "poor Mother," Bear notices something like an explosion somewhere in his soul. A mute, dazzling fire, a violent creak of happiness. "He does not arrive at his office before nine in the morning. At nine in the morning no one will know, ever, that Mario was on this island."

Kisses, kisses, kisses. Who might have invented this kind of effusiveness, kisses that sound like "chas" (like a frog squashed on one's cheeks) damp kisses that make a "mooah" sound, those squeezed together, or those others in the air, that go like "chees?" All kinds of kisses, Bear observes, can not be appreciated here, this morning. At least Beverly, among many other noticeable things, kept him from a similar, moderate cannibalism. An infinite range of lips, pucker up, imitate crumpled paper. Especially there, on the cheek (bag of years, wrinkled skin, flaccid); undaunted and passively tyrannical.

Mass has ended. At the far end of the room two altar boys, somewhat astounded, peep through the door of the oratory-study. The little one was on the point of stepping on his tunic. Looking at him Bear thinks of a childish and overblown parody of the King of Hearts. He carries a goblet, really, between his hands; which he must return to the family treasures, from which he took it; a goblet solemn and scarce (it is only used on red-letter and significant days such as this one). Bear still experiences a humid uneasiness, remembering the moment when the old woman, placed in the front row, has raised her hand, sharpened like a claw, to cut off the beginning of a harangue that began, more or less: "On this day, a symbol and a compendium of a long tradition of dignity and good fellowship...," to suffocate (with her strangely firm voice, almost impossible in that throat encircled by the velvet ribbon): "There is no sermon." Bear has contemplated the humiliated astonishment of the young and new parish priest of this place. (Inexperienced and peasant, shaved head and big feet.)

On the terrace the unreal cousins of the centenarian are waiting. Old, all of them, whatever their age might be. "As if they had given a holiday to a curious, luxurious and decrepit old people's home, a home for filthy and valuable sleepers; just like this chasuble that, according to what I hear, is worth a fortune. Although it has appeared to me only a dirty rag, covered with gold and roses."

It was very hot. "How hot it is, unheard of at this time of year." The sticky heat attracts an army of minute flying insects: golden green, iridescent, which throw themselves with pleasure, on foreheads dripping sweat. Bear looks at the sky: there are no clouds. Or, perhaps, the whole sky is only a big cloud, flat, smooth, which rubs out shadows and through which you could see a metallic brightness, a mixture of moon and sun. "Chas, chas"; now it is not kisses, it is the flat, bony hand of the old man with a collar of green velvet. He squeezes, with an infinite pleasure, with his eyes almost blank, a mosquito naively gluttonous for his yellow skull.

How strange, Mother was not here. Why is Mother not here? A slight irritation is born in Bear. Nor must Mother offer any discordant note. No one must attract the attention of anyone on a day like today. Mother must continue here, pathetic, quietly kind—some people believe mistakenly that Mother is proud—; a proper masquerade. Mother ought to be here, in her place. During the whole day she ought to remain in her place.

Only when the decisive hour arrives, will Bear leave here. (At that hour they will already be gathering up the leftover bones in plates and baskets, all the vast cemetery of birds and suckling pigs, of feathers; the yellow tablecloths, probably valuable; the porcelain, the crystal, the crumbs and the kisses.) Soon they will march by, in their beat-up cars or in those artifacts of an indefinable age and name in which they arrived, lay people, peasants and ecclesiastics. Bear contemplates sweaty foreheads, pinched necks, medals, jackets of Napoleonic cut; curious manifestations of affection and respect, in Recognized and Severe Authorities. "My great grandmother is worth a million," he thinks, in a contradictory resentment and respect. "A Totem, a Tower, an Army…" The goblets, blue, green, opaline, shine in a jumbled way, under the smooth sky. There is something infinitely inconvenient, on this broad terrace, from which one can not make out the sea. "Where could Mother have gone?"

Unexpectedly, Bear discovers eyes staring at him, luminous and grey, just like this sky. For the first time, perhaps—at least in his memory—Bear feels a trembling akin to terror, or repugnance, or an infinite astonishment. A pair of grey eyes—inhuman, savagely alive—are resurrected like two Lazarus, in a think, white, immobile face. "How can one have those eyes at a hundred years old?" he thinks; and it seems to him that those eyes are capable of paralyzing his hand: the glass from which he was going to drink has remained stuck to his lips. In the middle of the swarm— murmurs, soft laughs, admiring exclamations—a long silence opened a path, firm and hard, like a lance, between those eyes and Bear. "I have not kissed her yet," he says to himself, without knowing why. A puerile revolt fills him. "Nor will I kiss her. It will be the only discordant note: but, at least, I will not kiss her." Will this be the beginning of hate? He lowers his eyelids and sinks his glance in the golden, cool liquid, which is suddenly friendly. "I have never hated anyone. I have never hated anyone," he repeats to himself, in the monotonous stupor. A phrase, ironically deformed, arrives in the fog of another distant phrase: "This boy is now old enough to know his homeland. This boy is now old enough to know hate…" But this is not Bear's homeland, Bear does not have a homeland. Bear never talks about those things. He does not want to begin, suddenly, to say such things to himself.

"And, besides, where could Mother have gone?"

The noise—the creaking, the flattering exclamations, the old and undecipherable jokes, the culinary and ornamental work that makes up the noise of the house—has come together downstairs: between the big dining room, the terrace, and the service areas.

The staircase, solitary, brings him a silence which is not only the absence of noises or of voices, but something more dense, more unused: as if the silence which comes out from the old heart of the house (a grandfather's clock which has stopped), had been formed by the compendium of all the cries, of all the roars of the earth. A silence debased by the roar of centuries of laments and hollow words, by the long cries of desperation, love, abnegation, lust, obliges him to stop. He leans his hand on the wooden handrail, he thinks: "I don't have any reason to go and investigate where Mother went. What does it matter to me where she is. It is nothing important that..." But his steps continue, go up, they do not obey his reason. Only an obscure call (similar to another lacerating call, in some grey eyes, almost bestial through being human) which turns out impossible for him to identify. A trembling assails him. "Old rooms ought not to be opened, old and moldy locks ought not to be sprung. One must not penetrate polluted, dusty, decrepit rooms that a few men, a few mad men, got only for themselves; in order to hide, in order that no one should know the ultimate truth of their miserable helplessness..."

But he can not linger in premonitions, in absurd outbursts that never lead to any solution. Bear goes upstairs, opens doors, reaches the edge of the world where, minutes before (perhaps the same walls of the ruin, perhaps this swarm of desperate voices that now, within its clamor that nobody hears, and that is taken for silence) they warned him not to reveal it.

The heat has diminished, and in the confines of the land, of the trees, of the things, a perfumed night is announced. It is the moment in which surfeited weary, carried away by pleasures and confusion and complaints, the last redoubt of bands of revelers climb towards their nameless vehicles. Ghosts of some archaically boisterous holiday (with sailor clothes and sips of sarsaparilla). The old relatives, already forgotten by the recent and not yet ended festivity, leave again for the sleepy country from which they arrived. Towards patchy walls, pictures facing the wall, crafty

cats, substitutes for a scattered, fugitive or dead affection. Towards the sleepy Limbo of the shirking, tardy dead who had become blind, gluttons, deliriously magnificent.

Bear looks at his mother. Her silhouette seems strangely clear,
almost white, next to that silvery fig-tree where the last redoubt
of cousins exhales erratic kisses without any precise distinction,
happiness and praises dedicated to a ceremony that is already
mistaken for the last family funeral. They leave accompanied,
sustained, shoved by servants who appear sleepless, who are
grimly protective; mirages of some ultimate vanity gathered under the furniture, or at the back of an obscure drawer, like a forgotten piece of jewelry.

Mother and Uncle Borja, last sentinels of this Babylonian destruction, look firmly at the spectacle of intoxicated old people
and unusual tears, like those of that old cousin who is crying at
the death of the centenarian, convinced that she has attended her
burial; in place of her birthday. While she, the great, indifferent
protagonist, arm in arm with Antonia and Aunt Emilia, has again
climbed to the private rooms of her kingdom; her head tilted to
one side, her eyes fixed on her index finger where are strung
together four rings (too big for her).

A night like this, forgotten by the rancor of the sun, sweet-
ened by a vast, almost green, sky, is a strange night for revenge,
Bear thinks. But that is another one of the thousand farces woven in the vast bower of distrust, fears and terror that it is necessary to sweep from the earth. Revenge is not a way suitable for
this night. When did Bear hear that word? Was it perhaps announced during the long and elaborate program? Mario did not
pronounce it. He has never spoken of revenge. It is a word that is
permissible only to Gerardo. It would be an exact word for him,
although he might not pronounce it either. But it is a forbidden
word, for Mario and for Bear.

He goes towards the garage and the old car shakes and takes
off. Possibly no one has noticed him particularly. Although right
now it does not matter too much to him any more.

Behind the cloud of dust, the stuttering and quivering of the
last cousins, Bear believes that he is at the end of the comic-

pathetic retinue. "The last faithful ones," he says to himself, bitterly.

When at last, he comes out on the road, someplace, perhaps on the edge of the pines, perhaps over there, on the sea—the sun still has a gentle stretching out, a last glance of gold. "Perhaps he has realized that I am leaving." A frozen tranquility invades him almost physically. "What I most like about you," Mario has said on various occasions, although without the pride of the first time—is your self-control, your self-possession, your serenity…"

In the breeze, Bear smiles: "Your composure," Beverly used to say. "Bear, don't neglect your composure."

That stretch was not very crowded and he parked without difficulty. Upon parking the Citroen, suddenly, he seems to become a docile and marvellous precision instrument. "It will be necessary to reevaluate and discard so many things, so many things…" To begin again. That, now, was the only important thing. "It hardly seems possible how we can, so innocently, so smoothly, be mistaken, when reality is screaming in our ears its plain and very simple reason. It hardly seems possible how, so willingly, we can become deaf; we fight boldly and cruelly against our intimate and irreprochable truth."

Bear lowered the car window. On the sidewalk, on both sides of the door to the bar, little tables were lined up. The important table was still empty. Bear checked his watch: "There's still four, five minutes to go, at the most."

(At times, people seem eager to hurry their own downfall. Contrary to that was observed and scrupulously timed, days before, the man with the unvarying habits came along, down the street, today [striking his knee with the folded newspaper] four minutes earlier than other days. He turns around, draws near to his table, leaves his periodical on the marble top, and, with a very slight gesture, almost imperceptible, he lifts up the pant legs. "Baggy knees, pants out of shape, bother him. Take care of your suits. He is neat, methodical, severely exact." A weak sympathy, dead before its time, emerges somewhere, in some unthought of corner of Bear-Thought. But, now, Bear is one thing, his Thought another. Bear is a docile, submissive form, obeying only his thought that not even now does he feel to be his own: not even born from Bear. [In spite of everything and being Bear, only Bear, that Thought-Order.] That commanding voice, empty of all feeling, seems to constitute, now, the only form of life possible. "It is good to live quietly" a furtive little voice that still belongs, warmly, to the familiar and known Bear, slips out.

The man sat down slowly, carefully unfolded his newspaper on the marble top while the waiter drew close, and they spoke little. The man passed a flat finger over his eyebrow. Then he slipped his finger tip to the corner of his eye near his nose and held it there rubbing lightly some inopportune moment of discomfort. "Your last moment of discomfort," Bear-Thought decided. It was not necessary to get out of the car, nor to come near. Thus, peeping out of the car window from his seat at the steering wheel, he waited until the waiter had turned his back and had entered the bar once again. He took from his pocket the small package, the black and heavy weight, and raised it with an accuracy exactly like the precise and mathematical habits of the man. "Good-bye, baby-eyes." He bid him good-bye mechanically, in a perfectly audible voice.

The white hand stopped moving brusquely. It opened like a big fan, like an inoffensive little toad squashed in the middle of the road. His hand went up, still undecided, clumsy towards his forehead. His blue eyes, innocent, enormously round, remained placidly stupefied; perhaps at the gates of a remote pain, too fleeting to be understood. There was a little black and red hole— frankly proud in its precision and cleanness—above a glance, absolutely strange and ignorant of all that could stop it forever.

Flight was not even necessary, nor urgent. He was able to start the motor, pull out, disappear, come back.

A shot is something unusual. A man with a bullet in his forehead is not a frequent daily spectacle. Things scarcely happen: a passerby stops; a look of incredulity; a head that turns around and looks towards a place that is the place of the happening. The unusual situation, as one sees it, is something too brusque and inconceivable, too incomprehensible. There remains time to pull out and disappear in the first moment of astonishment or the first feeling of indignation.

(Not for fleeing, of course. Bear never flees, ever. Perhaps he would have preferred that they would not let him leave, just as they have left him: tranquil, almost gracefully; a look of surprise, of absolute stupefaction seized at the back of the neck. They have not had time, even, to lose their temper. "What a strange thing, truly, what a great imponderable thing, the human factor. In this, at least, Mario was right." The road cleared up under a clear luminosity, full of peace. "After this, the people of this country that Franc calls the Homeland, will define me in various ways. Mad, some will say. Others will say: What guts that little angel has; someone will think: what an S.O.B... So much inexactitude, to be truthful, in each affirmation. I do not possess even one blade of eccentricity so as to enter into madness; nor even the least trace of that paradoxical suicidal valor that animates those who love this life too much. And Mother is not a whore; only a good woman, solitary, useless.... She is really the woman for Mario in place of Isa...")

It was already dark night when he knocked on that door, with his knuckles. But he knew that she was not there. Therefore he pushed in the door and discovered, on the other side, the pink brightness of the lamp. It was not even a surprise that door (the other one, the one which guarded only an empty room at the far end of which another door opened and shut Mario's hiding place) half-opened, through the crack of which escaped the pink light of a globe of red crystal. The smell of mold, salt, dust, reached him with the disagreeable feeling that the first night produced in him and concealed. Only two nights had passed; since then, how strange it seemed that he had gone through a series of years, without days. Or a long day, like a year, without nights.

He entered the vacant room, and, in the light, the young men, daubed on the walls, uselessly obscene, awoke. Bear became aware of the noise, the surprise of the two beings who, suddenly, believe themselves to be surprised. He slowed down his movements; he advanced slowly, with the lamp in his hand. "Let them have time to pick up all that they have abandoned; that they can prepare the gestures, expressions, composure; that they can im-

provise some phrases, an attitude, a glance..." Now, yes, the
smile, difficult and uniquely solitary, arrived at without effort,
like something profoundly sure, real, even able to be shared.

He smiled when they appeared. He realized: "We met each
other here, in the empty room: not in Mario's hideout, nor in
Mother's bedroom. We have remained here, in the empty room,
with two half-rotten doors, one at my back, the other at his back."
He did not believe that the scene would originate there. "I imagined, I don't know why, that this meeting would take place between the bundles of papers and the dust, or in Mother's tempo-
rary bedroom."

But the three of them were there, comforting each other. Bear
observed the unquestionable and hazardous expression (of fright,
of irritation, or of severity, or of humiliation) that seemed to fill
them. Both of them, him and her. And, indeed, they both had the
vague air of having picked up something, forgotten, precipitously.
Something that was not clothes. (And he made fun of his own
innocence, he laughed at his own candor for having imagined
them to be cast down and naked like Adam and Eve.) Mario was
near him, having come forward, like someone who supposes that
he must take the reins of the unforeseen and the irremediable.
They did not seem to be stripped of clothes, but they were surely,
devastatingly, pathetically stripped of something very subtle,
vastly painful and lost. Something that he, Bear, had just consciously destroyed.

"Bear," Mario said. He noted the wavering of his voice, and
contemplated that hand which was raised, mechanically, towards
the center of his eyes (as if he grazed with his index finger the
imaginary bridge of inexistent glasses; that gesture that he knew
so well; Mario's gesture when he was looking for the solution to
a problem that was too complex.)

The total vacuum of feelings that, for an uncontrollable and
vast period of time (this can no longer be timed, as he might
have desired) impelled him to act, to speak, obliged him to focus
the lamp, with unenthusiastic curiosity, towards Mario's face.
And in the darkness floated a face, almost white, absolutely unknown. Then he directed the light towards the back, towards her

silhouette, she remained quiet. She seemed to be leaning on the wall, surrounded by faded ephebes. In her he surely discovered a very ancient face, in her he surely recognized, immediately, an infinity of faces, of voices, of words perhaps: obvious, however, visible and familiar. As though risen up from the mysterious trunk of memory (her memory, that she did not know to be so remote or not even to have happened). She seemed to lean on the naked torsos, flat and blushing, of some crazy boys. Her eyes offered a diaphanous sharpness, almost translucent, near the light. This quickened even more his curiosity: he did not turn the light away from her, as he heard Mario's voice. He listened to him, without looking at him, only looking at her. As though wondering about the reason for having been once, inside there, a nasty lump of tapioca.

Mario said:

"Listen to me, Bear."

But he did not let him continue.

"I know it already. It is not here that I am supposed to be now, but waiting for you in the street, inside the car, on the other side of the garden wall."

He was speaking to him, but not looking at him. Because his face no longer offered any interest to him. Only her face could still unveil some new, unknown country.

"Bear," Mario repeated. And he seemed, little by little, to regain a firmness which, really, no one needed anymore. "I should have said to you before, but you were not in the house, your mother did not find you. You left before the agreed upon hour; I wanted her to call you because I had to say it to you. I'm very sorry for what I have to tell you. Perhaps now you are not going to understand, but one day perhaps...."

"How is it possible," Bear said to himself, painfully, deeply amused. "How is it possible? Mario repeating the old, familiar phrases!"

"It is not going to happen," Mario continued. "I have desisted. Our plan is not going to be carried out. I can not explain to you more than that. But don't worry on my account."

He let him keep on with his explanation, useless now, unreasonable now: he let him continue.

"I'll go back alone, don't worry about me, forget everything, Bear. Forget me. I'm sorry, but..."

He turned around, slowly, and let the light of the lamp fall on him. On the face of his watch—a timepiece that never failed, because machines hardly fail—the hands ran inaudibly dizzily. He said to him:

"I'm not worried, it does not matter. It's already done."

Then he let the silence run down the walls, together with the almost invisible drops of dampness, upon the buttocks, the arms, the insolent smiles of the ephebes. That silence allowed him just the time to go forward to another commentary, more or less unsuitable, about Mario, about her.

"I knew that you would not do it, I have heard when you said so to Mother. I did not intend spying on you: Mother's private life, or yours, does not matter to me. But I was not able to avoid it, I heard it, when you said to her:

"Now nothing is going to happen. I will not do it. I'll tell Bear about it. I will not do it. Fine, you see, no need to worry. I did it alone."

He took his hand out of his pocket, and in the pinkish light, he showed the weapon. The one that Mario handed him (now that seemed a very long time ago), "because imponderables must not be forgotten." They then heard something that, truly, he did not expect. It was not a hysterical weeping, nor the moan of a hysterical woman, nor a repressed scream. It was a special sort of lowing, very gentle, that did not belong to a human being or to a known animal; a velvety, almost smooth lowing, infinitely more desperate, more desolate than the weeping. And that lowing caused an unusual question to arise in him. A question that seemed to drag itself along the floor, towards his feet. A cunning and extremely bitter question:

"But—have they seen you? Or did anyone see you?"

The stupor, immediately, tasting of salt, acrid, like the air that came in and corroded the bare room, frightened away his smile, made him go back towards the door, to stop on the threshold. He was slow in getting back his own voice.

"Yes, everyone saw me, because I did not hide from anyone."

"Soon they will no longer be necessary," he thought vaguely, while he returned the lamp to the floor, in a silence and a brightness that was turning, gradually, into something increasingly more unreal—the last shreds of being a gentleman, of chivalry, of honor, that Uncle Borja saves prudishly. "They are now no longer of any use to anyone."

Diary in Disorder

Here appears again this unfortunate notebook, these stupid words. Always the same notebook, this infinite disorder. But, had I not destroyed it, burned it, or thrown it away? It always appears, at the most inopportune moment. I read it, take it, write once more; and what I read, what I write, seems undecipherable to me. I read it again, and I do not understand a single one of these lines. As though it were written in an unknown language. I have thought, very often, that no one can write a diary, a real, serious, orderly diary. And here is this notebook, turning up when I am not looking for it, when I believe that, some time ago, I do not know when, I lost it.

I would have liked to write a good diary, something that could be read later; to live twice, as the ads for photograph cameras or books read. But, I have said it many times: no one can reconstruct, bit by bit, day by day, what happens to people. Because, afterwards, who is going to understand, decipher, a time that is already remote?

For example, Bear had big hands, gold, soft, beautiful boy's hands, I remember Bear's hands many times. But no matter how much I wrote in my diary: Bear, my son (I had a son called Bear: that is, Roger; or rather Little Bear because he looked like a teddy bear); well then, although I wrote here: Bear had beautiful hands incapable of hurting anyone, incapable of wrong; although I spoke, for days, years, pages and pages, about Bear's hands, or about my own little girl's hands, or about the hands of another boy (an unfortunate boy, a poor little boy, a silly creature, stupid creatures, wasting life in useless efforts, in useless gestures that are going to be of advantage to no one), nor even though I spoke for years and years about my hands, about the beautiful, dark, scratched hands of Manuel, or of Bear, who will give his hands or another's hands? Or my little girl's hands, along the jamb of the door, looking for a knot, a crack, a curve, gentle and polished like a child's skin…?

And Bear, where are you? Where are you now? Where are you going?

Barcelona—Bloomington (Indiana University)— Sitges.